The Madison Picker

The Picker Series

D1043212

by
Mark Clay Grove

Spitfire Publishing, LLC
Fairfax, Virginia

Mark C. Grove

Printed in South Carolina for Spitfire Publishing, LLC.

Publisher's Note: This is a work of fiction. Many names, characters, places, incidents, transactions, objects of interest, and tales of lore are the product of the author's experience and/or vivid imagination. Locales, businesses, products, services, and historic names mentioned herein are sometimes used for atmospheric purposes. Apologies in advance to anyone who might find fault; entertainment was the author's sole intent.

First edition   ©2014 :: ISBN 13: 978-1494786670
Large print edition ©2014 :: ISBN 13: 978-1495433214
Spanish edition   ©2014 :: ISBN 13: 978-1495461071

Library of Congress Control Number: 2014902355

Consulting editor: Sandra Haven www.sandrahaven.com
Copy editor: Carroll McNeill www.amatterofwords.com
Cover art by Jason Gaviria

FOR

MOM

THE ANGEL WHO TAUGHT ME
HOW TO PICK THE BEST

TABLE of CONTENTS

Prologue: Old Souls

I was living on a street in Coventry enjoying an ideal life with my lovely wife Rebecca and our two children when the blitz came; at least that is what I apparently reported to my nanny, more or less. I was five years old.

At first, my parents thought that I had contrived a family of imaginary English friends when I told them my story because I actually had been born in the UK and we had actually lived in Cambridge for a few months when I was an infant. They and the other adults that I had told about my English life were understandably puzzled. They would question me in detail but they could never accept the wartime facts I spouted as anything more than infantile babble. Understandably, it worried my parents, especially when I kept insisting that they should use my "real" name, Randolph West, instead of Charles Dawes. To add insult to injury, I also began prattling on about Mrs. West, my wife, our two children, and our pet dog. Eventually it became obvious to them that the sensation I was experiencing was something more than a young child's imagination; however, they didn't take action until I began complaining daily of a pain "on" my head. I'd point to where it hurt, in the back under my hair. My young mother would pet and kiss me and explain that birthmarks were not painful, but I knew better. Mine hurt.

My parents thought the worst; they thought perhaps that I was mad or going mad. So they took me to see the family doctor and he referred me to a pediatrician. Neither could explain the phenomenon. Everyone kept patting me on my head and telling my parents that I would outgrow it, whatever "it" was. In desperation, Mom and Dad shuttled me from one specialist to another for months. A platoon of psychologists and psychiatrists repeated what the others had told them until one day there came a knock at the door and Professor Stevenson walked into my life. Dr. Stevenson had heard of my affliction through professional channels. We were living on Capitol Hill at the time. He drove up from the University of Virginia and stayed with us for a couple of weeks. I remember him trying to explain to my parents what "it" was all about. But I already knew the whole story because I had lived "it" before, and I told him so in my little boy voice, but with an adult fluency that beguiled him.

He took copious notes, physically examined me, and directed one of his graduate staff researchers to verify the trail of facts that I had been prattling on about for some time. Professor Stevenson confirmed my story by documenting the facts, which only exchanged the worries my parents had for a new one: "He is an Old Soul," Stevenson said.

At such a young age, I was too immature to understand reincarnation, or so they thought, but I knew what it meant even though I couldn't pronounce the term. Dr. Stevenson started to explain the concept to me when we first sat down as a family but I stopped him. They later related how I'd held my palm forward and told him, "I already know *that*." It was the same story that I had been telling everyone all along, only now they were listening for the first time – and believing me. My parents were aghast. Dad put his arm around Mom as she bit her lip and cried. I fidgeted and looked out the open window at the kids playing hopscotch on the sidewalk as a streetcar rattled by and then I heard the neighbor's radio say that Hawaii had just become a state. It was 1959.

The staff researcher quickly verified that details of my story were factual. The address, the names, the descriptions – everything was true, she said. A man named Randolph West had existed, she told Dr. Stevenson, but I already knew that. I knew where I had lived, even the street address, the color of the house (red), and the gothic shape of the stained glass in the door. I cried when I remembered my young wife, Rebecca, and my two small children, and I told them that I missed my little white and brown Jack Russell terrier, Felix. "Can we go see them?" I asked, hopefully.

"No," they told me. "Sadly, they are all gone, Charlie."

"But gone *where?*

"They're with God, son," my dad explained, and I climbed into his arms to be held closely, and I wondered why.

When I was old enough, Dr. Stevenson explained everything. The home in which I had lived in my earlier incarnation was razed in a hail of Nazi bombs in 1942. We were casualties: Rebecca, the children, Felix, and I. I had died of a head injury. Professor Stevenson said the injury was "consistent with my birthmark," but even when I was a toddler, I already knew that.

My parents were relieved to be told that my Old Soul was not abnormal or even rare, and that it was actually common in certain parts of the world, India and Beirut. There was no remedy for my "situation" and I might or might not eventually outgrow "it." I never did. I still have love for Rebecca, Tom and Jane, and even little Felix. There's always been a hollow place inside me, as if it were a purposeful space kept ready for them. Sometimes I wonder to myself how many incarnations I have had. One day I hope to find out. Professor Stevenson kept tabs on me for twenty-some years.

1 Jerry's Game

I walked across the street from Bruno's shop to the antiques mall to peruse for sleepers. The Strasburg Emporium is one of the largest antiques malls on the mid-Atlantic seaboard. Somehow, the word had gotten across the street that I was in town with a load of Louis Vuitton, which can be a problem. More than once I have witnessed dealers rush around their booth changing prices *up* because I was headed down their aisle. Any dealer who raises their prices for that reason is a novice or a fool or both. Said fools will display the same level of stupidity at auctions that I attend, too. They'll run me up on a bid because they believe, incorrectly, that anything I bid on must be worth more than I am willing to pay, and so they bid higher. But no one really knows for sure what a bidder's motivation is, except the bidder.

In the early 1980's I ran a spongeware soap dish up at auction to $285 before I dropped out. At the time, it was worth less than a hundred, but I didn't know that and apparently neither did the high bidder. At that time, I was still a novice second-generation antiques dealer. The spongeware soap dish was the first that I had ever seen, and so I ran it up. Only later did I discover that the successful bidder was also a rookie. She got stuck with an $85 soap dish for which she paid too much. A few weeks later, I was a vendor at an antiques show in Manassas for a day. She was there, too, set up in a booth across from me. The contentious soap dish was on display in her booth for $285. I could tell from the dealer's sheepish behavior that by then she knew that she had paid too much. To make matters worse, the soap dish was shoplifted at the show. That dealer paid very high tuition to learn a cardinal rule: set your limit at auction and *never* exceed it no matter what. I do.

That incident was a long time ago. Now I'm a battle-scarred veteran in more ways than one. Dealers whisper when they see me shopping down an aisle or when I take a front seat at an auction. In a way, I'm the old sheriff in town and I have earned the right to wear my badge the hard way: I've lost fortunes and been lucky, but mostly lost fortunes because I take risks.

Such is the life of a picker.

The Strasburg Emporium is located at the junction of Interstate 81 and 66, in its namesake village. In the olden days, teamsters waylaid here overnight to rest their mules and oxen from transporting milled grains, timber, furs, pottery, and everything else grown or manufactured on the early American frontier. The Shenandoah River runs swiftly nearby and Signal Knob is its backdrop. This prominent mountain, a sharp endcap to the long and high Massanutten Ridge, was used by both Union and Confederate signal corps troops during the American Civil War. They would glass for opposing troop movements using collapsing brass telescopes and then signal to friendly forces what they saw. I had been told this story many times but by luck, I had also read about it in a cache of love letters written by a signalman to his sweetheart in 1863. He described a peculiar spyglass with 'two eyepieces bound together.'

His description set me on the hunt for what ultimately proved to be a prototype pair of binoculars made by the ocular innovator, Robert B. Tolles. As I walked around to the entrance of the place, my method of its discovery was still fresh and poignant.

Jerry Houff, the owner of The Strasburg Emporium, met me at the entrance in the gravel parking lot. "Hello again, Charles," he greeted me with a smile and a handshake.

I returned his strong grip and replied, "I was in town and thought maybe I should find something to pay for my gas." This is a colloquial expression amongst dealers indicating that we're looking to pick something with enough profit potential to offset the cost of gas for the day; a modest objective.

"Want to bet again, Charles?" he teased. "You know, to see if there's another sleeper as rich as the Tolles prototype?"

I shrugged confidently, pushed through the entrance doors, and replied, "It's your money."

Jerry and I engage in this sport that we call "Jerry's Game" whenever I visit The Emporium. How we got started doing it I don't remember, but it evolved into a marketing ploy on Jerry's part after the Tolles. Thereafter his objective was to get the "big dealer" (me) to buy something in his store so that his "little dealers" (his booth renters) would be impressed. It worked. His wait list doubled and I didn't mind because I made my gas money. If I lost the gambit by failing to find a sleeper (an undervalued object) for the agreed upon amount, then my obligation was to rent a small booth for three months. Either way, it was a marketing coup from Jerry's perspective, a win-win. For me the game was fun and the risk negligible. So far, I have never rented space in The Strasburg Emporium.

I asked him, "What's it going to be *this* time, Jerry?"

"Oh, I'll give you a ten minute window. How much gas do you need, Charles?"

Word had traveled. About eight or ten other dealers had gathered around to watch us, and also about half-a-dozen nosy customers who were trying to figure out what was going on. I could hear snippets of whispered comments.

"I looked all the way around the store, pirouetting, and then checked my watch. "Let's make it $150, or more, this time," I suggested nonchalantly.

"Alright." He looked at the clock on the wall. "Ten minutes ... starting ... *now.*"

Without missing so much as a beat or taking a step, I pointed and said, "I'll take the pair of ceramic owls behind you, Jerry, on the middle shelf."

He nearly jumped out of his handlebar mustache. "*What?*"

"You heard me, the owls." I tried my best to keep from grinning and poked with my index finger in the direction of the fifth shelf where a matched pair of Picasso chouette owls perched. Jerry had his own items for sale on display just inside the door behind the front reception desk, where we were standing.

"But, but you don't even know what I have on them."

He meant their price.

I kept a poker face. "I can see that the amount is three digits in the reflection of the price tag in the backmirror, so they can only be priced so high."

For a moment, he stood locked in place looking at them with his hands on his hips. He was wearing an argyle sweater vest, jeans, and white sneakers. Perhaps he was mentally willing them to fly away. Dejected, he finally forced himself, one by one, to place them on the counter. The advertised sticker price was $495 for the *pair*.

"You still have my current tax exempt form on file, right Jerry?"

His shoulders slumped. "Maybe," he faux-sulked.

I managed to keep my poker face even though inside I was hysterical. I knew Jerry well enough to know that he was elated and that he was working the crowd that had formed. I also knew that he was suffering more from having me find something under his very nose within five seconds of the start of *his* game, than for the loss of a higher profit. More onlookers had gathered around the counter to hear the details. By now, the rules of the game were known by all and everyone was waiting anxiously for me to reveal the details. I picked up one, then the other, and looked at each of their bottoms. Their bottoms were covered with green felt. An explanation was in order. The on-looking dealers were straining not to miss the lesson.

I explained, "Jerry, someone covered the hollow bottoms of the two figures with green felt. Because no one looked under the felt the pair remained unidentified until now." And with a thumb I pushed in the green felt, grabbed the loose edge, and gently pulled it away revealing clear markings. I lifted it for all to see.

"Picasso," the crowd whispered in unison in mutual epiphany, and then I lifted the other one. By the onlookers' reactions, Jerry realized that whatever he had lost by not identifying the two pieces as Picassos, he would gain back in PR. He had inadvertently tapped into the collective consciousness of his niche market: collectors and collectors who rent space. This particular episode of Jerry's Game would remain his favorite for years to come. Ultimately, it had wide-reaching effect. A couple of issues later in the year, this episode of the game appeared in the *Maine Antique Digest* as national news.

"What's it worth?" someone in the crowd asked. Others echoed the question within the noise of the general hubbub of excitement. Rather than be a curmudgeon and not disclose, I decided that the best course of action was to turn the event into a PR double whammy for both of us by teaching those present what I knew.

I answered the voice asking the question, "Well, at auction a matched pair of Picasso owls in this condition might fetch $10,000 dollars." More gallery noise erupted and subsided as they eagerly waited for additional information.

From the back someone hollered, "Is that retail or wholesale?"

I answered, "Retail. Many collectors buy at auction these days. That makes an auction result difficult to distinguish. Some hammer prices are retail and others are wholesale. In this case, $10,000 would be retail."

Someone else asked, "I didn't know he made ceramic pieces like these. So, how do you know it is really by Picasso?"

I nodded in the direction of the voice and thought of what to say, as I remembered the part that I couldn't tell them – that in my incarnation as Randolph West I had met Picasso in 1937 in a café in Montmartre. I was a war photographer fresh from the carnage at Guernica with a briefcase full of black and whites. What I showed him changed his life. What I told the group before me was just part of the story. "I was in Barcelona last year. They have a wonderful museum there dedicated to Picasso. I saw a lot of Picasso's work. Perusing museums might be time-consuming and expensive, but the payoff can be substantial, as you have witnessed with your own eyes here. Specimens like these were represented under a glass dome in the museum and there were thousands of other forms of his ceramics. Picasso had a relatively large line of ceramics: plates, bowls, figurines, vases, and other utility wares designed with the mass market in mind. Art was a business as well as a compulsion for Picasso. He was one of the few who made that combination successful, and that is rare. The key ingredients for success in the art world seem to be talent, business acumen, productivity, longevity, and a bit of luck. Picasso had all of the above in spades. And that, my friends, is the perfect transition I was looking for to present Jerry with a proposition," I turned to Jerry who had a what-the-heck look on his face.

"What proposition, Charles?" he asked quizzically. He was practically quivering.

"I want to set an example here with this episode of Jerry's Game," I turned to the audience, "as Jerry and I call it if you didn't already know." I looked around the room at all of the faces. They looked at me like deer in headlights not comprehending my next move.

2 Don't Glean the Field

A sizable crowd had gathered around the front counter at The Strasburg Emporium. They had just witnessed the latest episode of Jerry's Game. As usual, I had won and Jerry had lost. My profit advantage was an estimated $9,500 gross. I could have walked out the door with the Picasso owls and Jerry would have still been happy because the stunt had accomplished what he had designed it to do: to provide publicity for The Strasburg Emporium, which ensured that his wait list would remain long; however, there was, I perceived, a much larger public relations feat to be harvested on this occasion, although my motives included reasons other than publicity.

The world of antiques was changing rapidly and I felt like I had my foot caught in the gears as changes beyond my control swept over the trade and my life. It felt like I was already behind the ball even though I had just reinvented myself as an accredited appraiser. I hesitated a few moments thinking, and then figured my reputation as an appraiser could be strengthened by a bit of public teaching.

But that wasn't the whole of it.

There was yet another impetus and it was linked to my Old Soul thing. Even as a child, I had a sixth sense of understanding human nature beyond what others seemed to possess. I didn't really understand it. I still don't, but I have realized that when I teach others the act of sharing somehow opens channels in my mind. More of my past experiences flood in even as my *mouth* lectures. It's almost like an out-of-body experience, as if someone else is speaking as I watch. Sharing serves both the students and me. I have come to accept it as an obligation that has its genesis in an as-yet-unidentified Old Soul. Perhaps one day he will be revealed.

I explained to the onlookers, "This lesson is called, "Don't Glean the Field". I believe this ancient expression has its origin in agriculture. It was first mentioned in the Bible, but the lesson has been forgotten by our modern culture. The adage is simple: don't take it all. Leave something for others less fortunate."

Blank stares were aimed in my direction. I realized that if I went on for two more seconds half of them would tip over in a coma. My sermon was about to get spicier in just ten seconds more but it looked like they weren't going to be able to hold on even that long.

I fluctuated my intonation, leaning forward slightly and they responded in kind, leaning in as if anxious for some secret to be shared. "When you make a transaction in the antiques business, or ideally, *any* business, be fair. Be generous. And be thoughtful of others. Leave something in the field. A farmer's harvesting machine is imperfect; it fails to pick up every cob of dried corn. Thus, the machine's inherent imperfection leaves a tiny portion of the harvest in the field. Some farmers return to the field to glean what remains by hand, or they allow their livestock to graze the field after harvest. But the wise farmer intentionally leaves the un-gleaned portion of his crop in the field for wildlife, such as deer and Canada geese. In ancient times, an un-gleaned field would have benefitted the poor. People would be the gleaners, not geese. It was a form of welfare.

A voice said, "I don't get it, Mister. Why the Bible story when the topic is Picasso?"

I looked up and then around at the blank faces. Jerry was sitting on a tall stool, elbows on his glass countertop, hands holding up his head.

"Because, sir, I'm about to demonstrate my generosity, here and now." I looked to my friend. "Jerry?"

Jerry nearly fell off his stool. "Yes sir!" He stood, almost at attention and straightened his vest over his protruding belly.

I peeled off bills from roll of cash in my pocket. That woke up the coma-types. Color returned to all of the faces, and it was mostly green. "Here's full payment for the two ceramic figures, $495."

I looked at the faces.

"Notice, folks, that I did not ask for a dealer's discount even though by custom I am entitled to ask. *Not* asking for the discount is Part One of "The Glean Protocol." Its definition is: in the event of a large windfall, be a decent chap, don't strip the poor sod of a measly ten percent discount just because you can. You're about to rake in a big one. That's enough. The $495 owls are worth ten grand. Got it? Don't glean the field." There were a lot of understanding nods but there were also a few who shuffled their feet; I'd struck a chord. There was a general rumble of agreement interspersed with 'I-woulds' and 'why-nots?'

I pressed on with my philosophy.

"Now, Jerry, I want to do one more thing to make my 'Don't Glean the Field' point. We've been friends for decades, right?"

He nodded and shrugged his shoulders. One could hear a pin drop. An old lady jumped when a Coke machine compressor whirred on in the break area twenty feet to the side. Across the room, I saw a hula girl lamp from the early 50's suddenly do her thing amidst a collection of neon advertising signs.

"Yeah, sure Charles, I've known you a million years at least, it seems."

"Well, rather than scalp you on this transaction I want to include you in my harvest."

"Huh?" Jerry grunted quizzically.

"The Picassos, Jerry, I want you to sell them for me and we'll split the proceeds, 50-50." The crowd suddenly came alive in a rumble of surprise. I asked him before the hubbub subsided, "Are you OK with that?"

Jerry gulped down a large lump in his throat. "You don't have to do that, Charles."

"I know, Jerry, but I want to. Consider this action Part Two of The Glean Protocol."

He was nonplussed.

To lighten the mood of the moment I explained my attentions, "Since I have $495 in the two owls, any amount we net more than $495 we split down the middle. You broker them. Price them at $10k here in the mall and if they haven't sold by first frost, put them on eBay."

"Why not put them on eBay now?" someone asked.

I answered, "Spring is now in the air my friends. It's low season. This is the time of the year when people are falling back in love with their John Deere lawn mowers." People laughed and stirred. "If they're mowing, gardening, golfing, swimming, etc., then they're not in front of their computers bidding for eBay stuff. In effect, the eBay window narrows from April to first frost." I turned to Jerry, "You can log it in now, but set the start date on or about October fifteenth and run it for seven days. Starting bid, $300. Set the reserve at $9500. Winner pays for shipping, and insurance is mandatory. Make sense?"

"Yes sir," Jerry almost saluted.

I started to head out but the onlookers wanted more. "What other tips can you tell us?" someone asked.

Jerry's assistant blocked the exit by handing me a cup of coffee just the way I like it, two brown sugars and easy on the half-and-half. She winked at me and smiled when she detected the expression of resignation behind my eyes. "Like what?" I turned and replied in the general direction of the question. I took a sip and noticed that I had been tarrying for almost an hour. A chorus of questions from every direction ensued until I waved them to silence. "OK, OK, I see that you all like eBay. Probably many of you use it as a means to turn over slow-moving merch," heads nodded, "or esoteric stuff unsuitable to the local market," more heads wagged, "and of course there is always stuff of regional interest elsewhere. Am I right?"

Positive noise ensued as I made use of the moment to morph a Dunkin' Donuts coffee grimace into a grin. "OK, five minutes and then I have to push off."

There was general agreement: something is better than nothing.

"You all know the rule, 'Closest to Point of Origin,' right?" There were grunts of understanding but also a few blank stares. "OK, in case you don't…demand for something is always strongest the closer it is presented for sale to where it was made, because that is usually where the most number of collectors are." This time there were nods of understanding all around.

"OK, that's one," a voice said.

"Two, the esoteric stuff sells on eBay because the niche for it is narrow and probably not in your market. Hot water bottles with douche accessories mint in their original cardboard and cellophane box were once an example of the esoteric." A few of the ladies blushed. "Put that out on your table here in The Emporium and it'll turn to stone before it sells, but if you put it on eBay you'll have people fighting over it. Don't ask me why or we'll have to do CPR on one or two of you who don't get out much. Suffice it is to say that hot water bottles which I have sold always end up going to customers with addresses in San Francisco." That brought down the house. One or two initially blank faces guffawed late after someone explained my veiled meaning, but they all chuckled or tittered. "By the way, hot water bottles are passé, or so says an old army buddy of mine who I coached early-on in his addiction. They are no longer hot. Pardon the pun. I don't know what is hot right now in the esoteric line of collectibles."

Someone said, "Three."

I looked his way. "OK, three. Peak eBay season is from first frost to Pearl Harbor Day. After

December 7th people are too busy with the holiday, which causes demand on eBay to subside, but then it switches back on again after grandma's Christmas checks clear and trust fund babies have received their annual funding. That would be from around January 5th until they crank on their John Deere tractors in the springtime. Do keep in mind that this is a mid-Atlantic observation; other latitudes are different. The Rule varies with latitudinal location of the seller *and* the buyer." There were slow nods of comprehension and a few were jotting down notes.

"Four. Identify buyer distractions. What could they, the buyers, possibly be doing or be distracted by when your auction item matures? What distractions might there be scheduled on TV? You do not want the auction to mature right in the middle of the final episode of Dancing With the Stars, or some other foolish thing that might be distracting possible bidders.

"Five. This is the final tip because I have some work to do, folks. Take into account the age of the prospective buyer for whatever it is that you are trying to sell. For instance, nesting-age customers on the Left Coast should have put their kids to bed when your auction item ends. I'd give them a half hour or more to settle in and regain their enthusiasm before my items mature, if I were you." I looked at Jerry. "The Picasso auction needs to end at 9:30 PM on the west coast. Wednesday and Sundays are best, by the way. Got that, Jerry?"

"Sure Charles," he replied emphatically. "It makes perfect sense, right guys?" He raised both arms out, palms up. There was a general rush of approval and faces beamed in my direction.

"Folks, I need to hit the road again." I stood to excuse myself. A round of applause erupted from the crowd. I bowed slightly in acknowledgement as Jerry grabbed me with a bear hug.

The generosity I showed Jerry with the Picassos was repaid exponentially. I didn't realize it at the time, but Ken Neumann, a *Maine Antiques Digest* correspondent was present for the whole shebang. Normally a dealer avoids publicity because it can make dickering with sellers more difficult, but Jerry's Game benefited me as much as it did him because it went viral after Neumann's article. As a result of my one small act of kindness, according to Neumann's article in MAD, I have 'Unwittingly become a legend in my own time.' Ken may be right. Over the course of the next eighteen months, I engaged twenty-five to thirty different clients for appraisals and even more for consultations. Since I was edging my way out of the retail field and into appraisal work, this worked well for me as well.

More importantly though, the 'Don't Glean the Field' lesson became a much talked about concept. It transcended the antiques trade. My niece, Anna, a JMU Business School student, chose it for her thesis topic. A year later, a Hollywood screenwriter wrote a story based on her paper.

3 Inland Sea

"Charles! Hey Charles! Time to get up, now, Amor. Coffee's ready." With a familiar disappointment, I rolled out of bed to begin my morning routine; I pulled on my red, white, and blue sweat suit, shoved on my moccasin slippers, and shuffled my way to the coffee pot.

Emma smiled at me as she raised her cup of steaming Major Dickason's Blend. I poured some for myself and plunked down on the other side of our eight-foot heart-pine farm table. Grace, our old yellow Labrador retriever, greeted me with thumping tail and then laid herself down to peer at me from her usual spot, a heated pad by the stone hearth. Hickory wood popped loudly. I blinked out the window and rubbed the gray stubble on my chin.

"I was dreaming again," I groaned, as she pointed her dimples at me.

"Couldn't be worse than the last time, could it?"

I made an unintelligible sound.

She lowered her cup. "Well?"

Usually I don't remember my dreams, unless I'm startled awake. For some inexplicable reason, though, I'd been able to remember more of them recently. Not that I wanted to remember them, mind you. It just seemed to be a curious new personal phenomenon. My last dream was about rappelling out of a Blackhawk. Last night's was different.

"Actually, this one was one of my English dreams," I mumbled. "Kind of weird." The coffee was having the desired effect as I noticed a remnant of the morning's beautiful perigee moon disappearing behind white-capped Cowherd Mountain. The air looked still and cold. Large snowflakes were falling intermittently. *Beautiful,* I thought, *and in only another month May apples will begin to spring up from the forest floor … I'll want to get out my Tenkara rod again.*

"Well, let's hear all about it," Emma goaded me.

I looked at her with one eye. "Don't bodder me," I mimicked her Hispanic accent.

She giggled. "Amor, if you wait until later you won't remember anything at all."

My eyes glazed over trying to remember, my coffee cup at my lips. Remembering my dreams wasn't my favorite avocation; it was therapeutic, so said the V.A. doctors, but I wasn't a morning person. Well, actually I *was* a morning person but not when I felt restless and anxious, and I was restless and anxious. Our real estate agent had recently hooked a buyer interested in our two storefronts. We were experiencing the excruciatingly slow process of reeling him in. It couldn't happen soon enough, as far as I was concerned. While I had been away fighting the Iraq War, both of my family's businesses had suffered because of changing demographics. I had first felt these effects in 1991. I should have acted on my instincts then, but I was in Kuwait and then Iraq and Mom and Pop were in charge while I was away. I returned intact but the antiques business had changed for the worse. To recoup the losses I became a circuit rider: I did mostly antiques shows for a few years before 9-11, and then I was sent over there again, this time Afghanistan and then Iraq.

Emma set her red cup down and placed her hand on my arm. "Amor, what is it?"

I set down my blue ASA cup, with its Scales of Justice logo representing the professional society of appraisers to which I belonged, next to hers, and let her hold my hand so that it wouldn't tremble as much. "I was remembering when I first noticed how the antiques business changed, on my return from Desert Storm, and of my hypothesis then as to why the antiques trade was beginning to change." I looked out the window and silently re-examined my motives silently: why I had decided to sell the family business against my aging parents' wishes because of demographics that '*only I recognized*,' they said. I knew I had to reinvent myself. I could sense it. It wasn't the first time and it probably wouldn't be the last time either. And so I did what it took to become accredited and discovered a new hard row to hoe, just as difficult and a pain in the ass to achieve as was my first graduate degree.

I studied the logo on the cup avoiding Emma for the moment.

She realized the inner turmoil that I was going through. "It's OK, Amor, it's going to sell, and your parents will understand, eventually."

"Yeah, right."

My turmoil was real.

In the early 1990's, post-WWII collectors began to die off in increasing numbers and were bequeathing their stuff to us Boomers. Ten years later their tide of passing was even stronger and now we Boomers were downsizing in a massive wave never before seen; we already had too much of our own stuff, we didn't want our parents' stuff, and the younger generations didn't want anyone's stuff because '*they don't like old stuff*,' I tried to explain to Mom and Dad. In the antiques trade this combination of negative market factors is called a triple whammy.

I looked at Emma and saw the concern in her eyes. "It's never happened before. The majority of the dealers are in denial…."

"She'll sell it for us, Amor. Don't think about it."

"I can't help it. If the buyer she's got hooked realizes that there's a triple whammy in progress, then we're toast."

Emma leaned forward, "We don't know how the buyer is going to use the buildings. He might want to tear them down, for all we know."

I shrugged, "Good point, but still, "I can't help it. The bills are piling up and we haven't found anything of significance since the Picasso owls, last year! Maybe my divvy tingle has abandoned me." I held up my two little fingers for emphasis. It's an expression adopted immediately by the trade across the world from Jonathan Gash's *Lovejoy* series. A divvy is one who has the divine capability to detect quality. "Another couple of weeks of bad luck picking like this and we'll be all the way through our buffer, and our buffer is sacred." If it hadn't been for the appraisals I'd been contracted for over this last year— thanks in part to that owl article—we would already be through that buffer. But the appraisals were slowing down now too. In frustration I said, "I would sooner sell Grace…" Grace rolled over at hearing her name, exposing her belly in case someone wished to rub it. Emma squinted at me with one eye and gripped my hand with her fingernails, too hard. "Well, maybe not Grace," I winced.

I'm the worrywart in the family. Emma and Grace never worry about anything.

Emma prodded me, "Amor, you know it's feast or famine. You tell me this all of the time. Now, forget about the real estate and try to remember your dream from last night."

As usual, I resisted her request.

"I don't feel like it," I complained.

"Come on, give me the details." Maybe it was her way to distract me from the rattle in my head, but she loves to irritate me in the morning anyway.

I withdrew my hand, crossed my arms and concentrated. "I dreamt that I was searching for Felix."

"Hmmm, Felix again, huh?" Emma analyzed.

I kneaded my left temple. "Uh-huh."

She nodded patiently. "Where?"

"By the Hebron Lutheran Church ... during the flood."

"That's in Madison." She raised one eyebrow. "You're mixing reality with your Old Soul event, again." Emma has never had an Old Soul dream nor did she have a telltale birthmark so she really didn't understand how I felt, but she had read Tom Shroder's book, *Old Souls: The Scientific Evidence for Past Lives*. She'd also done her own research across the Web and spoken with Professor Stevenson personally. She understood my "affliction" on an intellectual level better than most.

I sighed. "I realize that I'm blending realities."

"Stevenson said that one day you might."

"Yeah, I know. Especially if I have a major event. Well, Fallujah was it, for sure, don'tcha think? The nut job almost killed me." Sometimes I have night sweats and wake up thrashing without remembering anything. Other times I remember: I flashback to Iraq or Panama or to some other of this life's experiences, or to Coventry.

"You've had plenty of major events, Charles. It's a wonder that it hasn't happened until now."

I made a thoughtful tisk-tisking sound by sucking my teeth. "Maybe it's why I merge different periods," I said, "like a time traveler, or something. This particular dream scrambled together the Coventry air raid, my combat experience, and the flood we had in Madison County in 1995." Emma waited patiently for me to think through my thoughts. "I dreamt about the Hebron Lutheran Church but it was in Coventry, not Virginia, and it was surrounded by water, and ah, I remember now, Felix was swimming toward me."

Emma studied me without comment and held my hand again when I reached for hers.

"It was weird," I concluded "and then I was looking down and floating above myself as I lay dying."

She raised one eyebrow. "As Randolph West?"

"Yeah, that's right, as Randolph West."

"What does the Hebron Church have to do with it, do you think?"

"I haven't the foggiest."

In 1995, mountainous Madison County experienced what the talking heads on local television had referred to as a flood of 'Biblical proportions.' One that 'occurred only every 800 years,' or so they said then, and then the following year it happened *again*, and the devastation was just as bad. Literally, it rained 24 hours a day for seven days. The destruction was horrendous. Landslides, crop damage, bridges washed out – everything one usually sees happening to California or New Orleans, only in '95 and '96 it was *our* turn. The Hebron Valley and all of the other river valleys in Madison and adjacent counties were turned into inland seas, and I'm not exaggerating. The giant round hay bales that dot farmers' pastures went bobbing like corks downstream with such force that they took out most of the guardrails on all our bridges. I remember being stranded east of the Rapidan at the Wolftown Mercantile Store. There was a bunch of us gaggling around, snacking on Dr. Pepper and nabs, when in rolled a shiny black Mercedes. A tall man stepped out and looked about. It was probably because Emma and I stood out from the locals that he asked us for directions. He was "headed to UVA hospital," he said, anxiously. I told him to take this and that route downstream where the water hadn't crested yet. I know that he did, too, because later that same day on the Charlottesville evening news, he told reporters that his brother Chris was in stable condition, but paralyzed. I felt sorry for him. Reeves made a good Superman.

The Corps of Engineers quickly made great improvement to the damaged areas. I had spent some of my middle formative years growing up in the county, out near Hood, back in the Kinderhook area, on a mostly mountainous farm next to Middle River. Funny, for some reason they changed its name to the Conway River, whoever "they" were, or are. Anyway, after the Corps of Engineers moved the car-sized boulders off the roads and reformed the riverbanks, to our great relief, the Fish and Wildlife folks restocked the tributaries with brookies and rainbows, but it's still not the same kind of fishing ten years later. I suppose that it'll never be the same again.

4 Picking the Valley

Emma looked at our green 1940's electric wall clock, and quickly gulped down the last of her coffee. She exclaimed, "Amor! It's time to get moving. We ought to be on the road by now. It's going to be a long day." So we hustled, dropped Grace off at her doggie camp, and were on the road again for Lexington, Virginia by way of Route 33.

We have regular scouting loops where we go to find stuff; the act of scouting is called picking. Along these loops, we stop at any and every place imaginable, but the pickings lately had been slim to nothing. As we usually do, we stopped by the Rolling Hills Antiques Mall in Harrisonburg. Emma picked a silver Navajo ring with turquoise stones and I added a reference book that I didn't already have in our vast library, but that was all. Then we drove past my Alma Mater, James Madison University, and got back in the loop headed south on Route 11, otherwise known as the Valley Pike.

Outside Staunton, the snow line fell behind us, a welcome sight. Interstate 81 is a fast way to travel the Valley of Virginia but it's never been my favorite route. That's why we take The Pike. It started out as a game trail that the Indians followed on foot. Later the Europeans converted it into a wagon trail, but sometime, and I don't know when, it was paralleled by Interstate 81. The Interstate is too fast and has too many big trucks going too fast on too few lanes. One day there'll be six lanes, or so rumor has it. No matter, we take Route 11.

By lunchtime we had made it to Lexington. I wound my way up a steep hill to a hilltop Howard Johnson's. This was one of our usual haunts where Emma ordered her usual twigs and seeds and I wolfed down my favorite: tuna fish on toasted wheat with a side of ripple fries. We said pleasantries to the familiar waitress, tipped her generously, and took off again on our pick.

On the way up the hill, we had noticed through the leafless trees an old Craftsman style bungalow, near ruin, that appeared to be a new attempt at our business: selling antiques. So on the way out from the restaurant we backtracked to check it out, hoping we'd find a sleeper. We must have driven by this small house without noticing it in the summertime when the trees were in full foliage. Now though, it was clearly visible.

On the porch sat a tattered upholstered sofa and a white wringer washer. One of my small fingers twitched as I got out of the car and set foot on the ground. Contact with the ground felt like spark from a dowsing rod. I uh-hummed to myself because a tingle sometimes portends a good find. It didn't take very long to look over what was in the old Sears house. Most of it was junk, Elvis records, milk bottles and so forth. We don't mind wading through mire like this in search of treasures. That's how we make our living. We're antiques dealers. And even if we had a lot of money, which we don't, we would still pick because we love it or perhaps because we're just a little nuts, or both. Yes, it's a hard life but *someone* has to save treasures from extinction. That's how most dealers perceive it; the "it" being the hunt.

After a few minutes pawing through pure crap armpit deep, I found a very fine first edition copy of *Post-Mortem*, by Patricia Cornwell. As soon as I touched it, the tingling stopped. From past experience I knew that Providence was momentarily satisfied. The book's dust jacket was in fine condition, too. I carefully opened the book part-way – about three inches wide – and it cracked audibly, which is what I had hoped. That meant that it was an unread copy, and then I continued my physical inspection. Next, was it a signed copy? I turned to the title page to see, but no, not this copy. Too bad. An author's signature improves the value of the book. I examined it for other things too, like remainder marks on the edges, none; and to see if the dust cover had a clipped price, none; and library stamps, none; so I figured, based on its condition and its other value attributes, that it was easily worth a day's wages for a tradesman in rural Virginia. I sighed. *It had been a really, really long dry spell. Maybe this is the icebreaker*, I thought to myself and rewarded the contributing digit with a gentle rub.

And then, Emma got lucky too, but I sensed that she didn't want to discuss it in front of the dealer. A few minutes later as we were driving away, she looked over her shoulder to be sure we were out of sight of the bungalow and then she went berserk. "Oh my god! Oh my god! Amor, oh my god!" This is how she normally acts when she finds a deep sleeper. "Do you have any idea what this is?" she chirruped at me, holding up the bracelet.

"Actually, yes," I replied calmly, "it's probably a Georg Jensen. You do realize that the book is worth a few hundred dollars, too, right?"

She nodded but she was too excited about the bracelet to talk about a dusty old book. "It's a Jensen, oh my god! It's worth a small fortune and it's in perfect condition, even the clasp. Just look how complicated it is, and the way it closes. You know how collectors value well-engineered fittings. Amor, this is the best find I've had in weeks! I love this business." She croons when she finds a real gem, although I never hear the end of it when business stinks; like how we should get *real jobs*, the way all of our geek friends have combined incomes in the six figures range, yet they only collect Flintstones soda glasses and live with new brown furniture which is circumstantial evidence that there is no God.

I interrupted her ecstasy. "You like it?" I asked rhetorically.

She gasped, "It's a Georg Jensen bracelet. Of course I like it. It's sterling and lapis lazuli." She was examining every link, stone, and mark with a loupe that she always keeps in her purse. "How old do you think it might be?"

"Oh, I'd say around 1912, by the looks of it," I replied nonchalantly.

"What do you suppose it is worth?" she panted. She was trembling from excitement while still examining each stone and fitting. Red blotches had appeared on her neck, like when she eats strawberries.

I shrugged. "You mean *if* we sell it, and we should because we need the money, Emma, but I know we won't because we have almost nothing in it, right?"

"Eighteen dollars," she beamed.

"We could use the $500 that we could get for it."

A very good find if one were to sell it, I thought to myself, but I knew it was a keeper, and that meant money had gone out and none had come in, yet. The likelihood of profit from this pick was certain since the bracelet only cost $18, but it was a delayed profit, one that might be years in the offing. Emma was ecstatic, though, and that was worth more than money, really. As for the book, well, it was only $5. A quick sale might return $500 but if I were patient and waited to take it to a Cornwell book signing, and had her sign it, well, that might double its value. I made a mental note to Google her later to see what she was up to, whether she was in Richmond or Malibu.

I drove slowly along winding country roads on top of packed snow the way I'd learned to years ago when I was at grad school in Idaho. The absence of wind turned the rolling landscape into a crystal wonderland, but Emma was too busy ogling her latest find to notice. My day plan was to drop in on David Gee, a dealer friend of ours who has a large shop in Brownsburg. I'd known David for years, ever since we'd first met at the Heart of Country Show in Nashville. A couple of years later, Emma introduced David to our travel agent, Greta, and the two of them have been together ever since. Greta looks kind of like a blonde version of Joyce DeWitt from Three's Company and David could be a very skinny Burl Ives with a full gray beard.

Greta was one of the first to move her travel business from a physical location to online. Now, from her home office in an antique log cabin across the street from David's shop, she runs both her travel agency and David's antiques website. David and Greta were one of Emma's few matchmaking success stories; most of the time Emma's schemes end in disaster. Theirs did not.

Next to David's man-cave antiques shop, Old South Antiques, is a tiny post office. It's probably been around for a hundred years or more. When I rounded the bend, I saw smoke drifting from its chimney. No other post office that I have ever been to has had a working, wood-burning fireplace. On this snowy day, nearly all the chimneys were smoking in the hamlet of not more than fifteen or twenty homes. What a sight!

I rolled the car to a stop in front of David's shop and turned the engine off. "Emma."

She looked up for the first time in minutes, and asked, "We're at David's?"

"We're at David's." I gestured with a nod in the appropriate direction, my wrists hung over the steering wheel, patiently.

"Oh, good. Help me put this on," she insisted. "I want to show them." She held her hand out and handed the bracelet to me to secure the clasp; it was so sophisticated that she needed help putting it on.

5 Digital Dowsing

We went inside and they greeted us. After some pleasantries, Emma showed off her new treasure and of course they both loved it. Who wouldn't?

"See, I told you so," she said.

I frowned with one side of my mouth and held my palms up. "I never said otherwise." The two ladies went off somewhere to look at smalls as David led me to what I like best: the heavy furniture pieces. He wanted to show me what he'd gotten in since our last visit, a pie safe.

It was a Wythe County pie safe, actually, and it just about knocked my socks off. I looked at his printed price tag to read the dimensions: It stood 54 inches in height, 72 inches wide, and 20 inches deep. The top was rectilinear with a molded edge, and sported a gallery with a central whale tail flourish and flanking dollop returns. I walked around it slowly absorbing the obvious details, obvious to any dilettante that is, and then I looked more closely.

David said, "I'm going to let you alone to do your thing."

I nodded to David and wondered why my divining rods were completely unresponsive in the presence of such a beautiful safe. David leaned against the warehouse-like wall and watched me studiously as he puffed on his pipe.

The safe appeared to be circa 1830's and primarily walnut. The secondary wood was mostly white pine, hickory, chestnut, and sycamore; the latter is otherwise known as river birch. It had two upper side-by-side drawers that were dovetailed in the front and in the back, and each had a chamfered chestnut bottom rabbeted in place. The dovetails were handmade, narrow, and elegant in the manner of the Federal Period. Under the drawers were two front doors. Each door and drawer sported a finely turned wooden pull. As usual for high-country cased furniture, construction was mortise and tenon and pegged. Interestingly, the pegs were square rather than round and probably hickory instead of walnut. In the back were narrow, vertical tongue-and-groove pine boards floating in place at the top and bottom in rabbeted horizontal rails. By the way, "cased furniture," means a piece of household furniture like a cabinet, as opposed to seating furniture or tables.

David asked with his pipe in his mouth, "Is it a Fleming, Charles?"

I looked his way without focusing, and then returned to the specimen without comment, thinking to myself.

Each of the two front doors was adorned with a single, flush-mounted vertical rectilinear pierced-decorated tin typical of the well-documented pie safe maker, Fleming Rich, from Wythe County, Virginia; he was prolific. One scholar has estimated that he may have produced two to three hundred pie safes in his time, from 1830 to the late 1840's. His cases were good, but he's remembered mostly for his tins which he typically decorated with a tall floral erupting from an ovoid collet-foot urn surrounded by other floriforms and large bellflower blossoms in all four corners. David's example stood majestically on four tall square tapered legs and the case appeared to have retained its original patina.

I thought to myself, *So much for kicking the tires*. I reached into my green Harris Tweed jacket and pulled out a small brown leather kit I always carry in my left inner pocket where a police officer might holster a revolver. It was now time to look under the hood. My kit includes a Leatherman's tool, a loupe, an earth magnet, a flashlight, a black light, and three or four things a savvy detective might construe as lock picking tools.

I continued to examine it in silence: all sides and from underneath, pulling both drawers, feeling for tool marks indiscernible to the eye and smelling surfaces for modern residues, scratching secondary wood surfaces with my fingernail and even stabbing it in a spot or two with the blade of the Leatherman to determine if what looked like chestnut was indeed chestnut or oak; a knife point will penetrate chestnut but not white oak.

David had relocated and was sitting patiently without comment by his wood-burning stove where he was nervously puffing on his meerschaum pipe as I went through my paces. Finally, I got up from underneath it, brushed myself off, and sat down beside him holding my palms to the heat of the stove.

"Have you purchased it yet?" I asked, still looking at the pie safe rather than at him.

He snapped his head in my direction and withdrew his figural pipe. "My gut knew it but my heart fell in love at first sight," he said in self-defense. "It's not right, is it?"

"Some of it is." I felt sorry for my friend. Without turning my head, I asked, "You want to guess or you want me to tell you?"

He sighed, plugged his pipe back into his gray beard, and then went over and put his right arm on top of it and stroked it as if it were his favorite horse. I knew what he was feeling. It's the way we collectors regard pedigreed pieces. He looked back at me through a puff of Davidoff red. "The picker said that it was a Fleming," he moaned to me.

I shook my head slowly, harrumphed, and deadpanned, "No, David, he probably said 'lemming.' " I opened the front door of his Vogelzang wood stove and shoved in a couple of pieces of hickory from a stack in a forty-gallon copper cauldron on the floor, then turned to face him, and smiled as the fire popped. I asked, "What's the damage?"

"Four grand," he puffed, holding the elbow of the arm holding his pipe in his maw. His body language made him look like a schoolboy in a principal's office.

I nodded once. "You know better than that, David."

"I shoulda called you sooner, darn it, but then it snowed and …yada, yada, yada."

"I would have been able to advise you had you sent me some pics, you know."

"That bad, is it?" He drew on his pipe making a gurgling sound without effect and then stuck its stem in the pencil pocket of his bib overalls with the ashes still in the bowl.

I prodded him a bit. "Greta knows how to email pics. She has a Blackberry."

"OK. Just tell me what's *not* right about it, and I'll deal with the picker later."

I kept my seat by the now too-hot stove, looked down at the worn floorboards, and closed my eyes to recite from memory what I had discovered by examining the pie safe in detail. I'm a little savant that way.

It's one of two of my uncanny traits: one, I never forget what I see and where it is when I see it – not ever. This does not, however, extend to remembering client names or where I have put the grocery list Emma sent with me to the store. The other trait that I seem to have, which I am not so sure about, is my tingling sensation – the divining thing going on with my small fingers. I experience a tingling sensation in my little fingers from time to time. My military docs attributed it to battle fatigue, but I knew it wasn't that because it began with puberty. Over time, I have come to associate the sensation with divining antiques and detecting trouble.

A tingle in one little finger usually signals that something old is inside of my sensory range. Two fingers tingling means that I'm very close or right on top of it. My memory trait never fails me, but the second trait is unreliable about half of the time, which is the same as a statistical equivalent. When I first noticed the sensation, Dr. Stevenson thought that it might be a rare form of synesthesia, which is when two senses are blended. An example of synesthesia would be smelling color or hearing smells. "Cilantro tastes like electricity to me," I told him, but at the time, he didn't think that I was serious. In recent years, synesthesia has become a widely accepted area of concentration in the academic and scientific community.

I didn't look at David. Instead, I looked at the offending piece of furniture and then at the floorboards at my feet. "David, it's a *made* piece." He knew what that meant. It was either a deliberate fake or it was reproduced to look like the real thing, but not necessarily with fraudulent intent. The extent of attention to detail in the execution of its manufacture usually determines if the creation of a piece is a deliberate attempt to fool the *initiated*, or not.

I explained: "Someone took two period Wythe tins off one piece and placed them on door frames from another period cased piece, also probably a pie safe but not a Fleming, by the looks of it, and the side tins are exact duplicates of the proper right front tin." I looked up from the warehouse floorboards to see David inspecting the wrong tin. "No David, the other one. The *proper* right."

"What's that mean?"

"The proper right headlight of an American car would be on the passenger's side."

The gears whirred inside of his head for a split second. "Oh. Got it." He knocked the ash out of his pipe against a vertical post holding up the building, harrumphed something unintelligible – which made me smile – and then re-stuffed his pipe from a round red tin he retrieved from his back pocket.

"What are you grinning at?" I asked.

"Nothin'." He walked back to the pie safe. I could tell that he was relishing my lesson despite the cost of his mistake. "What am I looking for in this *proper right* tin, dare I ask?" He was inspecting the pie safe's tin closely with his bifocals near the end of his nose.

I almost shrugged but chose to slightly raise one eyebrow instead. "The absence of rust and or patina *in all* of the holes." Over time, holes naturally fill with dust and rust on the cut edges.

David was bent over, looking at the holes. He turned his head to me. "You mean because he used an original tin as a template and re-punched through the original holes to make the side repro tins?"

"Correct, and the pierced holes should now be slightly larger, too, or very much larger if the perp wasn't careful."

He compared the piercings in the two front tins and then the two front tins to the two side tins. "This guy was careful. The holes are the same size but no longer plugged in the one front tin."

"That's the one he used to pattern the repro tins with. If he'd been very clever, he would have re-occluded the proper left one, and if he'd known enough to be that careful in covering his tracks, then he'd most likely have done them all."

David pointed with his pipe stem. "You mean, like with dirt?"

"Yeah, and shellac. Anything really. Over time the holes often get plugged."

"OK, so I have two antique tins in the front doors from some other cased piece. What about the rest of it?"

"It's a disassembled, cut down, larger piece of furniture. That's where the vertical and horizontal elements came from, and then there are bits and pieces from two other furniture pieces. For instance, the drawer fronts and their turned pulls are probably from a chest of drawers, and the backboards are from a pantry or porch ceiling in a late-Victorian house. Fleming would never have used those; they're from the 1890's. And the white pine was probably scavenged from a northern piece. Fleming would likely have used yellow pine, not white pine. Yellow pine and poplar were the most common secondary woods used in furniture in the mid-Atlantic backcountry, not white pine, although it is possible." David had relit his pipe and was standing obliquely so he could see the backboards and me at the same time.

He nodded. "Yeah, I see it now. But I don't see how he made the case."

"The stiles were heavier at one time." Stiles are vertical elements, usually corner posts. "Notice the difference in color on the two inside planes of the stiles when compared to the two outside surfaces."

"Wouldn't that be normal? I mean, its inside surfaces would be less exposed to UV light than the outside."

"True, but the difference here is from cutting a large square post into quarters resulting in each quarter having two fresh-cut surfaces, two original patina surfaces with one old edge and three new sharp edges. Notice the inside taper of the four legs; it is most noticeable below the inferior anterior and lateral rails external to the case. The three new edges are all too sharp to be original to the 1830's; they all should have wear consistent with age, from scuffing, mop slaps, and animal action."

David gave me a, "Huh?" look. I clarified the professional appraiser's terminology and pointed at the same time. "These are the lateral rails here on the sides, and this front rail is the anterior, and the term inferior means lower or bottom as opposed to upper or top, which would be called superior."

I could tell from his expression that he hadn't committed the terms to memory.

He replied, "You think he got the stiles from cutting down a bed?"

"Maybe, or from a big armoire. The wood is period and so are the tool marks. He used two different hand planes, a mortise gauge, and a chisel."

"So, he's a crook?"

I shrugged. "I don't know who you got this from, and I know that you're not going to tell me."

"I have to protect my sources," he said.

"Yeah, I know, and I respect that."

David cocked his head and added, "Though this source might need protection from me right now. You think he made this to deceive?"

"Maybe, or maybe he doesn't know any more than you do. Whoever did this was clever though. It's a B-minus on my grading scale."

"Only a B-minus?"

"And probably an American, probably from Tennessee."

"Good guess. Have you ever been fooled?"

I grimaced. "Oh, sure. There are plenty of people who are this good and a few in these parts who are as good as they get. It's been years now, but I once took a round tavern table with four tapered legs to a Brit I know here in Virginia, who will remain nameless by the way. The table had had its ankle stretcher cut away 150 years ago or so. I wanted them replaced so I could resell it and get more for it."

David waved the stem of his pipe. "Did you disclose it when you sold it?"

"Yes, of course," I replied. "It would have been an ethical violation had I not."

"OK, good. I figured as much."

"So, when I asked him, the Brit, how much it would cost, he gave me two prices: $750 or $2500."

"Jeez! That's quite a spread."

I nodded. "My reaction exactly. So I asked him why the big difference and he told me, 'For $750 you won't be able to tell that it has had its stretchers replaced.'"

"And for $2500?" David asked.

"He replied, '*I* won't be able to tell that they have been replaced.' " David laughed and I laughed with him.

"Did he give you examples of the difference?"

"I asked him that, too, of course, because I was baffled, and he told me that he would compensate for natural wood shrinkage over time, mimicking it, which makes the joints loose and the pegs proud, and he'd spend a considerable time on patina, like applying fly speck crap by the hundreds using a single horse hair, and he'd apply spider webs and mud dauber nests, and traces of mud dauber nests over nests, and stuff like that."

David shook his head in wonderment. "That's incredible!"

"I know."

We heard Emma and Greta come in through the back door. They were making shivering noises as they immediately made their way through the furniture to the stove. "What are you boys up to?" Greta asked sweetly.

David looked at me, withdrew his pipe, and turned to the girls. "We're just swapping war stories, that's all, honey."

I looked over at Emma to see if she was displaying another new acquisition that she might have bought from Greta's jewelry showcase, but I didn't see anything that I didn't recognize. "And what have you all been up to?" I asked, about the same moment that I noticed that the Jensen was now on Greta's wrist.

The two of them looked at each other and giggled. "Nothing," they said in unison.

6 Lexington

The Gees asked us if we'd care to join them for
dinner at a local Viennese restaurant just off Interstate
81, but we expressed our regrets and soon were on
the road again. It had warmed up a bit, enough for
the light snow to melt on the trees and the back roads
to have been mostly cleared. By early afternoon, after
a few more stops that proved fruitless, we made it to
Lexington before the sun set. I waited for Emma to
tell me that she had sold the bracelet to Greta, and
when I didn't bring it up after ten minutes or so, she
did.

"How much do you think I got for it?"
"You mean the Jensen?"
"Of course, Amor."
"Four hundred."
"Five," she squealed.
"Good job, Pretzel," I smiled.
"I love this job," she cooed.

***

Lexington, Virginia never ceases to charm us.
Rockbridge County is beautiful and the former home
county of more than a few celebrities most Americans
recognize by name, if they remember their history.
Sam Huston was born here, Stonewall Jackson taught
here at VMI before the war, and Robert E. Lee was
president of Washington University, later Washington

& Lee University, after the "War of Northern Aggression," as some people still remember it. The numerous little main street shops, the antebellum and Victorian architecture, and the mountain air make a perfect place for retirees to settle, and they do, in droves. It's one of our favorite places to visit and we've even considered moving to the area.

By the time we got to the room, my dogs were barking so loudly that I was afraid they'd wake the neighborhood. Despite my fatigue, I began my usual routine, which Emma complains is for no other purpose than to drive her crazy: I always arrange my toiletries in size order at the sink in a manner that would have made my drill sergeant proud. Unwittingly, as soon as I flop down on the bed to watch The Weather Channel, Emma begins *her* standard behavior pattern which drives *me* crazy; she talks on her cell and paces back and forth in front of the television creating a strobe-like effect. I compensate by pouring myself three fingers of Woodford Reserve over the last mountain of ice on the planet, and then I remembered that the front desk clerk had given us walking directions to a small restaurant nearby which had a European menu and purportedly did not use MSG, something I am allergic to. After what seemed like a half hour, Emma declared herself ready.

***

The meal was excellent and the wine even better, Emma thought, though I had none. Afterwards, we walked leisurely back to the hotel a different way. An old storefront with a new business sign caught our attention – an antiques storefront, of course. Naturally, at that hour it was closed, but the window display was very intriguing. It consisted of manly-man items in an arrangement that could have passed for a Ralph Lauren photo shoot, only better. My little fingers were drowning the symphony of my barking feet, but I couldn't tell which object was attracting their attention because the display was so diverse.

There were two old big-game single-shot breechloaders, old photographs of white hunters in the Belgian Congo when King Leopold was wreaking havoc, pith helmets, knives, cartridge belts, old books, you name it. It was one of the most fascinating displays of testosterone accouterments that we had ever seen in one window. It made Emma 'goose bumpy' and I couldn't take my eyes off of the arrangement. We made a point of jotting down the contact info in my Blackberry: the business hours, telephone number, and website of the shop. On the way back, we jabbered about what had been in the window and speculated about the possible sleepers that we'd find the next day. Neither of us slept very well because of those expectations.

***

We awoke early. By six, I had pulled on some clothes. Fifteen minutes later I was back from my coffee detail carrying the room tray piled high with huge Styrofoam cups, pastries, fruit, juice, and the morning paper. Emma had checked our email while I was gone. No overnight-website-sales, but our eBay posts were ratcheting up slowly. "No home runs yet," she chirped.

I usually let her do up her own coffee first: one fake cream, one brown sugar. Reaching between Emma and her caffeine early in the A.M. is not a wise move. However, two or three swallows are all it takes before her urge to amputate subsides and she remembers what last tactic we were on from the day before.

"Did you dream last night?" she asked.

"Not that I can remember."

"Too bad. Humor's the best way to start a day."

"Very funny." I rustled the local paper, The *News Gazette*, looking for yard sale opportunities while she munched and drank her coffee.

"Amor, why don't you give that shop a call?" she asked.

"It's too early. And the store hours are intermittent. 'By Chance,' remember? He probably doesn't come in 'till afternoon." As usual, the coffee was disappointing. I suppose it would have been all right to shave with it, the coffee, just because it was hot, but otherwise it was worthless. I missed Major Dickason.

"Call him anyway," insisted Emma, "leave a message on his machine. Besides, he might be an early bird." She can be annoyingly persistent.

"Oh, alright. Jeez, it's only 7:30," I said, shaking my head. I punched in the numbers that I had pecked into my cell the evening before. It rang four times before the machine picked up. I looked over at her. "See?" I said, "His machine came on , and it's telling me the same information that was on the door to his shop. It's too early." Emma sniffed. I left my name and phone number on the machine, and said that we'd be in town for the day.

MARK CLAY GROVE

"Well, maybe he'll call us back before we leave. Wasn't it open today?" she asked. Remembering the store window, I confirmed that it was and then urged her to get a move on so that we could see a little of the sights before leaving town. An hour later, just as we were picking up our gear to walk out, my cell rang.

"Hello," a southern drawl said, "this is Bubba Baxter from Southern Squire Antiques on Preston, are you the gentleman who called and left a message?"

Some southern accents are music to my ears, but not this one. "Yes, thanks for returning my call. We admired your window display last night. We're dealers from Madison, Virginia. Would it be possible to open for us now before we leave town?" I asked.

"Sure. Me and some of my buddies are at the shop now having coffee and Twinkies. Come on by."

I looked at Emma and said into the phone, "Gee, thanks, Bubba; we'll be there shortly," and then hung up.

Emma could sense that I was up to something; she looked up from what she was doing and said, "What?"

"Emma," I said facetiously, "I think you're going to like the proprietor of that nice manly-man shop."

"With a name like Bubba, I doubt it," she said.

"Yeah, that's his name alright," I said laughing, "and he sounds like a Bubba, too. Yep, you're going to like him, Emma." Emma is originally from Lima, Peru. Some of our North American accents are less pleasing to her ear than others, as she's told me on more than a few occasions in her sweet lilting Spanish, and I agree.

I met Emma on Match dot-com when I was temporarily attached as a liaison to Pakistan Special Forces in the second half of 2000. She was living in Harrisonburg, Virginia and I was freezing my ass off in Marine BDU's somewhere classified in the Hindu Kush. I read her profile online and it was love at first read. After corresponding for a couple of weeks, I finally convinced her that I was the real deal. It was another month before I could get to a landline. When she spoke for the first time I nearly dropped the receiver; I recognized her voice. Hers was the same voice that had been helping me learn Spanish by immersion for the past six months at Rosetta Stone.

7 A Day to Remember

We kept in touch almost daily via email and telephone but it was another six months before I could secure leave. I took her to my favorite resort on the Riviera Maya, The Grand Luxxe. Over the course of the next six months our relationship bloomed into what it has become – a natural bond. My divvy sense confirmed that it was meant to be. Emma was who I had been looking for in this life. Sometimes when I observe her as she lies sleeping or when I watch her moving about the kitchen, I muse: all I had to do was straddle a mountain ridge between Pakistan and Afghanistan to find her. I'm glad I did.

September is my birth month and my brother's, too. I always schedule my dental and medical checkups in September *and* satisfy part of my Individual Ready Reserve commitment, which can be anywhere my harebrained Uncle Sam wishes. In 2001, a General at The Pentagon selected me to be his gofer for a week. It was the first time that I had ever worked for one of the Joint Chiefs. Nothing eventful happened that week. He just needed help moving paper from one side of his desk to the other. He dismissed me late Thursday afternoon before he left on a scheduled junket to NATO headquarters.

I checked out of the BOQ and drove down from Washington very early Friday morning to my shop south of Madison on Route 29. There I quickly picked up a few belongings and rushed off again. I crossed the junction in front of my store and drove past "Spaceship Sheetz," as its critics call it, and headed due west on scenic Route 230 with the blush of a rising sun in my rearview. A few miles further, around a bend in the two-lane road, the thriving metropolis of Wolftown suddenly appeared on the horizon atop a hill, like a Madison version of Calvary. Ah, what memories it evoked of my early youth. This wide place on the Appian consists of Mr. Kite's Ham factory, two mom-and-pop country stores, the Cash 'n Carry, and Wolftown Mercantile, and about three dozen modest homes surrounded by pasture framed by forested mountains in the distance, which was where I was headed. As a boy I rode the five up-and-down miles on my rusty bicycle to buy Swisher Sweet cigars, fireballs, and bubblegum here in Wolftown so that Mr. Hood at Hood Store wouldn't tell on me; Hood Store was three miles closer to home. The candy and gum were to mask the smell of the tobacco but the ghastly combination made me sicker than a dog. I must have smelled like a brothel on Saturday night when I returned home, but my parents never said a word. The state of my tummy and color of my gills seemed punishment enough, they told me thirty years later.

Now, over the new bridge spanning the Rapidan River, I drove my gold-colored Volvo. On up the hill I reminisced as I passed Hood and turned down the Old Kinderhook to the family farm, Spring Hill. It was too early to call ahead; I knew they wouldn't be up yet. Since my folks were unaware of my arrival, I ran out to the henhouse to fetch a basket of fresh eggs, and by the time Mom and Dad appeared in the kitchen, I had the coffee was ready and the vittles spread out on a checkered cloth fit for a king. I briefed Dad, who had retired from the Air Force, and assured Mom that my mission this day was to spend time with Emma before shipping out Monday for a week of specialized training at Camp Lejeune. They enthusiastically agreed to tend the shop in my absence, which is our family business SOP.

I hugged the old folks good-bye and drove over the Blue Ridge as I have thousands of times. When a student, I commuted this route to James Madison University in Harrisonburg via Routes 230 and 33, but this time it was different; my pinkies were twitching to beat the band. Something was going to happen, they signaled. I presumed it was just the usual jitters before training, because a few days earlier I had shrugged off an early warning from a craggy old warrant officer I know at The Pentagon. He informed me that next week I'd be training with a SEAL team, which I told him I'd done before, but then he went on and divulged that we were to do "a new version of HALO which includes wearing some sort of flying squirrel suit," he whispered. And then he chuckled, "Bring an extra set of gonads, Sir, you're going to need 'em." I didn't know what he was talking about, except that all High Altitude-Low Opening parachute jumps always had its dangers. I told him that crusty old warrants from the Crimean War tend to exaggerate. He just guffawed knowingly and ambled off to the quartermaster.

But what I felt in my phalanges wasn't training jitters. It felt greater than that. It felt big, real big. Something was about to change my life and the others around me, and my perception of whatever "it" was went deeper than the norm. All six of my senses seemed more acute. As I drove the downhill side of big, Saddleback Mountain, *this time* I noticed the proverbial roses. Everything caught my attention. I consciously savored each mile, noticed every bird, every tree, and even every cloud in the blue sky. The extent and depth of their intensity affected me.

I almost cried.

A sudden ring in my shirt pocket nearly startled me off of the road. It was a call from Emma. She had saved me yet again. "Amor, where are you?" she said over the speaker. She sounded harried and on edge, and I knew that she probably was. This was at the height of immigration, legal and otherwise. Rockingham County is known for its poultry production and Spanish-speakers from all over Latin America worked in that industry. Many needed Emma's translation and interpretation assistance for various reasons. She had become the go-to gal for many of their concerns and she was completely swamped with work. Literally, during this period she worked from 0600 to midnight every day of the week – kind of like we Marines.

I snorted back to reality, "What? Not even an 'I love you, Amor' before inquiring about my coordinates?" I complained.

She giggled, "I love you Amor, but I don't have time for, how you say? Little talk?"

"Small talk," I supplied.

"That's what I said," she replied impatiently. "I have a crisis. My hot water doesn't work. Would you please fix it for me, Amor?"

Emma's office was on the eighth floor of a high-rise building. Surely they had a dedicated man for that sort of thing, I thought. I had forty-eight hours of freedom before I had to shove off. Plumbing of this sort is not what I had in mind.

I whined, "Tell Wilber. He's just down the hall from you. He's the owner of the building, for Pete's sake."

"*Amor*, at *home* is where I have no hot water."

I wasn't thinking clearly.

"Oh, of course. Alright. I'll head there first."

She made kissing noises in my ear. "I love you, Amor, bye."

She hung up before I had time to say anything else.

Emma's pale green stucco house was on a golf course with a near view of two ponds, a full up-close view of Virginia's equivalent of the Matterhorn, Massanutten Mountain, and a 180-degree view of the Skyline Drive atop the expansive Blue Ridge Mountains in the distance. That's the scenery I was relishing on the way over, and now it was in my rearview mirror as I passed McGaheysville with the Matterhorn on my right. Emma's house was in a new subdivision at the Cross Keys junction on Route 33 up ahead. I was glad that she had called me before rather than after I had passed it so that I wouldn't have to backpedal.

I hung a left and wound my way around the neighborhood streets to her pale pastel house which the neighbors had had a collective coronary over because Emma had *not* painted it beige as all of the other new homes were in the subdivision, and for that matter, most of Rockingham County. When she first built it, she said that the neighbors were aghast at the color. "I think it looks just fine," I told her, "and if it had been me and I had known what their reaction was going to be, I might have painted it fire engine red." We both laughed.

But now I was not laughing. I had plumbing to do and I'd rather be doing just about anything else, and so I did what I usually do under similarly unpleasant circumstances: I look to see if the darn thing is plugged in – and it was – and then I call someone, which I did. Problem solved, or so I thought.

The plumber showed up by himself, diagnosed her dilemma as a faulty hot water tank, and promptly dashed off in the direction of the nearest home improvement store for a replacement, while I waited patiently reading *Neon Rain* by James Lee Burke. My fingers continued their little fandango, so I figured the hot water crisis wasn't the issue. Long story short, on his return I had to change into my holey-knee jeans and dirty gardening sneakers to help him remove the old tank which must have weighed as much as a Bradley Fighting Vehicle. By the time we had loaded the leaking majesty upon his truck, I looked like a trampled jockey on a thoroughbred race track. That's when Emma called with yet another emergency.

"Amor, the Ford dealer still has my car. It needs something. I can't have it back until after five o'clock. Please, would you take me to the insane asylum," she said.

My natural response: "Huh?"

"*Please*, I have a hearing to attend. It's important in a political way."

"Sure," I acquiesced. "Why not? I'll try almost anything once."

"Come get me in one hour, please," she said, and then hung up. I looked at and flexed my hands. My phalanges weren't twanging with any greater fervor than before her call, so I figured something had gotten lost in translation and that I shouldn't worry any more than I usually do.

I washed up but didn't bother to change, drove into town and parked the car in the metered lot across the street from Emma's building. *There's plenty of time*, I thought to myself, before going to the nuthouse, *and I'm right here and the court is right there. Why not reconnoiter?* And so I walked across the square to the County courthouse to inquire about the legal necessaries of matrimony, which the two of us had been discussing since The Riviera Maya. Emma's intention was more immediate than mine. My plan was to tie the knot in about six months on February 14th so that *I* might always remember the annual event. A logical assumption, my male Marine brain had concluded and I agreed with it.

And so I casually made my way to the appropriate office where I was informed by one of the assistants to the County Clerk that all it took any longer to become married in The Old Dominion was $20 and my John Hancock on a form that looked to be no greater in dimension than the ubiquitous W2.

"You're kidding, right, Ma'am?" I asked, surprised.

She smiled, "Nope. That's all there is to it."

"OK, let's do it," said I, as I handed the young lady a wadded $20 bill that I had removed from the bottom of my front jeans pocket. She sniffed her disdain for currency in such a state, holding it by a corner as if it were a mouse as she dropped it in a drawer with denominations of the flatter sort. I filled out and signed the W2 lookalike and handed it back to her, whereupon she unceremoniously hammered it with a hand-held, red ink stamper-thingy that all officials the world over seem to be in charge of, and then ripped off the yellow copy with a flare of clerical power and tossed it into a wooden inbox meant for just this single purpose. She then returned her attention to me, the mouseketeer of money, and was about to shove the top copy in my direction when she realized who I was from a glance at our names on the form, and then all hell broke loose. She let out a whoop and a squeal with zeal the way I'd imagine she might have if I'd given her a ticket to see Oprah.

"You're Emma's *boyfriend*!"

She exclaimed at a decibel level so great that it actually startled me, and no doubt also most of the geese on the ponds across the county. I was instantly aghast, positively mortified from embarrassment and momentarily so petrified by her sudden transformation that I was made speechless, and I, who had not a qualm in my usually un-quavering body that could easily address Congress or bellow the National Anthem at the Super Bowl at the drop of a hat. *Surely*, I thought, the heat in my face will set off the overhead sprinklers! But, alas, from much practice being around Emma and her Latina *camaradas* who all lack even the smallest modicum of self-consciousness, I soon brought my thermal radiation under control, and croaked modestly, "Yes, ma'am, I am."

"So, *you're* the famous war hero, Major Dawes!" another female in the office burst out from the other side of the cavernous room. Soon I had a flock of admirers plying me with questions from where I had been in the world, why I wasn't in dress blues instead of the rags I had on, what I liked for breakfast, drank at dinner, and so on. Even a squad of uniformed male bailiffs huddled in an overwatch position to one side. Obviously, Emma's frequent involvement in courthouse proceedings as an interpreter had won her many friends. Emma works at this and other courts across the state. She's very popular and a well-respected professional in her field. Before she became a certified interpreter, she held an executive position in the local cathedral and from that position many across the Valley got to know her well.

Time was running short I realized. "Thank you all, folks, but Emma needs me to take her somewhere, I know not where." I glanced at the tiger's eye *Philip Patek* wrist watch on my arm, and said, "Sorry everyone, love to stay longer and thank you for your help, but I must get a move on."

The same official who only a moment earlier demonstrated impatience grabbed the sleeve of my polo shirt and looked up at me adoringly. "Major," she cooed.

I tugged on my sleeve and looked at her over my shoulder. "Ma'am?" I sighed.

She gripped tighter and wet her lips. "Wilber Harrington has the authority to marry people," she told me in the midst of a covey of adorers.

Puzzled, I regarded her talons clutching my sleeve before returning my gaze to her. "I've known Wilber for years. Why would he?"

She nodded. "The court designated him at a time when there were a lot of requests. So now he can perform civil weddings," she verily cooed her response.

"I see. OK, w-well uh thank you, ma'am, very much," I stammered and extracted myself from government control. "I'll keep that in mind. Now, I really must not keep Emma waiting. Surely you know how she is when she's in a hurry."

And they all did, too, because Emma works at this and other courts across the state. She's very popular and a well-respected professional in her field. Before she became a certified interpreter, she held an executive position in the local cathedral and from that position many across the Valley got to know her well.

I almost backed out of the courthouse to get away. Luckily my cell rang as I made my escape and it was Emma. "I'm leaving the courthouse now," I said, before she could even speak.

***

"Where are we going?" I asked, as I pointed the car east in the direction of I81.

"Western State Hospital, Staunton," was her answer as I enviously watched her do more than one task at a time.

"You have a commitment hearing to do, you said?" I inquired.

"Yes Amor," she replied but continued doing something administrative with various paper forms and her phone. "He's in solitary and wants to be released into the general population inside the hospital. There is a solidarity group in D.C. trying to get him his freedom. They are pressuring the media to force the politicians to act. It's become an international cause."

"Good grief. You mean they want him out of the hospital altogether?"

"No, no just out of his padded room so that he can talk and interact with the other patients."

I shrugged a whatever. "What can I do to help you, Babe?"

She shook her head, "Amor, you *are* helping me by driving me there so that I can conclude this other business that I have here," she motioned to what was in her lap, "and make a few calls on the way to the hearing. When we arrive, just wait in the car, please."

"OK."

"Do you have something to read?"

"Yes. *Neon Rain.*"

"Haven't you read it before?"

"Yeah, but I like how Burke writes. I've read his *Black Cherry Blues* four times."

"Wasn't that one an *Edgar* winner?"

I nodded, "Yep, and *Neon Rain* should have been, too, I think."

We arrived on time to what appeared to be the 1950's institutional equivalent of a brick Quonset hut. Emma pecked me on the cheek as I pulled up to the curb. Other professionals who she recognized as a judge and a psychiatrist were in discussion in front of the building. I waved bye as she egressed the car and then I rolled the station wagon around to the side under the shade of a tree with a view of the entrance and its wire-grated doors.

Hearings usually take minutes. This one exceeded the norm. After reading three chapters I became impatient. Twenty more minutes passed and suddenly a Virginia State Trooper's blue and gray cruiser screeched to a halt in front of the building with its blue strobe lights on. Two large uniformed troopers dashed to the entrance and were immediately let inside.

That, I figured, must be my cue.

I got out of the car, ran over and pulled on the locked door. No one let me in so I peered through the heavy wire grate bolted over the glass to see a dozen or so people milling around Emma who was spread-eagled on the floor with a bandage on her chest as large as my open hand. The two troopers inside leapt to restrict my frantic pounding on the door but from her supine position I could see from her actions that she was explaining to the trooper who I was. They stood down but still, they viewed me with suspicion and wouldn't let me in. After a minute, however, they did let Emma out with a white-clad orderly holding onto each of her trembling arms.

"*What* happened?" I croaked. Her makeup was streaming, her hair was awry, and the bandage on her chest was stained red. The troopers must have sensed that I was on the edge because they stood within arm's reach on either side of *me*.

"He *attacked* me, Amor!" she said, almost in tears.

I clenched both fists. "Who attacked you?"

"The patient," she whined.

Stunned, I just looked at her uncomprehendingly with my mouth open and then around at the others who appeared embarrassed and wouldn't make eye contact. The two troopers shrugged. One of them explained, "We arrived *after* the fact."

One of the other professionals said in their collective defense, "It happened so fast!"

Emma explained quickly as I helped her toward the car because she could see I was about to jump on someone's case. "Amor, he pretended that he couldn't hear from inside his room, so he had me come closer."

I was puzzled. "What? He was inside his cell when he attacked you?"

"Yes Amor," Emma continued explaining, as we walked to the car with my arm around her. "When I came close enough, he reached through the food tray slot in the door and grabbed me by my front. I dropped my Blackberry," she showed me the disassembled parts in one hand, "and my pearl necklace went flying all over." She showed me a handful of loose pearls in the other hand. "Look. He tore my favorite blue dress and scratched my chest," she sobbed.

I felt helpless as I opened her car door and assisted her gingerly. The other professionals had disappeared. "What can I do?" I asked as I got behind the wheel.

"I need a tetanus injection," she replied.

I blinked. "You mean a tetanus shot?"

"Yes, Amor. We need to go to my GP in Harrisonburg."

***

By the time we got through the doc's office, it must have been 1400 hours. We were starved. Emma had a fresh, more professional-looking bandage that detached less often than the original as we were seated in our favorite Mexican restaurant, El Charro's. The staff swarmed Emma and me when they saw what state of disrepair their beloved Emma was in. Salted margaritas appeared without asking and salsa with corn chips. Since I was driving I drank a third of mine. Emma had hers and the rest of mine. By the time we had finished our late lunch, it was a quarter after four when I got her back to her office. Again Emma was swarmed, this time by her half-dozen coed beauties. I stepped back, leaned against the doorjamb, and watched them spoil her. A couple of young guys who had been dallying in the hall *because* of Emma's beauties found other places to be when I gave them a stern look.

Wilber stepped out into the hall to see what all the commotion was. He recognized me and sauntered over. I began explaining the day's ordeal as we shook hands.

"Oh, Wilber, you have a minute?" I motioned to his office.

"Yeah, sure. Come on down."

Wilber is one of the local real estate magnates in the county and an avid collector of silver jewelry, as am I, and Art Deco stuff. Neither of us wears jewelry other than a watch, but we collect it and appreciate it for the miniature sculpture that it is. I tend to collect Spratling and Jensen. Wilber prefers American Indian and obscure designer jewelry like Chayat from the first half of the 20th century. Whenever either of us finds something excellent that might be of interest to the other, we buy it and use it to swap. At the moment swapping wasn't on my mind, I told him.

"What *is* on your mind, Charles?" he asked, as I sat in a brown leather deco club chair by the side window next to his desk. In the distance I could see the Appalachians and down below I heard a siren Doppler away from us.

"Earlier t-today," I stuttered, "before all of this drama, I was told by a clerk across the way that you have the a-authority to perform ceremonies of the matrimonial type." He nodded as I said, "I didn't know that."

"Yes, indeed that is true," he confirmed. The twinkle in his eye corroborated what my phalanges were already signaling me: that intel had recently been tweeted to Wilber from one of the a little clerical birds from across the way. I wouldn't be surprised if he had actually heard the one's exclamations, she had been so loud. "Have you filled out the standard form at the Clerk's Office?"

"Yes," I replied.

"Let's have a look."

I extracted it from my wallet and handed it to Wilber across his mahogany desk. He scanned it briefly and asked, "So, when's the big day?"

I shrugged. "I don't know. Monday I ship out for a week of training at Lejeune. I had in mind next Valentine's Day – "

He cut me off. "How about now?"

My attention snapped to him, but all I managed was a noise, "...uhh-buuu…"

"No time like the present!" he cheerfully exclaimed. "Hey, you might bite the bullet on this training exercise. You never know."

I gulped and knew I looked like a cloven-hoofed creature in headlights and that I had become a blathering idiot all of a sudden. I gazed at Wilber who had steered hapless mammals to the slaughter on numerous occasions. My mind was bleating like Bambi as my mouth turned to cotton. He was measuring me, like a haberdasher on a tailor's plinth. "Well? What do you say we ask Emma, huh?"

I croaked, "OK," stood and allowed him to steer me from behind to his open office door where he encouraged me with a poke of his elbow. I hollered, "*Emma!*"

We heard the chatter of the beauties cease. Suddenly a chair screeched and Emma peered from her doorway. "What?" she said, and then sipped on a straw. All I could see of her was her head and shoulders and half of her white bandage as she leaned into the hallway.

I asked timidly, "You wanna get married?"

She blinked, took a gurgle, and replied, "When?"

"Right now," I said confidently.

Wilber was next to me. With a gesture he waved her over.

She disappeared.

I looked at Wilber. He looked at me. We shrugged in unison and then we turned in the direction of an ensemble of giggles followed by the sight of Emma and her trailing entourage striding towards me wearing the biggest margarita grin an exultant man had ever seen. Despite all of the drama, September 7th 2001 was the happiest and most memorable day in my life.

Still, on Monday I shipped out for my HALO exercises.

And on Tuesday my pinkies finally stopped tingling, and I knew why. A day later I learned that the desk that I had been flying at The Pentagon only the Friday before was ground zero for American Airlines Flight 77.

8 Flying Tigers

The pins and needles sensation in my little phalanges intensified as the overhead clangor-bell sounded when we opened the door to the narrow but deep antebellum period store. Boisterous conversation near the rear of the shop came to an abrupt halt. There was a faint smell of coal smoke in the air from a stove. I noticed in the back of the store a vertical round tin pipe take a right angle into a flue in the red brick wall, where silence now reigned. Adjustable stacked-board shelves on all three sides went up the walls, from floor to nearly the ceiling, behind low yellow pine counters. Victorian glass showcases that once displayed islands of dry goods filled the space between the counters. It reminded me of the general store in the old Gunsmoke TV show episodes.

We knew that we were expected and we had heard the bell that had announced our arrival, but we waited momentarily near the door to be greeted.

Someone had converted the purpose of the store from what had no doubt been a dry goods store back in the day, to an antique and vintage weapons store. Inventory was nicely arranged, but clutter had begun lapping up the sides of the counters, which is a sure sign that the manly-man concept had been going on for some time. I suppose that the store had gone unnoticed by us because the proprietor didn't advertise or we would have checked it out immediately, and too, it was off our usual beaten scouting path.

Most of what was on display was vintage and antique: sporting long guns, edged weapons, advertising, and there was a huge amount of dug Civil War items, which I've never been able to appreciate. About seventy-five percent of the overall collection followed a hunting-related theme. I knew right away that it would be tough to find any hunting-related sleeper in there, but he might have hoarded things outside of his primary area of expertise. And that's what we always look for: sleepers.

One of our strategies is to stop at specialty shops like this one where we expect the 'Packrat Syndrome' to prevail. Chronic collectors never throw anything out; they just keep on collecting and collecting, hence the Packrat Syndrome. Bubba's shop turned out to be no different than ninety percent of the other specialty shops that we had been in over the years throughout the country and abroad. By shopping such places we'd found some drop-dead killer sleepers.

Noisily, a huge man emerged from what probably was a back office or storeroom and walked the length of the store behind the counter to greet us. When the curtain to the back opened, I noticed a clutch of old men in varying states of physical disrepair. Five pairs of bloodshot eyes swiveled in our direction without actually making eye contact with us. Me, they gave a onceover and then ignored. But they lingered on Emma, and seemed pretty much intent on visually piercing through Emma's cashmere sweater; the ones who were able to, that is. She has always been rather popular because of her wit and accent, but it looked like these good ol' boys had already developed a shine for her without benefit of hearing her speak. One struggled tying the curtains back, another geezer was frantically cleaning his spectacles, and I saw a third old timer insert his dentures, and then smile at Emma.

"Hello there!" the proprietor striding toward us called out. He was red-faced and morbidly obese. Sweat stood out on his forehead. His old multi-pocketed fishing vest sported NRA patches: Emma's least favorite nonprofit organization. "What kin we do you in for, folks?" he bellowed good-naturedly. Without looking, I imagined Emma rolling her eyes.

I was born in the UK, but I grew up in Delaware where I absorbed my neutral American accent. But I also spent some of my middle formative years in rural Virginia after Dad retired from the Air Force. I was used to the many accents of The Old South, and when I'm around one, I 'revert back to my Confederate roots,' or so Emma says. "Nonsense," I tell her each time. "I haven't the foggiest idea what you mean. I was born an Englishman. *Y'all* don't know what you're talking about."

She ignores me, mostly.

I stepped toward Bubba and informed him, "We're the Dawes'." I made a back-and-'forth hand motion to include Emma as we shook hands. "We called earlier from the hotel here in Lexington." Emma stood behind me. I could sense her apprehension at being in this boy's club. She crossed her arms under her breasts and put me between her and the trolls.

"I thought it was you-all," he said. "Come on in and have a look-see. When you have a question just holler at me and I'll be glad ta hep y'all." The other five pairs of eyes ignored me entirely to follow Emma. I poked around the shop in one direction and Emma went another as Bubba answered the phone a couple of times, all the while talking with a Twinkie in his mouth. I slowly worked my way around the place taking it all in: his prices, his descriptions, and the details, stealing with my eyes as my noble Austrian grandmother called it. Smart dealers learn from their mistakes and do their best to minimize risk. It's not just a fundamental tenant of business, 'it is just good common sense,' as my dad used to say. Risk is a great motivator. You wouldn't believe the fortunes I've gone through to earn my stripes in this business. After about five minutes in his store, I could tell I was wearing more stripes than Bubba. Under one island counter I spotted a footlocker with a patch sewn on brown leather inside, which made my paresthesia kick in big-time.

I looked his way. "Hey Bubba, what's in the wooden box over here?" I asked. He thundered over, shaking the whole building, and replied, "Well, let's have a look, Mr. Dawes." He pulled out the box, lifted it effortlessly onto the countertop, and invited me to have a look inside for myself while he stood by. I was correct in my initial impression that the brown leather was a WWII Army Air Corps aviator's jacket, though I wouldn't have guessed I'd be lucky enough to find one sporting a "Flying Tigers" patch. I knew that Walt Disney had designed this particular version. The wooden box, as it turned out, was a standard-issue footlocker filled with all the paraphernalia of a well-decorated CBI Tiger, a squadron in the China-Burma-India Theater of operations during the Second World War.

A poker face is essential at times like these and I'm a master at it. "Bubba, what'll you take for the box and contents?" My pulse leaped as my mind calculated and my hands committed themselves to a washing motion for several moments before I noticed.

He took a step closer, peeked inside unnecessarily, and said, "Well, I don't rightly know. What'll you give me for it, sir?"

"You're the seller, Bubba. So what's it going to be?" I tossed the ball back into his court as a matter of protocol. The seller always sets the price because it would be unethical for a dealer to make an offer to a seller; an offer is a de facto appraisal, and to buy something one has appraised would be a conflict of interest. This conundrum is less of an issue when the haggle is between dealers of equal stature, but still, he knew that I knew that setting the price was incumbent upon him, not me.

"I ain't had it too long and I ain't done all the research on it either, who it mighta belonged to and all, but I do know that bomber jackets fetch a pretty penny."

"Yes," I said, "and I'm prepared to pay a fair price. So what's it going to be?" I repeated calmly without showing anxiety.

"Four grand," he blurted out. I was sure that he was fishing. His red handkerchief couldn't keep up with his heavy perspiration. He swabbed his face and neck constantly.

I rubbed my whiskers thoughtfully. Emma was off rummaging by herself to one side. "We're a bit short on cash at the moment, Bubba. May I take a photo of it and send it off to a colleague?"

He nodded. "Sure. Take all the photos you want, Mr. Dawes."

"What's your best price for the footlocker and contents, Bubba, very best?"

While he contemplated, I took a few pics of the green box, the jacket, the patch on the jacket, some of the paper ephemera, and other things and emailed them off to a buddy of mine who might appreciate all of it as an archive. That's what something like this is called; an archive is a bunch of stuff that is all related to one person or event.

Bubba pondered a while and responded, "My best price is three grand. That's it."

"Let me see what my buddy thinks of it," I replied.

"No problem, Mr. Dawes," he said. "Take all the time you need."

Emma had watched from afar. She walked over to have a look but in a way that kept me between her and the line of sight of the five goobers. They hadn't relented on staring at her from their seats by the stove. She sensed something big was in the works. One thing about Emma that endears her to me, she never interferes at times like this.

She whispered, "How are your hands, Amor?"

I stuffed them in my back pockets and replied, "I'm OK, Babe," I whispered back.

"You're not acting OK," she signaled with a lift of her chin.

"One other thing caught my eye, Bubba, over there; the old tintype in the window." I motioned in the direction of the hard image that was propped upright; its leather case just barely opened enough for me to see it. Photographs on metal, glass, and ceramics are referred to as *hard images*. A friend of mine from my college days taught me all about photos. It was one of the first categories that I learned to collect.

"Oh yeah, that's a really big one, iddenit?" He handed me the full-plate leather case closed. When I opened it, the image stunned me as I realized I was looking at the best daguerreotype – not a tintype – that I'd seen in at least ten years. It was a J.H. Whitehurst whole-plate, housed in a fine leather case featuring an image of a small boy holding a toy rifle and a girl clutching a pull-toy horse in one hand and a fancy doll in the other. Its condition was absolutely pristine.

"How much for this, Bubba?" My voice nearly squeaked. I could've used a spot of tea about then or anything else to wet my whistle.

"Need fifteen hundred for that and I cain't take no less on account it ain't mine. My granny's best friend, who's also kin to me somehow, she used to live down in Norfolk, Virginia, she up and consigned it to me cuz she know'd I have this here store."

"Alright Bubba, you have a deal on the photo," I said. "Emma, have you found anything yet?"

"As a matter of fact, I did," she piped up for the first time. "I like these. What do you think, Charles?" She stepped around to an oak bookcase. Bubba seemed to be enchanted by Emma's ability to speak, or maybe it was her Hispanic accent. And the goobers suddenly become animated, stretching their scrawny chicken necks like turtles reaching out of their shells.

I walked over to the bookcase, reached in and took out what she was pointing to, a set of six Audubon books, "Birds of America". "Well, Emma, they're kinda nice," I managed to say, knowing full well that the Audubons were worth a lot more than what they were marked.

"Bubba, how much can we have these for? I see that they're marked $1,000," I said.

"Them bird books? They's real nice, ain't they? Well, since you done bought sumpin' already, I reckon I'll let them go for five hundred. The pretty lady ought to be entitled to something she likes if'n her husband is buying' all of this for hisself. Where in Virginia are you all from, anyway?" he asked.

"We used to have an open shop and antiques center about twenty-five miles north of Charlottesville near Madison," Emma said with a twinkle in her eye, bringing a bit more sweat to Bubba's brow. "But we closed them after twenty-five years and have them for sale. We live nearby in Barboursville, although most people still think of Charles as a Madisonian."

Bubba thought for a moment, kneading his chins, and then said, "Would your shop be at the end of the Wolftown-Hood Road where a Sheetz gas station is now by a new traffic light? Cuz heard tell of a man known as the Madison picker."

I answered for Emma who was talking too much in the middle of business. "Yes, that's my shop and I guess I'm the one. Okay, Bubba, add that to our pile, too," I told him.

He nodded to himself for his accurate deduction, forced himself away from Emma's charming effect, and flapped his jowls back to the task at hand. He was really grinning now. I imagined that he was probably calculating to himself how many handkerchiefs or maybe of all of the Twinkies he'd be able to buy with the proceeds.

"Y'all been dealin' long?" he asked not remembering what Emma had told him a moment earlier. She has that effect on men.

"Charles grew up in the business," Emma replied and sort of gave me a look. "But I'm new to the business," turning her perfect smile at him, causing him to steady himself on a glass showcase. It creaked.

"Bubba, do you have anything that might have its origins from our area in Virginia?" I asked. He ruminated a moment, his jowls quivering. He thought hard while once again mopping the back of his neck and folds with his red bandanna. "Yeah, just a minute and I'll go get what I got." He was only gone a minute. When he came back, he was carrying a rocking chair with the rockers pointed away from his girth. I noticed that there was a shoebox on its seat. "Here you go. I bought these from an old lady and her daughter in Culpeper. They told me that the rocker belonged to her great-grandfather and that he fought in the Civil War, on our side."

The old lady was right about the rocker being from our area. I recognized it as being by the hand of a regionally acclaimed legend. I kept on my best poker face and asked him, "How much?"

He made a sucking noise with his teeth and replied, "It'd be $400 and I'll throw in this box of Kodak photographs that came with it. There's some papers in that there box, too," Bubba exhaled laboriously.

His body language indicated that he thought that he was asking too much and that he expected me to counter offer, but I didn't. "Okay, we'll take that, too. Anything else?" I asked.

He blinked at the immediate sale and thought a second. "I'd love ta sell you all some more, but I cain't think of nuthin' else right now." He started to make a wide turn the way I imagined an oil tanker might but then paused halfway through before committing the energy. "I'll go add it up if'n you's ready?"

I nodded to him. He shoved off. I motioned to Emma and we stepped to the side to chat privately. "I don't understand it," I spoke softly.

"What do you mean?" she replied, turning her back to her onlookers.

"Well, we scout Lexington at least twice a year, right? Why haven't we stumbled upon this place before now? It's practically virgin territory. This shop hasn't been picked in quite some time, if ever." Through clenched teeth, I added, "Periwinkle, this pick is going to make our cash flow troubles go away!"

"Just how well *have* we done?" She kept a straight face as if we were discussing tire pressure. "I know the Audubons gotta be big bucks. What about the other stuff?" She was becoming excited and looked at me expectantly as we strolled arm-in-arm farther off to one side.

"You know the bomber jacket, right?"

"Yeah, yeah."

"It looks like it was a jacket worn by a special unit in WWII that is very popular. They called themselves the Flying Tigers."

"How good is that?"

I stopped, looked incredulously at her. "It doesn't get *better*! It's CBI," I said through clenched teeth, again.

"*Alright*, be patient with me. I didn't grow up in this country. What's CBI?"

I relaxed a bit and apologized. "CBI stands for China-Burma-India. It was a theatre of war during WWII, the same way Europe and the Pacific were theatres. The bomber jacket was in the pilot's US Army Air Corps footlocker and it is all there: his flight cap, goggles, leather helmet, army papers, chits, maps, all of his stuff."

"Wow! That's great, Amor. But who will want to buy it?"

"*Everyone*, but I'm going to let Fleet have first dibs. I emailed him some pics. He'll jump at the opportunity to add this archive to the Confederate Air Force's air museum. If Fleet buys, and I'm sure he will, we'll make a small profit but I'll have returned his favor once and for all and still managed to get a short profit turnaround. On the open market I'd be able to ask a lot more."

She was excited. "And Fleet will know that, right?"

"Yes, on the open market the jacket and other stuff could get into the mid six figures because of whom it all belonged to. After this Fleet is going to owe *us* a favor. It's that big."

Her eyes bugged out at the thought of Easy Street. She replied haltingly, "Amor – "

I cut her off, "Babe, this is a point of honor I have with Fleet. Profit takes a back seat."

She moved closer, looked up at me adoringly and put her palms and forearms on my chest. "What I was going to ask you about, Amor, was the dag," she purred understandingly, knowing me full well and how I think. Honor, integrity, fidelity, and all of my other "T's" as I call them, are what matter most to me. I know how corny it sounds in the modern lexicon, but I don't really give a damn what other people think or do. It's the only way I know how to live and it's worth dying for, as far as I'm concerned. Only the intangibles are what really matter. My parents first instilled them in me and later the Boy Scouts and The Service, too. And then I taught others as I have learned.

She sighed.

I changed mental gears, put my hands on top of hers, and whispered. "The whole plate dag is superb, Pretzel. I'll give Rick Waggener in Gaithersburg a call later and offer it to him."

"For how much?" I took her hand and we sat on a deacon's bench Bubba had in front of one of the front display windows. The day was going to be sunny and I was getting hungry, again. Emma's stomach growled just then as if our two digestive organs were communicating. I thought a moment about all of the hard images that had passed through my hands over the years, many of which I'd love to have back. "I think $2500 is a fair price, which means we'll make a thousand. That'll still leave him with a thousand left in it. He ought to go for the deal without too much squawking. Rick can flip it fast. He always does."

She nodded and asked, "What do you have in mind for the old rocker. You know rockers don't sell well. People don't sit in them or they're afraid that their cat's tail or kid's toes will be run over."

I'd taught Emma well. She had just then recited what she'd heard me tell a score of pickers trying to foist off their rocking chairs on us. "Periwinkle, this one is different. It's a rare Albert Aylor rocker and one of the better sort, probably circa 1880's, and it's not like the one we have at home. It's as good as the one Mrs. Payne owns. I offered her $3000 for it twenty years ago and she wouldn't even budge. Until this one, I didn't think that any others as good were extant. It's a keeper, Emma. We'll sell the other one we have when we get home."

"And the box that came with it?"

I hadn't really given the box any thought. "I haven't—"

Bubba interrupted, "Mr. Dawes, I've got it all added up." We stopped talking and moved over to his checkout counter, which had been made in the 1870's, by the looks of it. It had an incised ball-and-stick design in all of the right places typical of a period American Aesthetic Movement piece. Next to the brass cash register was an oak O.N.T. spool cabinet, and overhead hung a converted brass oil lamp from a patterned tin ceiling. "It comes to $7900, Mr. Dawes," he said as he handed me the bill of sale hesitantly.

At the time, *that* amount of money seemed like a lot. We just didn't have the cash flow. Yet I knew there was money to be made. I wanted it all, especially the bomber jacket, badly. So I called Fleet, but got his voicemail. In frustration, I sent him a text message.

He answered right away by text message: "in meetin how $"

I replied back, "$4k"

"tkx wilco dep b4 1700hrs yur act# wch bank?"

I answered back, "wlls frgo tks" and the account number.

I looked up from the Blackberry at Bubba, "Looks like we have a deal if you can hold our check until after 2:00 PM tomorrow?"

"You betcha, podner," he replied, and then he did his best to get us to stay longer. He even offered to take us 'to lunch up the street a ways,' but we told him that we wanted to hit the road again because the day was still young.

Emma replied, "We'll be back. We love Lexington, and your shop gives us a third reason to visit."

"A third reason?" he looked at Emma.

She replied sweetly, "Yes, the town's scenic beauty, the local history … and now Bubba's place."

Bubba's mass threatened to collapse as he chortled his approval. He guffawed a reply, "It's been a real pleasure doing business with you and if'n I ever git up to Madison, I'll be sure to stop in and see ya'll." Bubba picked up the rocker and handed it to me. Emma grabbed the shoebox and the dag. I carried the Audubons and Bubba carried the footlocker containing the bomber jacket and related ephemera. We all streamed out to the Volvo. Bubba asked, "You-all headed back to Madison?"

"Actually, Bubba, we're headed south," I answered. "Probably as far as Roanoke today before heading back home."

"Roanoke's a nice town. Look up my nephew, Mott Perry. He's a good kid, a former SFPD. Tell 'em I sent you and he might give you a free beer. He owns the Valley Bar & Grill on Delancey."

"Thanks for the tip, Bubba. Maybe we'll run into him one day," Emma said, as she climbed behind the wheel. I closed the tailgate, hopped in, and we both waved goodbye as he watched us pull away from the curve feeling very good about our luck. I shoved an Eagles CD into the dash and tapped my foot to the rhythm. There were periods of silence as we zoned out on music, followed by periods of excited conversation about what had just been purchased as the Lexington countryside fell behind us. From time to time, we stopped to check out the occasional antiques shop along the way. After a while, we stopped at a deli in Troutville, a wide place along Route 11, and made a tailgate picnic from the back of the car by a little brook. I opened the hatch and spread a blanket across the bumper. The air was brisk and still but the sun was warm and bright, and here there was no snow.

9 Back on Track

We sat together on a quilted packing blanket and carefully looked over the set of books for the first time. Emma looked them up on LiveAuctioneers dot-com, a free database that every appraiser, auctioneer, dealer, and picker uses. A minute passed before she reacted.

"Amor, what did we pay for the set of Audubons, five hundred, right?"

"Yep. Why?" The breeze was blowing her curly black hair all over the place. Her 'possum grin was contagious. I looked at what she was showing me and it confirmed what I had recalled from memory: that sets of Audubon books were strong in the marketplace.

"We're going to double, at least, from what it looks like here."

"I figured as much," I replied, smiling. "Probably triple, actually."

"Who do you have in mind on the client list for them?"

"Well, I think we ought to give Peter Shupp a call right now to tell him what we think we've found."

"He's in Monterey, right?"

"No, Santa Barbara. We can trust him to evaluate them for us and find a private buyer. If we run the set through auction it'll take longer and the payoff wouldn't necessarily be any more or quicker." Private buyers like to buy fresh merch so they can brag to their buddies about their good fortune.

"Okay, let's do it," she said excitedly and tossed me my cell. I can remember when she fussed at me for buying the stupid thing, telling me that I was one step away from Yuppyhood. Now for both of us our cell phones were practically our entire office; everything was on it. I scanned its database and punched in his number from the client list. Peter answered on my first try. I told him what I had, but he was with a celebrity, so he said he'd return my call in half an hour, if possible.

"Peter's busy with some Hollywood celeb named Scarlet," I told Emma. "So I'll give Rick a call to see if we can unload the dag quickly."

The conversation with Rick was short and to the point. My description of the dag sounded fantastic to him, but, as is customary, he needed to see it before he'd commit. So I emailed him a pic, and he bought it for $2500, plus $50 for shipping. Like my transaction with Fleet, he promised to deposit the cash into my Wells Fargo account before five o'clock and I promised to FedEx it overnight. I can't remember how I executed quick sales before cell phones and the Internet.

I was glancing at the beauty of the Audubon prints in the set of books when the phone rang. "Charles, its Peter." He's rather flamboyant, transplanted from Philly, rich, gay, monogamous, brilliant, the top book dealer in the country, knows everybody who is anybody on the Left Coast, and we've been friends since he was one of my ROTC instructors at JMU.

"Thanks for returning my call, Peter. How's Thackery?" Thack is Peter's husband or whatever. I can't seem to get used to the permutation of traditional relationships.

"Oh, he's very fine, thank you. How's Emma, we miss her soooo very much," crooned Peter.

"I'm hardly behaving myself, Peter." She leaned over the phone and blasted him with a greeting.

"Ooooh, she sounds healthy, doesn't she? Balanced food will do it every time. You should listen to your Periwinkle and try to be more conscious of what you eat, Charles. You'd feel better and live longer," he lectured.

"Peter, if I felt any better I wouldn't be able to stand it. I don't have an inherent cholesterol problem like Emma. Now, what do you think about the Audubons? Want in?"

"I'd have to look them over to be sure, but it sounds like you've found the real McCoy, my boy," he laughed at his little rhyme. "How about FedExing them as soon as possible?"

I'm used to Peter's silliness and ignore it. "Alright. I'll have them double-boxed and send them right off. After you're scheduled to receive them I'll call to hear what your opinion is. We can talk some more then. If they're what we think they are, then I think I'd like *you* to act as broker in a private sale. Would you be agreeable to that?"

"Why yes, of course, Charles. You know we always accommodate you guys. We love you two soooo much. I'll keep a lookout for the shipment and then I'll call you." He rattled on a minute or so more and asked to be handed over to Emma, and then they went on for a few more minutes.

In the meantime, I went through the contents of the Allen Edmonds shoe box we'd acquired with the rocker. I spilled it out on the blanket so that I could paw through the wreckage while the two of them prattled. There were numerous letters, notes, receipts, and several late cabinet card photographs of landmarks I recognized as being in Madison County, Graves Mill, and the Madison Court House. There were also tintype images of men in dark clothes posing beside horse and buggies tied to hitching posts, a leather-bound photo album with double metal clasps, a spring clamp paper holder in the form of a duck's head, old Harding and FDR political buttons, bits and pieces of jewelry, and sundry other ephemera.

Emma hung up, peered over the pile, and reached for a piece of jewelry. "Look Amor, Miriam Haskell," Emma said, while holding out her arm for me to inspect a heavy copper bracelet.

"That's nice."

I reached for the cabinet cards and began scrutinizing them. I asked her, testing. "How good is it?"

She scrutinized its mark, and replied, "Uh, maybe $50 to $75. It's not bad. Crystal will like it. Her collection is really getting to be extensive." Crystal is the wife of a Charlottesville picker we know.

"Okay, then let's swing back that way if we have the time," I suggested.

"You know, only a couple of days ago I'd have gone through the roof if I'd found this. After today at Bubba's, this is anticlimactic," she sighed.

"Yeah, I know what you mean. The cabinet cards are worth some money, too, but I think I'll just give them to the Kemper Mansion instead." I picked up the cell phone again and began punching in another number.

"Who're you calling now?" she asked.

"General Pride." It rang twice and then a staff sergeant answered for the general's office. He told me that the general was due back in ten minutes and would return my call ASAP. We're on the best of terms.

I guess I've known him for ten or fifteen years or so. He's a leaner version of the actor from the Quaker Oats commercials. He earned his star after Desert Storm, where, as a Marine jet pilot, he was one of the few to be shot down. Anyway, Fleetwood Pride pulled my proverbial nuts out of a very hot fire a couple of years ago in Iraq and I've been beholden to him ever since. He's retired now and runs a museum of vintage WWII military aircraft that still fly. Donations of time and capital from aviation enthusiasts keep the squadron aloft. It's called The Confederate Air Force and it's unbelievably cool. And so is Fleet.

I'm kind of a lone wolf, which is not the best trait to have if you're a military type, especially a Recon Marine. Fleet recognized that in me, and instead of attacking me for having that weakness, he mentored me and showed me how to use my streak of individuality to benefit the Corps. For Fleet it was always about the Corps. Fleet is like a father figure to me.

"Emma, he's not in. The staff sergeant said he'd be back in a few minutes. Let's wait awhile. I'd like to touch base with him about the jacket," I said.

"This photo album is pretty interesting, Charles. It even has black people from Madison."

"That doesn't surprise me. After all, the cabinet cards are of Madison sites and the Albert Aylor rocker is definitely from there because Madison is where Aylor lived and worked. Actually, he lived out a ways in Haywood. What timeframe is the photo album from?"

"I can't tell," she replied, handing it to me.

"It's from the 1860's to the early, ah, maybe 19-teens." The phone rang and I picked it up. "Hello," I said.

"Charles, this is Fleet. How are you doing, Major?" I had long since retired from the Individual Ready Reserve, but Fleet still addressed me by my last rank. He was probably fifteen years my senior and he had such a commanding presence that everyone always rendered deferential respect to the old warrior, including me. To him I'd always be the young butter-bar that flew back seat to his maple leaf before becoming Recon. To me he'd always be General.

"Semper Fi, sir. I'm doing just fine. Have you given up flying yet, sir?"

"Never, boy, never. I'll go down in one before I give it up."

"That's the spirit, Fleet. So how's the financial condition of the Confederate Air Force?" I could feel him buckle his armor. The Brigadier always straps on his formalities when he thinks I'm about to reach into his pocket, whereupon he reminds me of my loyalties.

"What have you found for me now, Major? A CBI cache?"

"Looks that way, sir," I said.

"Charles, it looks like a real find from the photos you sent. Thanks for offering it to us first."

"You're very welcome, General."

"How do you come up with these gems, and always when our budget is just about shot?"

"A lot of miles, General. We're on the road all the time since we closed our antique shop. Besides, I've made it my mission in life to bankrupt the Confederate Air Museum." We both laughed.

"I'm very excited. When can you ship it all?"

"I'm headed to FedEx now, sir."

"Charles, I know you could have made a killing out there on these items." I could tell from his tone that Fleet was a little misty. "The Confederate Air Force and I are deeply grateful that you came to us first instead of offering it on the open market. Thank you ever so much."

"You're welcome, General. I figured that I still owed you one for the time you saved my sorry ass."

"Naw. You don't owe me a thing. I'd help out a fellow spec-op anytime. And you're even-steven with the C.A.F., too. In fact, we owe you a big one. When the moment comes, just say the word and I'll put the full might of the membership of the C.A.F. at your disposal."

"Thanks, Fleet, but I'll try to stay out of trouble so you won't have to bother."

He chuckled in his Wilford Brimley kind of way. "Give my regards to your lovely wife, Em, and drop in on us when you get a chance. Mrs. Pride asks about you-all often."

I told him I would and did and then we were on the road again.

***

When Emma asked me if we were going on to Roanoke, I surprised myself. I told her, "I would prefer it if we slept in our own bed tonight. Things are turning around for us," I explained. "Our karma is back on track and I don't want to disturb the cosmic forces by picking too far afield, if you know what I mean."

She contemplated that philosophy for a moment, and replied, "I thought you might say that," and smiled as I pulled the car onto the ramp to Interstate 81 to take the fast way home through Charlottesville. She reclined her seat, pushed her brown fedora over her eyes and slept as I thought about calling a picker friend of mine by the name of Jazzman Fry.

10 Jazzman

My family moved to Madison County in 1965 when I was not yet twelve. By then I had stopped fretting about my past life as Randolph West, although it was still just as clear to me. I suppose fitting in to a peer group for a boy of that age was far more important than trying to resolve the inexplicable. Not attracting attention to oneself became part of the solution. Besides, there was so much distraction on the farm that I went weeks at a time without giving it a thought.

Dad had bought a farm three years earlier in preparation for his retirement from the Air Force. On the last day in July we piled into our 1961 Ford Falcon and an old 1949 Ford pickup truck and left Dover for the last time, or so I thought. I remember it distinctly because President Johnson was on the radio talking about troops going to a place called Viet Nam, and Suzie, our beagle, peed on my lap as we were driving through the town of Warrenton. I haven't liked Warrenton since. Dog pee is very hot.

Our farm in Madison County was a much different place to live than our townhome on Circle Drive on Dover Air Force Base. There weren't any Negroes nearby our place in Virginia, nor Asians, nor Catholics, or Jews. There were only nice WASPy country folks who would and did come when needed. The day we arrived, Mom was thirty-three years old and had four kids in tow. When we rolled up the driveway, she cried. The house was a wreck: unpainted, falling apart, the lawn unmowed for two years, the roof leaked, the electricity was off, and there was no water because the well pump was electric. The movie "Deliverance" hadn't been made yet, but it was like that. Mom begged Dad to take us all to a hotel, or anyplace else, but then Providence supplied us with Mr. and Mrs. Yowell who arrived with bulging picnic baskets full of hot biscuits, sweet corn, egg salad, and the like. Mr. Yowell even brought two push lawn mowers and helped Dad clear enough so my young sisters wouldn't get lost in the weeds in the front yard. My playground was now three-hundred acres in size, much to my delight.

Many of our neighbors were the unfortunate victims of the Shenandoah National Park being established a generation earlier. They were still bitter about their forced evictions. And then, that same summer, legislation was passed declaring racial integration the new law of the land. Virginia had a big problem with that. The Civil War was a hundred years over in 1965, but no one would admit it; not here.

I hadn't realized that the Madison school system wasn't integrated until school opened in the fall and I witnessed some of the kids making fun of a pretty little Negro girl named Lisa Blue. She was the only Negro integrated into the white system that year. I didn't understand what integration was because I had grown up on military bases where everyone lived together peacefully. Just before we left base housing, I'd had my first crush. It was for a charming Amerasian girl named Linda of about my age. Then one day she didn't come to school — she'd died of a brain aneurism. That news severely traumatized me. I thought I'd understood death but I'd viewed it as an old person's problem. Suddenly all life seemed tentative. Plus, I had no one to talk to about those kinds of feelings because revealing I'd had a crush on a girl wasn't an admission for a boy just shy of twelve years. It was my first experience with grief.

Social tension became almost measurable in Madison County as the adults' expectations of full integration loomed on their psychological horizons. Their anxiety was definitely palpable. It hung in the air like static in a blanket.

The following year, many more black kids were integrated and the tension escalated into fights between a few troublemakers and a few victims. One such incident happened on my school bus when three rednecks punched and knifed a Negro boy who had refused to engage them in verbal banter. I was stunned by the incident and immediately told my parents who telephoned the school system. The white boys were suspended, and I was bullied at school the next day. My parents received threats against their property for weeks and, as a result, Dad switched us from a party line to a private phone line. For the first night of threats, both Dad and I stood guard in the dark outside on the porch with loaded shotguns. Every time a car passed he raised his weapon to his shoulder, and I raised mine. I was barely twelve at the time but that period had a lasting effect. It may have been the spark that led me later onto a martial path.

I wonder.

A few weeks later, a group of rednecks cornered me on the playground and proceeded to beat the tar out of me. But Jazzman Fry came to my rescue. He was two grades higher and thirty pounds heavier than the biggest of my assailants and one of the new Negroes in the school. Jazz grabbed the largest one and used him as a plunger to bash the others. No one bothered me, or for that matter, anyone else on the playground again. Jazz and I have been friends ever since.

Jazz graduated two years earlier than I did and then he went away to Southeast Asia, but we kept in touch as best as GIs could in those days. Years later, he told me that he didn't like combat, but that he had liked his career in Army CID, Criminal Investigation Department. After twenty years of faithful service he retired, and soon after, he looked me up. It was I who had gotten him into the antiques business, he accused, but what I hadn't realized was how advanced a collector he had become. Jazz turned out to be a packrat of Hollywood proportions. He comes up with the most unusual things, too; many of which he offers to me first. They're sometimes so good that I just can't turn them down.

Jazz now owns and operates a small shop in the nearby town of Culpeper, about thirty miles away from our home in Barboursville. After some initial hesitation, the conservative antiques community embraced him as one of their own. He's one of the very few blacks in the antiques business anywhere that I know of, and his pet peeve is being referred to as "African American." Jazz figures himself an American. *Period.* "You-all want to call me something? Call me *sir!*" he says. Over and over again he says that to different people, and Jazz is big. He only has to tell a person that once before it takes hold.

Occasionally, Jazz is called upon to do some private undercover investigative work for individuals and various law enforcement agencies in the region because of his background and because he can access certain sectors more easily than most everyone else in uniform in Culpeper and its bordering counties.

"Jazz, it's Charles. How're you doing?"

"Heeeey Charles! I'm doing great, man. I got into a humdinger of a house yesterday. You should see the stuff I got." Like me, and now Emma, Jazz is a diehard collector at heart who loves the chase as well as anyone, and that's always the first thing we talk about if we haven't spoken in a while.

"Like what?" I asked.

"Well, like a spiked German helmet, a full kit and uniform of a WWI Army light colonel, an eight-foot scrubbed three-board top farm table with a pigeon blood skirt and tapered legs, a Federal Pembroke table with an end drawer, a Biedermeier-leg server with ormolu mounts, a two-drawer work table with a Sheraton leg, a reeded leg work table with ovolo corners, boxes of first editions with dust jackets, breakables out the freaking wazoo, and lord knows what else. Man, I'm telling you I haven't had such a find in years!"

"Very cool, Jazz, sounds like a lot of fun," I was genuinely impressed and interested. "What's the wood on the eight-footer?"

"Heart pine scrub-top, chestnut legs and skirt, breadboard ends with canted dovetail corners. Beautiful!"

"And the clearance?"

"Twenty-four inches from the floor to the skirt. Twenty-nine to the top."

"Does it need anything?" I quizzed.

"Nuthin', it was in use where I found it. When I hang up, I'll email you some pics."

"How much to me?"

"A grand."

"Save it for me. Can you take a video with your cell phone?"

"No problem," Jazz calculated. "Uh-huh, just a second." I could hear him scribble on the little spiral flip pad that he always keeps in his back pocket. It's his office.

"I have an idea, Jazz."

"What's that?"

"You have video capability on your cell phone?"

"Yeah."

"Where do you have all of this stuff?"

"In the middle of my house, like always. Don't have no room in my shop right now. Jammed to the rafters. I need a bigger shop *and* house, looks like," he laughed. "What idea?"

"Stand in the middle of your room and do a pirouette with your video camera on."

"Do a *what?* Charles, I speak Vietnamese, Spanish, and a little English, but I got no big degrees like you."

I laughed. Jazz is the smartest person I've ever met, and one of the best actors. He was pulling my leg, of course. He knew what I meant but I explained it to him anyway because I found the image in my mind amusing. "*Pirouette*, like a ballerina, turn slowly in a circle with your *camera on* and speak into the mic about what you're pointing at with the viewfinder, explaining all the while to the viewer about what you're filming."

It's advice I sometimes give to my clients when they can't afford a formal appraisal report. I tell them to film their whole house using the pirouette method and then stash the disc in a safe deposit box, or at any location other than the domicile. In case something should happen, the disc is somewhere else. It sounds simple enough, but it's the last part that makes all the difference. Every year I get between two and five calls from clients who have suffered some sort of catastrophe and want me to reconstruct from thin air what they need in order to satisfy a Damage and Loss claim, and I just cannot do it. The first responsibility of an accredited appraiser is to witness.

"Uh-huh," Jazz harrumphed. "I kin already imagine my cracker neighbors on Oak Park Road peeking through their blinds at my six-foot-six skinny-ass frame, *pirouetting*."

We both cracked up.

"Jazz, *enough*," I gasped. My sides were splitting. "Tell me about the fancy piece."

He chuckled, but then returned to seriousness. "You mean the one with the Biedermeier leg? Oh, I'd say it's probably Norfolk circa 1795 by the looks of it, or maybe a Tom Day piece if it isn't. It's got that kind of look: flame mahogany and bookmatched veneer along the frieze, original finish and fine hardware, brass sabots, two side-by-side drawers over three long graduated drawers that need resoling, and the runners need replacing. Some of the cockbeading is gone in places. Lumps and bumps consistent with a piece this old and still in use."

I had taught Jazz how to describe an object well, but it was easy, really. He was already a trained investigator. A picture was developing in my mind.

"Well, it's not a Tom Day piece if it has brass sabots, Jazz," I explained. And it probably had a pile of silver weighing down its two side-by-side drawers if their runners are worn so badly that they need work."

He uh-hummed a reply. "That was my thought, too, but there wasn't any in the house, silver, that is. They must have liquidated it all."

"Price?" I queried.

"Fifteen hundred."

"Save it. What about the books, Jazz?"

"Lots of books. This family has been literate since they fell off of the boat in 1740, or so I'm told. You name it and it'll probably be here; maybe eight hundred titles altogether. Lots of leather, some leather sets, too, and not that fake stuff, the real deal. Even three fore-edged decorated books, lots of literary firsts from about 1910 until through the '50's, Burroughs, H.G. Wells, Zane Grey, Tolkien, Twain, Faulkner, Steinbeck, Hemmingway, Stein, Fitzgerald, Woolf, Mailer, Thompson, Kerouac, man, I could go on and on. You're the bookman; I only read the titles and look 'em up on Bookfinder dot-com."

It sounded like Jazz had found a dream cache. "What about their condition, Jazz?"

"Very fine to very good I'd say, using *Firsts Magazine* as a guideline."

"And they're all firsts?"

"Yep, I think so."

"Are you sure that they're not book club editions, Jazz?"

"I'm going to pretend you didn't just insult me, Major."

"Ok, sorry. Jazz, what'dja give for the whole house?" Pickers and dealers never reveal their sources; or their purchase price. It would be like telling everyone where your favorite fishing hole is or revealing Coca-Cola's special recipe.

"Hey! That's not nice," he laughed with false indignation.

"Just testing my student," I grinned. "How much do you want for all the books; the whole lot?"

"Jeez, I don't know, Charles, I've only had 'em for five days and haven't had time to do anything with them yet."

I interrupted. "I'll take all the books off your hands, sight unseen. You won't have to think about it anymore. Name your price."

"Six thousand."

"Done."

"Are you sure?" I could hear him almost choke on whatever he had taken a sip of. "Man, that's a lot of moolah!"

"Yeah, I'm sure. I'll talk to my banker and see if I have anything left on my line of credit tomorrow. Just hold it for me: the books, the farm table, and the Norfolk server. Box up all the books and keep them in a safe place. If they're in the way, put them in an environmentally conditioned rental unit until I can get to them."

"No, I'll send them over to you. I know you're good for it. Where the hell are you anyway? Where's Emma? I can usually hear her singing in the background."

"At home. We just got back from picking."

"I see," he said chuckling, "I'd heard you're serious about selling the antiques center."

"Yeah, we are, and the shop, too. It can't happen soon enough."

"Oh," he said. I could hear the resignation in his voice. "Those were some good times before the recession, weren't they?" For a while before he opened his own shop in Culpeper, Jazz had rented space from us at our Madison Antiques Center. I modeled the center after the best of its kind, one that I had seen in West Townsend, Massachusetts. This was long before Emma.

I sighed, "Yes, they were my friend."

"Look," he said, and got back on track. "I'll send Harry over with the books, table, and server." Culpeper has very few taxi drivers. Harry Watts is the one Jazz uses for odd jobs. He'll do pretty much any kind of thing, and he's completely dependable. "Whenever you're flush, send me a check and I'll do the pirouetting thing first chance and email it."

"Sounds fine, thanks, Jazz."

After I hung up, I went into the kitchen. "I told Jazz that we are serious about selling the buildings."

Emma's hands continued with the task that she was doing. "That's good. Did he have anything interesting?"

"Great stuff, actually. I bought an eight-foot farm table, a Norfolk server, and some first editions."

She looked over at me from the kitchen island sink. "How's Jazz?"

"Sounds fine. Real busy with what he just got. This family where all the loot came from has been in Virginia since 1740."

She looked at me suspiciously. "How much did you spend?" she asked, noticing I'd left that bit of information out.

"Eighty-five hundred."

"*What?*"

"There were eight hundred-some books," I explained in my defense, "all firsts, literary, early scifi, fantasy, mysteries, leather, fore-edge decorated books, all in very good to very fine shape."

"But we don't —"

I interrupted, "Emma, you've been worried for weeks that we haven't found anything to sell. Well, the dry spell is over. We're now in a wet spell. We'll just have to use the line of credit."

She chopped a head of lettuce in half loud enough to make Grace flinch.

11 The Devil is in the Details

A few minutes after we hung up, Jazz sent me the video of what Harry would deliver early next morning: boxes of the books, the pigeon blood farm table, and the Norfolk server. The books were in forty-three small cardboard boxes, and they were as Jazz had described them, mostly firsts, with not-clipped jackets, and almost all were of marketable genres. Such a huge number of books represented days of work cataloguing, wrapping, loading into our business website, eBay store, ABE, and Amazon. It was tedious, mind-bending work. Neither of us could stand it for more than four or five hours a day. But it was profitable and a part of our job description.

The farm table was so perfect that Emma and I had Harry help us swap it out for the one that we were presently using in our dining room. Swapping is a common practice. Collectors upgrade constantly. It's one of the reasons that when a collector's estate sells at auction, it brings more than estates of non-collectors: one, because the quality of the collection has ratcheted up the quality scale, and two, the notoriety and/or celebrity of the collector becomes a value attribute in itself. Celebrity enhances provenance and provenance enhances value because collectors love a good story. The devil is in the details, so to speak.

The server that I had bought sight-unseen from Jazz was *not* made in Norfolk, Virginia, circa 1795.

Anthony Quervelle made it in Philadelphia in the 1830's. Both time periods produced Fancy Furniture, which is a recognized subcategory, and so it was understandable to me why Jazz hadn't recognized the difference. Quervelle is to American Fancy Furniture as Rolls Royce is to motorcars. It doesn't get any better in *each* respective niche.

Jazz's mistake was all in my favor.

If I didn't reveal his error now, then one day in the future he would discover his mistake, smile at the memory of my poker face, and probably order a book on the famous maker the way he did for Tom Day before. It was years ago, but I had learned the same lesson the same way and I have no doubt that I will again, and again.

Most pickers and dealers handle exchange situations such as this one almost on a daily basis and they *do not* reveal their superior knowledge. As crooked to the uninitiated as it may seem, not revealing one's superior knowledge *is* ethical in the antiques trade. An equivalent example outside the trade would be if you hired a lawyer to create a corporation. I did for my first company, and my lawyer eagerly reached into my pocket for three hundred dollars. It was his job. That's how he made his living, *and*, I asked him to do it. But what he didn't reveal to me was how simple it was for anyone to go online and create their own corporation, or Limited Liability Company (LLC), with a few dozen keystrokes and about a hundred bucks.

There is, however, a tricky part to all of this in 'The Trade,' and it is when a dealer with superior knowledge makes a very low offer to buy something from an ignorant non-dealer seller; and, do be mindful that the term 'ignorant' is not necessarily an indicator of stupidity, merely a lack of knowledge. If a dealer were to make a very low offer to a non-dealer, and the offer was accepted, then the dealer would be vulnerable to litigation if the seller were to make the discovery and sue for damages. There are precedents on the books and they are a perennial amusement to read about in the *Maine Antique Digest*.

My buying the Quervelle server from Jazz was safe because Jazz set the price, I accepted the unseen risk, and we are both dealers; but it's not how I do business. My ethics rule.

I called him and revealed. Jazz listened patiently while I briefed him on Quervelle, pointing out one or two tell-tale indicators as best as I could over the phone, and then he stopped me from going on. "Charles, you bought it at my asking price over the phone, sight unseen. It's yours, Major, and that's all there is to it. I may've learned something valuable and you can rest assured that I will study up on him later, but you don't owe me nothin'."

"Jazz," I said, "it's worth *a lot*."

"Don't matter, Major," and he recited the rules of the trade back to me -- the same ones that I once had taught him many years ago.

My hand hurt from my involuntary reflex to crush the Blackberry in my fist, I was so frustrated, but he wouldn't let me get a word in edgewise. "*Jazz!*" I shouted at the phone. He stopped for a breath. And I revealed, "It's probably worth thirty or forty thousand dollars." Finally, I had silenced him. "Well?" I prompted after a dozen heartbeats. "What do you have to say about it now?"

His final reply: "It must be some kind of good."

Emma liked the Quervelle server, too, so we decided to keep it, but she didn't have a clue about what she was looking at. Like Jazz, she lacks the depth of knowledge that I have. I informed Emma of our luck and how scarce Quervelle pieces are, but she still wasn't any more enthusiastic. Heavy stuff just isn't her thing.

12 A Pox on Sprint

We worked until noon, had a sandwich, and then rolled down 33 to the roundabout in Gordonsville taking Route 231 south into Charlottesville. It's a beautiful scenic drive through Keswick hunt country where old estates line the serpentine road all of the way into Shadwell.

On our agenda for the afternoon was to visit another picker, Lenny. He is a character who takes some getting used to. Usually we call ahead anytime we decide to visit someone, but with Lenny that courtesy is no longer possible; he doesn't own a telephone. Long story short, Sprint gave him such a hard time one day that he yanked his phone out of the wall, chucked it into the street – in front of a couple of CPD officers *and* a judge, whereupon he was almost arrested for conduct unbecoming an ex-con. Luckily, Judge Derry had a similar opinion of the service provider; he let Lenny off with a stern warning and ordered him to retrieve his "junk in the street." Lenny hasn't used *any* telephone since. The absence of the ubiquitous modern convenience apparently has not had an adverse effect on his business, or so he claims, which is probably true because he continues to find us good stuff.

I parked the Volvo in the 11th Street garage, and took the ticket with us to have Lenny stamp it for two hours of free parking. Holding hands, we strode uphill to the edge of the reviving Belmont neighborhood towards several commercial storefronts on the other side of the tracks. As I stepped over the second set of *Amtrak* rails one of my little fingers began to tingle and curl all of its own. I ignored the sensation and put that hand in my pocket. Emma didn't notice.

"Hello Lenny," I said as we walked through his doorway, a clangor bell rattling our presence. My other small digit suddenly had a sympathetic reaction to its cousin. This time Emma did notice. She made a hand washing motion. I frowned but relented to keep the peace. Sometimes it does help. That's what Lenny saw me doing when the little guy bounced in energetically.

"Charles and Emma!" he exclaimed, eyeing my movement to hide my hands. "It's good to see you guys, where've you been?" He pronounced 'been' with three E's, shook my hand in a way not to disturb my smallest phalange, and then disengaged to give Emma a big hug. Emma indulges Lenny's fantasy: she's tall, he's short, and his face is about eye level with two of her better assets. I ignored his cheekiness and Emma's tolerance. "We've been working too hard, Lenny, but we have good news: we may have a buyer for our antiques shop and the antiques center," I said, to distract him from noticing my still moving hands. It worked.

"That's terrific, guys," Lenny said, genuinely glad. "What are you going to do with all that money?"

Soberly, I replied, "We're not going to have a lot left over after the mortgage and line of credit is satisfied, Lenny."

Emma changed the topic. "We needed a break from the mundane task of cataloguing, so we came here to bug you."

Lenny got the message. "Good, I like bugs," he smiled. "May I get you something to drink? Coffee, hot tea, iced tea, Snapple?"

"Ice tea would be nice, Lenny," Emma said. I echoed her request. He told us how things were going, how he liked *not* having a parole officer anymore, and that he really loved how his *sixth* marriage was going. When he first informed me of his latest marriage a few months earlier, I told him that more than three makes a collection. He replied that he was 'a connoisseur, not a collector.'

Lenny's a retired late-middle-aged second-story man who swears up and down that he never ever carried a gun on a caper, and only took from the super-rich when they pissed him off, which was, according to Lenny himself, often. He probably got caught at it about as many times as he'd been married. For three years since his return, Lenny has operated a coin and stamp shop downtown on the mall in Charlottesville, legitimately. Originally from Las Vegas, he wears too much gold and diamond jewelry, spends a lot of time at the track in Charlestown, West Virginia and picks like there is no tomorrow. He knows what we like and, when he finds it, he sets it aside until we visit, which is about every two or three weeks.

After some more pleasantries, I suggested, "Let's have a look at what you have saved for us, Lenny."

"Charles, Emma, I've got great stuff for you guys, as usual," he said all excited. "Just a minute while I go get it." From a distance, Lenny's small stature made the box he brought back appear deceptively large.

"Any jewelry for me?" Emma asked, trying her best to peek.

"Oh, just this little thing," he reached in and handed her a blue velvet bag that once held a bottle of Crown Royal.

She opened the drawstring and poured out a spectacular piece that took our breaths away. "William Spratling, 1938, the *god* of Taxco designers," Emma whispered to herself in awe; her black, almond-shaped eyes were as large as saucers. It was a magnificent brooch. She was beginning her strawberry blotch thing again; I could tell. And my two fingers were singing to one another like a pair of tuning forks.

Spratling was an adventurous American designer with an extraordinary facility for organizing people. Most dealers don't know this but he was responsible for curating Diego Rivera's infamous exhibit at The Metropolitan in New York, which is an interesting story by itself. From his commission for that job, Spratling purchased a small house in the mountain village of Taxco. It was rural and a relatively unknown dot on the global atlas then, except for mining. For 400 years, the region was known for its silver ore but the humble indigenous people had not benefited in any meaningful way. They were dirt poor. Spratling changed all of that in the early 1930's by employing local maestro goldsmiths to work silver into designs that he adapted from the local tribal cultures. Single-handedly, and virtually overnight, he transformed the marketplace by encouraging local designers and smiths to get involved making jewelry and decorative utilitarian wares that appealed to tourists. At the time, droves of them were pouring in from North America and Western Europe, and there was little for them to buy. Spratling proved to be Taxco's most ingenious innovator. Serious collectors of Mexican silver consider Spratling to be second-to-none.

"Emma, don't you know better than to show enthusiasm in front of a seller?" I reprimanded her, but couldn't help laughing. Lenny laughed too.

"It's tortoiseshell and ivory, Charles. I didn't know he worked with those materials. Besides you can't expect me to keep a poker face with something like this. As you know, both tortoiseshell and ivory are now protected by law, so this can't go anywhere but up in value, right Amor?"

I studied it under my loupe and then thought for a moment before answering Emma's questions in order: "Yes, it's ivory and tortoiseshell alright but not ordinary ivory."

They both looked at me expectantly.

"It's either mammoth or mastodon ivory," I explained, looking at it under magnification, "which means that it's old enough to be exempt from the Endangered Species Act."

"How can you tell the difference?" asked Lenny.

"Yeah," Emma said, "you've explained it to me several times, but I don't remember which way it is."

I looked at Lenny. "She means the grain lines. Look." I held it for the two of them to see what I was pointing to with a pencil. "See how the grain lines are steep like the pyramids of Egypt?"

They both, "Uh-huhed" me.

"That's ancient ivory. Now, if the lines were rounded like a camel's hump, then it would mean that it was modern ivory."

Lenny looked up at me, over his half rims, and asked, "Is there a difference between African and Asian ivory?"

"No," I shook my head.

"What about mastodon and mammoth ivory?" he pursued his questioning.

Again, I shook my head. "No."

Emma gave me a wise guy look. "I knew it was good," she murmured, and purred herself over to a window with the brooch, pushing her loupe into her eye socket in order to capture the natural light.

Lenny and I observed how delighted she was with the brooch. We probably both thought how nice it is to make a woman happy – and then I snapped out of it. "What's your best on the Spratling, Lenny?" I asked.

"I have to have $1000," he said, lifting his chin in defiance.

We usually haggle over everything, but since we were *going* to be very flush soon (knock on wood) because of the pending sale of our real estate and some of our recent finds, which were also not paid for, the rational part of my mind reminded me, I decided to throw him off balance and accept *his* price without hesitation. "Okay, we'll take it," I agreed. He looked nonplussed for a moment but quickly regained his composure. "What do you have for *me*, Lenny?" I asked, hiding my hands in the tight back pockets of my jeans.

The little giant walked around the end of his counter and reached for something down on a lower shelf. It was about a yard long and wrapped in burlap that had begun its life as an old feed sack. With a calculated degree of drama, Lenny unfurled the sack and handed me something that I had been searching for, well, for just about forever. As soon as I had it in my hands, my fingers relaxed to normal.

"Charles, you'll like *this* sword, I believe."

I don't collect militaria; most blooded warriors usually don't. The wannabe warriors that have never worn a uniform and never been to war are the collectors. Swords, as a subcategory of militaria, are at top of the category's food chain, too. They can be broadly categorized as functional swords, meaning the ones actually used in combat, or presentation swords, used ceremonially. This specimen now in my well-behaved hands was of the latter sort. Its most significant value attribute was the fact so few were made and that they were made for the Confederacy in the South, as opposed to being manufactured by the French or English for the South.

In contrast to the simplicity of a battle sword, a fancy, etched and gilded presentation sword with a clear provenance can be worth hundreds of thousands of dollars. Some swords are legendary or have become mythical over time because of the tall tales that grow taller as "his-stories" are passed down from father to son. However most histories have been lost to time; the provenance is unknown. What lay in my grasp was not a fancy presentation sword with provenance, nor would it have any sort of notoriety if taken away from the immediate region, and it wasn't even particularly attractive; in fact, it was rather featureless. But, once I saw the mark on its ricasso, just above the handle, I was as pleased with it as Emma was with her Spratling. I examined it and the scabbard that sheathed it as my heart pounded.

Emma stood beside me. "It was this thing, wasn't it?" She glanced from my hands clutching the weapon to my eyes.

I hoped that her question was rhetorical.

"Lenny, how *much*?"

He grinned like a Cheshire cat. "It's a Charlottesville sword," he pointed out.

"*Yeah*, I know. You know that I've been looking for one."

"For as long as we've known each other, too, right?"

Lenny was agonizingly rubbing salt into my anticipation. "Yes. *How much?*"

"It's yours," he gestured his generosity with a dramatic sweep of his arm and a grin. Emma had come over next to me in support and watched the drama unfold as I unsheathed the blade and read the crude acid-etched script on both sides of the blade, "7 McKennie & Co. Charlottesville Va." It had a distinctly French appearance with unstopped large fullers on both sides. Little is known of Charlottesville swords. The manufacturer began operations in July of 1861; just three months after the first shots were fired at Ft. Sumter, South Carolina. Only four hands worked the forge. They probably only turned out a half dozen blades a week, if that many. Mine would be the fourth identified example.

"Oh no it isn't, either. How *much*?" I insisted.

"Lenny, what's going on?" asked Emma.

Lenny chimed, "Remember when Charles got me out of that jam a while back? Well, let's just say that I'm very grateful."

She acknowledged with a head motion, took a stem to stern gander at the edged weapon, and declared, "But it's ugly, Lenny."

Lenny made a face and snorted at her female aptitude.

"Lenny, I can't accept this. It's too valuable. Besides, I would have done the same for anyone."

About three years ago, I vouched for Lenny's whereabouts when he was a chief suspect in a series of jewelry heists that had a similar MO to his. They hauled Lenny in for questioning. I stepped up and told them that he was with me during the time one of the jobs went down. Which was true, but then that made *me* a suspect, too. Law enforcement sees black and white sometimes. I didn't hold it against CPD; they were just doing their job. Luckily, the real culprit was caught in the act while they had us in a holding pattern. Emma was bonkers during the whole episode, and I had one continuous migraine. Afterwards I bought stock in the pharmaceutical company that manufactures Fiorinal; it's the only thing that'll kill my monster headaches. The stock has since split two-for-one, twice. I had figured that Lenny and I were even because of that and had forgotten all about it.

"Lenny, Charles's right, I think," she said, and from the quizzical expression on her face, I could tell that she was outside of her comfort zone on the topic of militaria. "How much is it worth?"

I shrugged. "I don't know, actually. I've known about these swords for fifteen years or more. I saw one that a dealer had long ago and he wanted $6000. A small Albemarle County foundry made only six or seven of these swords weekly for the Confederacy.

About a half dozen are known to have survived. Like this specimen, typically they're not particularly beautiful, just from Charlottesville. I collect stuff from Charlottesville, that's all. And there are other collectors who do, too. Collecting regional things is common, just as common as collecting anything Spratling or anything by Faberge."

Emma shrugged her acceptance at me and then looked at Lenny.

"What do you have in it, Lenny?" I asked, seeking an honorable way to pay Lenny for what he was prepared to give me outright.

He sighed and resigned. "Five hundred,"

"Let me give you that much for it, at least, and I'll release you from your ill-perceived obligation."

"He's not obligated!" exclaimed Emma.

"Lenny knows that," I laughed.

Lenny laughed, too. "Okay, it's a deal," he said, and we shook hands.

"Alright, what else do you have?" I asked.

"Just these," he pulled three books out of the box, two with Mylar protectors already on their dust jackets, and the third a spiral spine book. A book's cover, or jacket, comprises most of the value of a rare book. Without its jacket, a modern first edition isn't worth the ink it's printed with. These three were mint and sported wonderfully bright jackets unaffected by the effects of U.V. light.

"Let's see the spiral one," I said. "Wow! We have James Lee Burke's *Half of Paradise*. That's the last one I don't have of his as a first edition. Terrific! How much?" I was gleeful, completely ignoring my own rule not to show enthusiasm.

"That's $750," said Lenny. A bargain easily worth $4000, I thought. I put it aside and looked at the next jewel that I would add to my collection now that I could afford to keep the good stuff.

Tarzan of the Apes, by Edgar Rice Burroughs, first edition, very good with a very good but clipped dust jacket, bumped corners, spine sunning, top pull, some minor shelf wear, …OK," I murmured to myself in front of Lenny. "I read this book the summer between ninth and tenth grades. My English teacher, Mr. Pond, loaned all of his paperback Tarzan novels to me over the summer; all twenty-four of them. Very, very nice, Lenny. And the price for this one?"

Books were my weakness; Lenny knew that full well. I have a handful of other Achilles weaknesses, too: dimples and hats on pretty woman, schnitzel, coffee ice cream, and the National Anthem. When any of those things are present, heaven can wait.

"Twenty-five hundred, Charles," he replied.

"How about two grand?"

Lenny squirmed but finally agreed to my offer after a bit more haggling and then was annoyed when I asked him to hold all of it for me until I had a chance to speak to my banker.

"*What?*" he nearly shrieked.

"Sorry, Lenny, but times are tight, our cash isn't flowing. We have some things in the works but they haven't come to fruition."

"Charles, it's not good form to chisel and then ask for a layaway. Professionals don't do that and I just gave you a sword, too," he reminded me.

I felt the heat in my face. I had violated dealer protocol. As a dealer myself, I had more than once thrown a retail jerk out of my booth or shop for the same thoughtless action. Asking for a discount is OK, but to combine a discount with a credit card sale, which costs the merchant a percentage, with a free delivery, and/or with an advertised sale is beyond the pale.

"I am very sorry, Lenny, I apologize." I looked at Emma. "I'll go around the corner to Wells Fargo and get some cash. Emma will wait here as a hostage."

She tilted her head and peered at me with one eye nearly closed, but didn't argue.

Apologetically, I backed out of the store accidently rattling the overhead door clangor, which made a frightful racket. That mishap heightened my already scarlet composure. I walked the hundred yards or so to the bank, staring at my Blackberry as a means of disguise. Closing time was in a half hour. I hoped there might be enough time left in the day to move some money around. Before I got in line, I slipped in an ear bud and plugged the other end into the phone so that I wouldn't disturb anyone. There were a couple of messages that I had to act on. The delay that two customers ahead of me in queue provided was sufficient to listen to Rick Waggener's message; his was the oldest. Rick was delighted with the dag, and he said that he had already made a direct deposit into my account. And then I texted Peter Shupp, hoping that he'd already received the Audubon set by FedEx, which he had five minutes earlier, as I discovered. We exchanged texts and I learned that he'd already begun looking them over, but that he'd need a couple of days more to complete his analysis. Emma texted me to hurry up because Lenny wanted to take us down the street for a bite. Five minutes before security shut the building I finally got to speak with a teller. He confirmed Rick's and Fleet's cash deposits, and then I had him move $5000 from the line of credit to the business checking. I walked back to Lenny's feeling much relieved.

"Thanks, Charles," Lenny said. "You're a standup guy."

I looked at him sheepishly. "Yeah, I know. Thanks for your patience."

"Let's go eat at the C&O, Charles," Emma pleaded.

13 The So-Married Man

"Alright, let's go," I urged.

But just then a yuppie couple in tweeds parallel parked a red BMW in front of his shop. Emma made a face. I couldn't very well encourage Lenny to shoo them away so I made the best of the delay. "Where's your wife, Lenny?" I asked, as we waited patiently for the customers to come in.

"Crystal's at a class studying forensic anthropology." Lenny's sixth wife is a perpetual student. She has three undergrad degrees, plus two Master's, a JD, and an MD. Some people collect personal property, some are connoisseurs of wives, and others collect degrees.

When the couple was all the way in the back looking at something, Lenny whispered, "Should've flipped the open sign. You can bet they won't buy anything."

Sure enough, they looked around a few minutes and then left without buying a thing.

"How'd you know they weren't going to buy anything," asked Emma.

"People who drive red cars never buy anything," he complained.

Emma and I looked at each other with our eyebrows raised, and said simultaneously, "You're right!" We all laughed. Crystal joined us in the nick of time just as Lenny was locking up and the four of us chatted as we walked to the C&O Restaurant. Lenny was friendly with the staff. They assigned us a good table right away.

The C&O, known for its fine cuisine, is named after the nearby train depot by the same name. I decided to order two appetizers instead of one appetizer with an entrée. The mushroom and oyster chowder sounded perfect, as did the puy lentil tortelloni with crisp prosciutto and Parmigiano reggiano. That and a beer with a bib lettuce house salad followed by one of their famous desserts would be enough.

Emma chose a warm butternut squash tart as an appetizer and a wonderful entre of horseradish-crusted salmon and creamed spinach in a spiced pinot noir reduction. As usual when we dine out, I wished I had chosen what Emma had ordered. And while I'm busy inspecting Emma's plate, she proceeded to eat stuff off of my plate before I even had a chance to nibble. I gave her my usual look of disapproval for foraging beyond the boundary and got her usual response: "Delicious, Darling," as she smiled sweetly.

I returned her an expressionless look of the, So-Married Man, a term that she had coined flippantly early on in our union when I came home unexpectedly in the middle of one of her laundry days. Draped all over the house like a Macy's Day Parade were what appeared to be her entire collection of still damp, newly washed delicates. And I am quite certain it was her entire assembly, because not a square foot remained where a tired man could rest, lean, or otherwise travel safely across the expanse of any room in the house. I stood from the threshold aghast, having never before witnessed an interior decorated in such a manner. Momentarily, it was an incomprehensible situation for me. Her reply, when I croaked my astonishment, was: "You're *so* married, Amor."

"Indeed," I muttered. And so I have been known within my own castle ever since as the 'So-Married Man.'

Crystal and Lenny mirrored our dinner selections; Lenny ordered what Emma chose and Crystal ordered what I got. The three of them split a nice cabernet franc from Barboursville Vineyards, which I was envious of, but the sulfites in wine induce massive migraines in me, whereas beer does not. I had my favorite, Dos Equis.

I thought, *Everything could not be more excellent: the food, the service, the company — ah, what a nice moment in our lives.* As we settled back from our plates, satisfied with the meal and the day, I asked, "So, Lenny, what other insights have you observed over time? Other than the fact that drivers of red cars don't buy much of anything in antiques shops?"

"Plenty," he replied evenly.

"Like what?" Emma asked.

"Well, for instance, people who drive Camaros, Firebirds, Corvettes, or convertibles usually don't buy anything, either, no matter their color," he added.

Emma and I looked at each other for confirmation. "We've noticed that phenomenon, too," I said, nodding, for both of us.

Lenny continued. "Here's another one. People who pick up free literature from the wall rack on the way *into* the shop, never buy anything either. I suppose it's a signal that they're most likely cheapskates." We all began laughing at the same time as the waiter came for our after-dinner drink orders.

Emma added, "If they're sixty or older they don't buy anything,"

I nodded. "That's because they don't need anything anymore. Heck, they're trying to get rid of their stuff, not acquire more. That's why the antiques trade weakened in the early '90's: the WWII generation, who had been strong collectors, went over the hill."

Lenny chuckled and nodded in agreement, as he sipped a fine Armagnac, a Baron De Lustrac, 1980. That evening I chose the valiant efforts of Chateau de Tariquet XO, a Bas-Armagnac, and probably the better of the two. Both ladies enjoyed champagne cocktails and our banter.

Not to be outdone Emma chimed in, "Groups of women that enter our shop seldom spend any money either because there always seems to be one in their group to tell all of the others not to buy."

Lenny laughed his agreement and added, "And, any group of people that includes parents and adult children usually won't buy anything because the parents reminisce to their kids how they bought the same thing for a song thirty years earlier."

"If you don't mind my saying so, I couldn't help but overhear you," a distinguished looking gentleman seated next to us at a table by himself said, with a Peter O'Toole accent. We turned toward his voice. "I might add that people who whistle never buy anything, either." That remark had us nearly rolling in the aisle; it was so unexpected. The gentleman introduced himself as Fred Hoar, and told us that he had a rare bookshop in London and offices elsewhere. We introduced ourselves, invited him to our table for an after-dinner brandy, and discovered a funny man.

"So Fred, what brings you to Charlottesville," I asked.

"It should be obvious, old chap, eight rare bookshops."

Lenny asked, "Which one in particular?"

He replied, "Actually two: Blue Whale Books and the Virginia Book Shop. Also, it's very pleasant here, though a bit chilly in the winter, and there are so many very lovely ladies," he flirted with Emma. I couldn't help but think that Fred looked a bit like Eric Clapton, and Clapton is the one person who really flips Emma's wig, but I'm not the envious or jealous sort. Needless to say, she was enjoying being charmed. Fred told us that he liked to winter in Naples and Palm Springs, scouting books between the two.

"What other retail observations do you have, Fred," I asked leaning back in my seat.

"In the UK," he continued, "I don't have many people driving American sports cars stopping by the shop, but I have noticed that the experience Lenny described of the car types phenomena holds true in Britain as well." We were delighted to discover a comrade-in-arms, so to speak. "Also, a majority of people under about twenty-five years of age rarely buy anything of consequence, mostly, I presume, because they're not yet well established."

Emma added, "I've noticed that smokers don't buy very much unless they're dealers, and a lot of dealers are smokers."

"This business causes bad habits," Lenny confirmed.

"That used to be the case," I said.

By this point in the evening we were all a bit schnockered and enjoying the trading of antiques war stories.

"What about your pet business peeves," I asked everyone.

"Ahh, now that's a lengthy list, isn't it?" Fred quipped.

"Yeah, everything pisses Charles off," Emma giggled.

"Me too," Lenny chuckled, and Fred laughed.

They looked to me. I thought for a second. "For me, I'm most peeved when people ask me *where* I get my things. It makes me see red. Now *really*, do they think I'm going to tell them my *sources*?"

Lenny commented, "They always assume we get things from auctions, anyway."

Fred nodded sagely. "Even if you told them that it takes years to establish a supply network of pickers and wholesalers, they wouldn't be able to comprehend it all. They just don't have a clue, Charles."

"And knowing what to buy and to whom to sell it, and when, is the other side of the equation," Emma added.

"What do you tell them when they ask how you know a particular book is valuable?" Lenny asked Fred.

Fred thought for a moment and then expounded, "I tell them that it takes years of experience which may or may not develop into useful knowledge that may eventually become a talent for discerning nuances for any single set of objects, and each set has its own subset of definitive variables which are subject to an individual's learning curve."

I noticed Lenny seemed to be taking mental notes.

"What?" Emma chirped. Between Fred's gobbledygook, the cultural differences, and the two cocktails that she'd had, I don't think anything registered.

I clarified for Emma's sake, "Over time the collector, who is likely to be narrow in scope, will become more proficient in his field than the dealer, who is more likely to be a generalist than a specialist."

"Correct," Fred said, "that was very succinct, Charles."

His phone began ringing from inside his Harris Tweed sports jacket. Fred excused himself from the conversation and walked away to the lobby for a few minutes. We were content at small talk while he was away and silenced our chatter when he approached to rejoin us.

"That was a bit of good news, my new friends." Fred seemed to have something exciting to tell us. "My New York office has located a rare set of Audubon books in California. I'll be leaving first thing in the morning for Santa Barbara."

Emma gave a little gasp.

"That sounds great, Fred." I sounded hopeful. "Do you have a buyer lined up for the Audubons?"

"For really fine items there are always buyers readily available, as all of you well know. Unfortunately, though, because of my early departure, I must bid you all farewell at this time and take my leave," he said, and we men stood to shake his hand. "I have enjoyed the evening's conversation," Fred continued. "Perhaps we can get together again soon. Oh, and here's my card. And if I may contribute to the evening's damages." He put some folded money under the edge of his plate. We were sad to see him go.

"Charles, what – ," Emma started to say something.

"We'll talk about it later, Emma." I quieted her. Lenny pretended to ignore us, perhaps thinking it was a personal thing due to Fred Hoar's obvious flirting earlier. And that must have been enough impetus to make Lenny say he thought they'd call it a night.

"Well, I guess we'd better be off, too, Lenny," I said. "We'll have a long day tomorrow with all of this neat stuff to research."

We went back to Lenny's shop, loaded the day's spoils into the Volvo and said our good-byes promising to drop in on him another time. I got behind the wheel and we began our drive back to Barboursville. *What a lovely evening,* I thought, but I could tell Emma had something on her mind.

"Amor," she asked, "why didn't you want Fred to know that we were the ones who owned the Audubon books?"

I tilted my head and raised an eyebrow before I spoke. "He looked excited. I didn't want to rain on his parade, in a manner of speaking. And, it may have spooked him. We could have lost a sale."

"Oh, I see. Well, I wouldn't have said anything without checking with you first."

"I know, dear. When and if it becomes necessary to tell him that the books really belonged to us, and that Peter is only the broker, then he'll be told. Besides, we have to respect the confidentiality of the brokering agreement. Peter is responsible for his check clearing and the shipping arrangements; two fewer things for us to worry about."

I contemplated for a second. "There is one other reason as well." Emma looked at me. "Revealing our connection might spoil the chase for him, my dear. Half of the fun for us dealers is the chase." At that Emma nodded, pacified by my logical explanations. I found myself falling silent as well but for another reason — selling our businesses would never stop me from picking. I had private collectors, and a whole bevy of dealers to continue to work with, plus my appraisal business and show circuit. But closing the stores would change the chase in certain ways. Would I find the same satisfaction without our retail shops to display and sell our various finds? Time would tell.

14 The Turkey Sag Facility

It was dark by the time we took Route 231 north of Charlottesville.

At Cash's Store I hung a left onto Turkey Sag Road and drove up the side of the slippery mountain past miles of white board fences marking the boundary of the humongous Albemarle County estate, Castle Hill. At one of its farm entrances there is a gate constructed of boards that I always admire for its design merit as I drive past. Opposite the estate, at the foot of what passes for a mountain in central Virginia, is a segment of chain link fence marking an open entrance to a paved road that winds its way up Peters Mountain. Rumor has it that somewhere past the large sign, "Do Not Enter -- AT&T" at the entrance, there's a deep bunker for Federal elites. Vice President Cheney is rumored to have retreated there on 9-11.

I checked Google maps. There is a bunker. I've seen it. I asked myself, *Why would AT&T need a bunker? And why is there a huge white AT&T logo painted on a round helipad up there? Not a Huey-sized pad, but one big enough for four or five Blackhawks or maybe a couple of Chinooks. Uh-huh, AT&T. Sure. And Catherine Zeta Jones is going to kick in my door one day, too.*

Anyone ignoring the AT&T sign is politely escorted downhill by armed men in black camouflage, or so I was told by one of my horsey friends. She was tempted one day to ride her horse up the manicured path, but she didn't get very far. Two men ordered her to dismount and then they escorted her out on foot.

Since when does AT&T employ commandos? I always think, as we drive past the entrance to pick up Grace from her doggie camp on the other side of the mountain.

Unusual activity happens in this neck of the woods. Last year I witnessed a parade of four or five shiny black Suburbans race past Grace's camp. The sight of blacked-out windows made me wonder. I felt both of my little fingers twitch and I knew it wasn't because the Suburbans were a great find; something was going on. That kind of activity is hard to miss in a bucolic country setting.

Periodically, when I stop by Cash's Store, or when I'm on the other side of Peters Mountain at Bobby's Store, I ask the locals about the goings on at 'The Facility', and they're eager to talk. Over the last few years, a dozen sources have corroborated the mystery. The only consensus is that there is something going on up on Peters Mountain, but no one seems to know what it is.

One old guy that I asked, a fur trapper, who works the area, told me that on September 12th 2001 – the day after terrorists knocked down the Twin Towers – a flatbed tractor trailer truck hauling what would pass for artillery went through the entrance and never came back out. Some people in nearby Gordonsville claim that at night the hilltop is sometimes lit brightly with blue lights. I've looked, but cannot confirm that.

On past the macadam where Turkey Sag Road degrades into a rough gravel road there's a big, 500-

acre-plus farm on the right side that encompasses the entire sag, or natural bowl in the landscape surrounded by a ridge; that's what a sag is. The natural feature is visible from a wide gap along the road, and Tom Tanner's log cabin is too. It's up high on the side of the tree-cleared ridge. I visit Tom two or three times a year whenever I find the one thing that he avidly collects: turkey calls. I bet that I have sold him a hundred and forty or fifty in the past twenty-five years. He credits me with building his collection and likes to show them to me each time I visit. Tom looks a bit like Grandpa on the television show, The Waltons; the actor's name is Will Geer.

From his front porch, he can see all the way to the women's correctional facility, some twenty miles away, and well beyond to a branch of the Southwest Mountains so distant that I don't even know them by name. We were sitting in rocking chairs on his front porch one day not that long ago talking about his collection when he told me something that I will always remember. It was springtime. The redbud was rioting and there was a blush on the maples and tulip poplars. My mind had drifted to morel hunting because Tom's voice was gentle and had a calming effect on me, and then he surprised me.

"Charles," he began, "you know I'm an ex-Green Beret, dontcha?"

"Yeah, I remember."

"I saw something that I cannot explain," he said.

I perked up. "When?"

"It was about three months after 9-11," he told me.

"What did you see?"

He continued, "It was nighttime, around 2300 hours, I suppose. I went down the steps into my yard over there to take a leak." He pointed to a small patch of mowed grass by a meter-sized millstone lying on its side. Yellow daffodils sprouted from the square hole in the stone's center. "As I was doing my business, I looked at the starry night sky and counted the aviation traffic. I counted seventeen different aircraft moving along routinely in their usual corridors. Seventeen is a lot. Ten to twelve is typical. I saw one craft approaching me slightly off center at about my eleven o'clock position. It wasn't strobing. It was a plain white light and not like a landing light either, and it wasn't blinking. I thought that it was a satellite. It got to my twelve o'clock high position, which would be practically dead center on Peters Mountain, and then it zoomed away at an unearthly rate of acceleration." He saw a question on my lips but managed to answer it before I could utter a sound. "And, no, there was no noise, no sonic boom, no nothin'." That's all he said about it. He wouldn't elaborate or speculate when I prodded, so I dropped it. He just seemed to need to tell someone. Later that day, I bade my farewell to him but always recalled his words when we drove by this way.

Grace was delighted to see us, but the lady at the doggie camp seemed sad. When Emma asked her if everything was OK, she broke into tears and sobbed in Emma's arms. I don't know what to do when women cry for no apparent reason. After some commotion she calmed down, used a few Kleenex's, and told us that her drinking buddy had just died the day before. I offered her my condolences immediately, of course, and asked her what had happened.

She replied, "He was walking his dog in the field in front of his property and just dropped dead."

I felt a lump in my throat.

"Who?" Emma asked.

She sobbed, "Tom Tanner."

15 Bombay Hook

After picking so much recently, and buying, there was a lot of catching up to do. We were both behind because the new acquisitions needed processing and mail needed tending to, so we got to work. Emma paid the paper bills and I answered the email: Peter and Thack wanted to come for a visit. "...Saturday evening...," I told Emma. "Peter wants to bring us a check for the Audubons."

Emma cooed her delight and dove into the chores at hand: cleaning and repairing jewelry and logging it into our Microsoft Access database and into our eBay store. By the time she was done with the jewelry, I was done with the furniture pieces. Then both of us started on the pile of books. I triage faster than she does, so I made the categorical cuts: the eBay sell pile, the ABE pile, the keeper pile, and the toss pile that goes to the local Goodwill. Which pile a book lands on is on a book-by-book basis and dependent on the respective book's potentially numerous value attributes. As I graded for condition, Emma covered the valuable books with Mylar, the way librarians do, all 788 of them.

Books are tedious to buy and sell if you don't know much about them. Condition grading and Mylaring is just the prep; then comes the research, pricing, logging, full written description, marketing, packaging, and shipping. Marketing means placing them in the most appropriate venue for sale, which is yet another type of triage, and just like anything else for sale, presentation and condition are everything. To do it right takes a lot of time, diligence, and experience. When those three elements are lacking, it shows aesthetically and is reflected on the bottom line. As with other categories of inventory, diligent work upfront is rewarded on the back end with a greater return. After two days of grinding away at cataloging, we were ready to hit the road again on one of our easterly loops.

We went off to see the picker, John Arnold.

I met John at the Tobacco Barn Antiques Show in 1989, I think. That was ten years or more before Emma. It was a show that had been sponsored by the St. Thomas Episcopal Parish Church in Upper Marlborough since 1959. To be invited was a feather in a dealer's cap. He and I were assigned booths across from each other. It was his first time, too.

As we set up our booths, we got to talking and soon learned of our similar backgrounds: he was a retired Marine colonel and I was still a Ready Reserve Marine aviator. At that time, John handled only Oriental tribal rugs, and I handled Americana. After a few years of knowing each other, we agreed to keep a lookout for each other's interests. Occasionally I pick for him and he returns the favor when he finds my kind of stuff. This was one of those times; he had something for me, so off we went to see him.

Four hours later, we were approaching our scheduled meeting place: Sambo's, a tavern in Leipzig, Delaware. I told Emma how I remembered it from the early 1970's from when I used to come here in my youth with my parents; nearby Dover Air Force Base was my dad's last assignment. To get a rise out of

Emma, I exaggerated how I remembered its dilapidated state.

"Like a crab shack on a bayou," I reminisced as we pulled off the freeway onto a narrow country road that passed through the tidal marshlands. I told her, "Cane reeds grow all around the thatched hooch and the air holds marsh muck odors, like this." I rolled the windows down. She gave me a look and I rolled them back up. I chuckled at the way she wrinkled her pert nose, and then continued, "Darling, I remember there used to be an old hand-lettered sign that read 'Fresh Crabs Sold Her,' over there somewhere by that tree." I pointed to a lone tree we were approaching. "And thousands of bottle caps and cigarette butts littered the oyster shell parking lot back then. Of course, now I'm sure that it's been paved over. Oh, and seagulls flew overhead by the dozens making their dutiful contributions to the organic viability of the natural environment."

"Alright, Charles, that's enough," she snapped. "Do you suppose they might be sophisticated enough to have a bathroom?"

"Sure, they're bound to have a hole cut in the floor in the ladies' room." I snickered.

She was not amused. "I wouldn't be surprised," she snorted and looked out her window. She gets cranky when she's been in the car too long.

Sambo's was named Sambo's long before a name like that could have caused such uproar in a politically sensitive society. Another restaurant chain with the same name had yielded to public opinion, this Sambo's had not. The name was still the same when we rounded the bend in this sleepy hamlet, but like I saw online before leaving, someone had given it a makeover Oprah would have been proud of. Emma was visibly relieved.

She laughed, "You were, how you say it, Amor? Putting me over?"

"'Putting me on,' Periwinkle." I get a kick out of making Emma laugh.

Grace needed to be let out, so we walked her around a few minutes, to her delight, but then we had a heck of a time convincing her to get back in the Volvo; we used cookie bribery to do so. When we opened the folk art painted screen door, it was like time traveling back to the 1950's. The clock had stopped for these folks about the same year Buddy Holly died, give or take. Coca-Cola advertisements of the period were everywhere, including the apron of the red-haired girl who came to serve us.

"Hi," she greeted us with a smile and an open pad, "what can we do for you today?"

"Where's your bathroom, please?" Emma asked right away, and then left in the direction the girl pointed. I asked for a few minutes and the waitress went to help two of the other tables.

Fresh crab, fish, shrimp, clams, oysters, and crawfish seemed to be emphasized more than anything else on the menu. I waited until Emma came back to hear her hygiene critique of the restroom.

"Clean facilities," Emma declared on returning with a thumb up. She paused and gestured to the door that we'd just entered. "I like the front door, Amor."

I turned around, "Nice isn't it. There are a lot of them in Baltimore."

"Why Baltimore?"

"Around the 19-teens a new immigrant to Baltimore, a Czech grocer named William Oktavec, was the first to paint door screens. He first decorated his own red bungalow and then his neighbors'. Soon it became a trendy thing that took off down the block in both directions, and eventually the idea spread all over the region. East-side Baltimore has the most, but there're probably hundreds of examples remaining throughout the area. Baltimoreans consider their screens living history. They even have a Baltimore Painted Screen Society. Shortly before we met I gave one to Jazz."

Emma stepped closer to the door, examining it from the inside, and then from the outside. "I can't see the picture from the inside," she said.

"Yep, that's the intent. Passersby can't see in but people inside can see out. Tourists get to enjoy all sorts of colorful landscape, animal, and whimsical scenes while the view from inside is unobstructed."

"How do you know so much about them, Amor?"

"They're folk art, Babe. One of my appraiser certifications is folk art, so I have a need to know. Besides, I like them. I've met a couple of the contemporary screen artists, including one of the descendants of the original Czech man, and he's still carrying on his grandfather's tradition."

She smiled delightfully and snuggled her hand underneath mine on the table.

The redheaded waitress, in her early twenties ,returned. "Have you been to Sambo's before?" she asked.

Before I could answer, John Arnold rounded the bend in his fancy white Mercedes.

"One moment, please," I told the waitress, and pointed to the approaching sloop with a license plate that read, Hooker. "Our other party is arriving to join us now," I said to the girl. She glanced out the window at the car parking, smiled, and then drifted away again to another table. John oozed from the McLaren as if it were a scabbard. He was wearing his favorite full-quill ostrich boots, jeans, red plaid flannel shirt, and a sheepskin coat. John's about six foot six, two-hundred-fifty hard pounds, and looks kind of like Johnny Depp.

As he squeezed through the ample doorway with a grocery bag in one hand, my pinkies curled like fern fronds, a clear indicator something of consequence was within my proximity receptors. The way I was tingling, I figured he must have a dinosaur bone in that sack, but I kept my patience.

John roared, "Charles, you old Leatherneck! How's it hanging?" My normal man-sized fist all but disappeared in his monstrous grasp. "And Emma my darling, *good god*! You are as gorgeous as ever." The seagulls outside circling the parking lot flared away at his tempest. He then planted an ever-so-delicate peck on Emma's cheek. She sniffed his cologne and thanked him with the usual body language he evokes in women wherever he goes.

The waitress sidled over again when we were all seated, and attempted to gain our attention. With a curious glint in her eye, she seemed to be paying especially close attention to John, which was no surprise. I'd seen him in non-combat action before. He's quite deft. I smiled at the scene unfolding before me and assumed the position of grasshopper in the presence of a maestro, while Emma reacted predictably to John's charms; she blushed and fanned the heat away with a laminated menu.

The waitress approached us with a, "Howdy, folks, have you ever been to Sambo's before?"

"Yes, we have," I answered the same question again, and attempted to focus my group by ordering first. "I'll have an order of...."

But Emma interrupted, pointing to her menu, "Charles, don't you *dare* order those nauseating frog legs."

"...a dozen jumbo blue crabs, please," I completed my sentence with one eyebrow raised in Emma's direction. Chesapeake blue point crabs are the best, especially the jumbo-sized ones.

The waitress responded, "OK, and I recommend clams as well."

"I'll have some of my husband's," said Emma. "And water, too, please."

John grinned at the pretty girl with the fiery steampunk hairdo. "I'll have a dozen jumbos and three dozen clams, too," he charmed. The two exchanged mental memos that no doubt would lead to greater expectations, knowing John the way I do.

"Charles, Emma, you're going to love this little gem," and he withdrew a splendid key basket from his brown paper bag.

Key baskets are from the 19th century. They're usually made of leather and are elongated in shape with rounded ends and a round-wrapped, fixed-loop handle. The depth of the side is typically four inches in height, the flat bottom eight inches long and five inches wide. Key baskets were a gift given to a young bride in which she kept all of the household keys. Plain key baskets are relatively scarce; fancy-tooled and painted specimens are rare. This one was as good as or better than the world auction record, the Deyerle key basket. It sold at a Charlottesville auction in 1995 for about $36,000.

I held the one John brought like a preemie infant, and sighed in relief as my tuning forks unfurled. Its paint was bright, its tooling was superb, and its condition was excellent. "John, we'd love to take it off your hands outright, but I am afraid that we just can't afford it," I said.

John looked surprised. "But I haven't even told you what I want for it."

"You don't have to. It's the best that I have ever seen. We can't afford it."

John looked at Emma and then at me as the waitress returned with a large tray mounded with jumbo crabs before she made separate trips for the clams and more beer. John carefully set the basket aside, and we took a few minutes to settle into the routine of cracking and picking crabs before John resumed the discussion. "Charles, the price is $20,000."

"No way José," I shook my head and cracked open another pincer in a practiced way hoping to be rewarded with the whole piece.

Emma just watched the drama unfold as we hemmed and hawed for a minute before John said, "Look, you have a buyer, right?"

I shrugged affirmatively but said, "Sell it at auction. It'll easily fetch $20,000."

He spat a shell fragment onto his newspaper and replied, "No, I want *you* to sell it. I know that you have powerful clients. Besides, I trust you with the transaction; you send me twenty grand when it goes through. Whatever you get over that, you keep."

I looked to Emma for approval because of the high amount. She just shrugged the ball back to me and smashed a claw too hard.

"See there," John said, "I knew we'd come to an understanding. Thank you Emma for your input." He drained the last of his beer and smiled satisfactorily. "We have a deal."

I said, "Agreed."

She looked at him and then at me with her mouth open. "What'd I do?"

John used a wet wipe to clean his hands before setting the gem back in the bag. Then we went back to our crab cracking until all of the jumbos were finished. For a while, we enjoyed swapping antiques stories with each other and bringing Emma up to speed. We listed our almost finds, too-late misses, and then our attention settled on the array of Coca-Cola collectibles on the walls of Sambo's. Each booth, including the one we were occupying, had a countertop Wurlitzer #61 jukebox mounted on the wall-end of the table and there were at least three items on the walls that I liked.

When the girl brought us key lime pie and coffee with the bill, I asked if the jukeboxes and Coca-Cola memorabilia were for sale. She didn't know, but she had the owner come to our table. A tall skinny guy, about thirty years old, sat down at our request and introduced himself as Henry Compton. He told us that he'd inherited the place two months earlier from his father who'd just passed away. He was not averse to selling anything because business hadn't been that great since the last hurricane. As it turned out, he didn't have a clue as to value of anything.

"What do you think?" I asked Emma and John.

"Not my thing, Charles, you handle it," said John.

"Let's broker it if we can," encouraged Emma. "I like advertising."

So, on a pad of paper I made a few calculations while the others waited patiently.

"Okay, Henry," I said, "here's the plan if you're interested. We're here on temporary business for the day and wouldn't have the room in our station wagon to take all of what we'd like to buy from you anyway, but this is what I'll do. I have a friend in Atlanta who has a truck that will come up here to get the jukeboxes, calendars, signs, postcards, thermometers, and all of the other stuff the day after tomorrow. He's a nice guy and can pay you in cash for all of it. Anything in mint condition, he'll pay you half of book price and he'll bring a copy of this year's price guide with him to show you what the book rates are for each piece he wants to buy. Items in less than mint condition, he'll pay you less than half of book value. His name is Randal Cunningham. He deals exclusively in advertising items and things like jukeboxes. Do you understand what I've told you so far?"

"Yes sir. How much do you think all this will bring me?" asked Henry. He seemed to have some difficulty keeping up with the information stream.

I replied, "My guess is somewhere around forty to fifty thousand dollars."

John piped up. "That's a fair amount, my boy."

"Oh, dear," The young waitress had joined Henry and appeared to have emotional ties to the young man. We learned later that she was his cousin.

"You've got some good stuff here Henry," I advised. "It'll bring you enough money to get you a solid start in the restaurant business so that you won't have to worry about the little things anymore. Be sure to check with your accountant about the tax liability."

Henry gulped, "Jeez, OK. I can pay off my debts, get some new equipment for the kitchen, a new outboard motor, and a better car, too." Henry was moving from being dumbfounded to joy and he was already spending his chickens before they hatched.

I handed him my card and said, "We're Charles & Emma. Our company is Spring Hill Farm Antiques, LLC. We'll be in the area at these mobile numbers," and I pointed to our phone numbers on the card, "in the meantime, Henry, I don't want you to sell any of this to anyone and I don't want you to do anything to it at all. Don't clean it or anything. Just leave it alone and wait for Mr. Cunningham. You got that?"

"Yes sir." He and his redheaded cousin looked at each other.

"When Cunningham gets here," I explained, he'll show you his identification, probably a Georgia driver's license, and he'll want you to close the place, or if you don't want to close, then he'll wait until closing time so he won't disturb your patrons. Okay?"

"Yes sir. No problem, I'll close as soon as possible."

"Good. If at any time you get cold feet or if for some reason you don't like Mr. Cunningham you can call me at those numbers I just gave you."

"Yes sir, I will," Henry said.

"Yes sir, he will," said the girl.

"One more thing," I said, "in case you're wondering, Cunningham will pay me a finder's fee to me on top of what I've told you he will pay you. I want you to realize that for me this is a business transaction, Henry. It seems like a favor to you, but this is how I make my living. I find what other people want and see that they get it. Do you understand?"

"Yes sir I do," he gulped.

"Do you still want to do this?"

"Yes sir." He nodded his head rapidly.

"Then we have an agreement," I said as we shook hands. John insisted on paying for the meal. I picked up one of Henry's cards, took a half-dozen photos with my cell phone, and we all said our goodbyes. John climbed back into his humongously expensive vehicle and led the way.

This time Emma drove. On the way I emailed the photos of the Coca-Cola stuff to Cunningham. He responded immediately with a call and grilled me about the discovery. I filled him in on the particulars and how to proceed. He thanked me and told me that he'd get back to me after he had assessed the collection.

John's second home is near Bombay Hook Wildlife Refuge. That's why his license plate reads "Hooker". I smile to myself at the thought of what most peoples' thoughts might be when they first see it, and then my mind reminisces elsewhere. I have memories of coming here when I was a young man. Sometimes I came here to shoot photographs of the waterfowl in the autumn during migration season, and at other times I would come to show off how much I knew about nature to my dates. Bombay Hook wasn't just a nature preserve to me; it was where I went to take refuge from whatever it was that was bothering me. All young people have things that bother them. It's how they deal with their bothers that determines if they avoid the abyss or not. Some escape in a bad way. I escaped here. Bombay Hook, to me, is as peaceful a place as Sedona, Arizona. But unlike Sedona, here it is unspoiled by commercial enterprise, white-socked tourists, and tattooed hippies.

From atop pilings, his shingle-style mansion has a sweeping vista of the marshland. Muskrat huts dot the landscape giving it a visual texture similar to John's full-quill boots. What I enjoy most about his place is the waterfowl migration in the fall. You have to experience it yourself in order to comprehend how loud, beautiful, and awesome it is. There must be millions of ducks and geese and swans and other birds all flying about at once in every direction in flocks and V formations, and from tree-top level to so high as to be nearly out of sight. I wished it was the migration season now, but spring is pretty here too. Spring is always pretty everywhere.

Emma gave Grace a long walk before joining John and me inside. She refused a drink, but I accepted the Armagnac that he handed me before he launched a refresher course on the value attributes of Oriental rugs in his paneled trophy room which was plastered with mounted game heads and full-body mounts including, lions and tigers and bears. Grace followed our voices and came bounding in. As soon as she realized that she was literally in a lion's den, she yelped and fled back to the kitchen to Emma.

John made a motion with the glass in his hand, "So much for the ferocious guard dog you have there, Charles."

I turned when I heard the patter of Emma's shoes behind me.

"Oh my," Emma murmured, looking all around the room. She had never been in John's trophy room before. She complained to John, "Your aneemals scared Grace."

"Come on you guys, ain't it great? I bagged all of these trophies myself over the years. Some are Boone and Crocket records. That hartebeest and this Cape buffalo are my most recent acquisitions." John tried to justify his trophies to Emma before she could marshal her usual argument against his favorite sport. She doesn't like hunting trophies and never hesitates to proselytize against hunting.

I laughed. "I'll excuse myself if you guys don't mind while you two butt heads; I need to check my messages." I went off to John's sunroom and took a seat in a comfortable red leather club chair with a gas fireplace behind me and a view of the marsh at dusk.

Peter had left a message. He asked if we had room to put them up tomorrow evening. I texted him, *"yes & we wish u-all safe trip."*

Next, I took a look at our eBay sales to see how they had done for the day, and as usual of late, they were dismal and our website sales were worse. Plus, we had a return; a customer returning merchandise is worse than a day of no sales, and we had one. I learned that a belligerent customer who had purchased a $500 crock last week had returned it without prior approval. In an email I reiterated our written policy but approved the return because it is good business to be accommodating, and I very nicely told him that I hoped that he had double-boxed it and insured it for the full amount, because if it arrived damaged, there would be no refund. The jerk emailed me a picture of his longest finger. I emailed back to him a picture I pulled from Google Images of a horse's ass.

This business sucks, I thought, and took another sip of my Armagnac.

I felt like crap for having stooped as low as the ungrateful client. I also could feel my blood pressure rising, so I distracted myself from wanting to murder someone by sending a photo of the key basket to one of my client friends down in Richmond, Virginia. Richmond is where many of these key baskets were made by an unidentified saddler in the middle of the 1800's. People who worked leather into useful objects are called saddlers. In Virginia's capitol city there are four or five serious collectors of key baskets as fine as the one John asked us to broker. I gave celebrity plastic surgeon, Marshall Evans Crawford, first dibs. His response was immediate: he bought it for $35,000, and asked me to deliver it tomorrow as soon as possible so that he could pose with it for a photo shoot that he planned to send to the *Maine Antique Digest* in time to make the next deadline. I agreed to deliver it post-haste, of course, as long as I didn't have to be in the photograph. Celebrity is not a useful condition in the picking business. A low profile is much more desirable. I have enough trouble bidding at auctions as it is.

This business is great, I thought to myself, and then took another sip of my Armagnac.

16 Bookman's Feast

Our ride back to Barboursville by way of Richmond to drop off the key basket was uneventful except for the predictable traffic jam on the Chesapeake Bay Bridge and another jam on the DC beltway at the Interstate 95 south junction that lasted all the way to Fredericksburg. Normally a four-hour trip, our return took nearly all of the next day. By the time we got home, it was dark. No sooner had I fed Grace and built a fire, than there was a knock at the door.

"Charles! Emma! We're soooo glad to see you guys," oozed Peter as he hugged each of us in turn. Thack filled the doorway, acting as rear guard, and greeted me with an enveloping handshake while patiently bending down to receive Emma's peck and hug. Grace stirred from her favorite spot just long enough to sniff the new crotches and then conked out again.

"I see you have found your way here," I greeted them.

"No problem at all," replied Thack. Emma took their coats and put them away while Thack went to the kitchen to place on the counter a half case of cold champagne that they had brought with them.

"Well Charles, we sold the Audubon set for you," Peter announced, throwing his chewing gum into the burning fireplace.

"Are we all rich?" I asked.

"Hardly, darling," Peter said. "However $9000 is better than no thousand."

"Indeed," I replied. "Let's celebrate! I said, extending my arm to retrieve one of the bottles from the partitioned cardboard box, which was the cue for Emma to fetch four tall flutes from the Shaker-style cherry cabinets. I deftly removed the cork and allowed it to ricochet off one of the fir beams overhead with a pop! That startled Grace. Emma and Peter both sidled over to me holding the bottle over the island sink so as to be the first to harvest the suds.

Thack smiled good-naturedly, "Me, too, I need it. Been hanging with Pete all day! You know how taxing that is."

Peter pretended he didn't hear him.

I declared, "Cheers!" and the four of us clinked glasses as we stood around the fireplace.

"Nice find, Charles," Thack said.

"Actually Emma made the pick," I credited.

"Em, you're *so* clever!" Peter crooned, sidled up against her, and immediately launched a new topic. "God, what a wonderful old Sears house you have here darlings!"

We were both flattered that Peter would think our humble abode charming. "Thank you so much," Emma said, enjoying the moment. The two of them immediately began yacking at each other unmindful of my desire to know about the Audubon deal. It would have been futile to try to butt in, I realized, so I turned to Thack for man-talk.

He's only thirty-five years old, six feet six, two hundred eighty-five pounds, Irish-Mormon background, with a physics degree from Yale. After only three seasons, he washed out of pro football due to injuries. I met him through Peter. The two of them met online and they've been an item for six and a half years. I'd lost touch with Peter but accidently got reacquainted with him at a book fair in Denver, before the two met. Peter looked familiar to me when I saw him set up at the book show, so I introduced myself. Almost immediately, we both realized that he had been one of my ROTC instructors at JMU. Fancy that. What a small world all of us live in. I motioned Thack toward the living room so we'd have a view of the Blue Ridge Mountains.

I said to Thack, "It seems like you're getting bigger every time we see you."

He was flattered that I noticed, and swaggered a bit. "Yeah, thanks Charles. I've been working out more, actually."

"What, not giving up on returning to the NFL?"

"No more football for me, Charles, too much knee damage. But I've been trying to break into the muscle market. That's still a possibility for me."

"You mean competitive weight lifting?"

"No, my knees can't take the weight. I mean bodybuilding, like Schwarzenegger."

"Oh, I see." I gave him the once-over.

He grinned with one side of his mouth. "I've already competed in a couple of meets."

I nodded, "Really?"

I knew little to nothing about either sport, and as far as sports are concerned, I am not the least bit interested, and never have been. It's a family tradition, actually. My father, brother, sisters – no one ever watched sports or participated in them. *My* sport was fishing, but I never belittle others for their interests. I always keep my opinion to myself in trite matters, and

I am fully aware that many would consider outwitting a trout to be just as foolish as I find following a tiny white ball over hills and dales.

Thack explained, "Yeah, I'm serious about this. It's a serious sport, you know. I actually took second place at both meets. They say I could make money at it if I continue to improve."

Again, I nodded my approval. "Well, that's great, Thack. I know it's a very lucrative field based on what Schwarzenegger has been able to accomplish with it," I said, offering my encouragement.

Emma and Peter had migrated to the kitchen. I could hear her describing how she had made the best soufflé just last week. Peter was effusive with praise of her accomplishment, occasionally interjecting words of wisdom as only a gourmet cook would know. After the army, he dabbled in the restaurant business in Miami before he contracted book fever. With his business savvy, and Thack's nest egg, Peter built the strongest name in rare books on the West Coast. I could hear him as he and Emma approached. They were discussing the details of interior decorating as they sashayed over to us.

Peter suggested drunkenly, "Let's go out to the Palladio at the Barboursville Vineyard. I have read online that it is wonderful!"

I tried to rein him in a bit. "It is," I explained, "a five-star restaurant, Peter, but we would need reservations."

Thack recognized a cue when he heard one. He said firmly to Peter, "Emma's too tired to go elsewhere and so am I."

Emma entwined her arm with Peter's. "We just got back from Delaware and it took all day because of the awful traffic," she confirmed, and then batted her eyes at Peter for sympathy.

"Oh, you poor dears," Peter consoled, ushering Emma to a leather sofa, his attention momentarily diverted. "You sit down dearie. Open another bottle of champagne, Thackery! And throw a log onto the fire, Charles, while I cook a fabulous meal in this wonderful kitchen of Emma's. You can tell us all about it after dinner." Before Emma realized, Peter had stormed off to the kitchen with his old mission-importance. The rest of us resigned ourselves to our assigned tasks. I fed the fire with what was left in the copper caldron by the hearth while Thack brought in an armload of wood, and then opened a new bottle and poured some bubbly into all of our glasses. From the kitchen, Peter yoo-hooed at us every time he took a sip as he made a racket that sounded like he was turning the fridge, pantry, and all of the copper pots upside down. Occasionally we could hear him say something like, "Yes!" as he found whatever it was that he was looking for, or "Perfect! This'll do…and where's the Phyllo dough? Ah, that's it…Charles is just going to *love* this, he-he," he'd chuckle to himself.

I sat comfortably in an antique Gustav Stickley 332I. Its sturdy, squared form with worn leather cushions a stabilizing comfort after a long road trip. I leaned back in satisfaction as dinner preparations continued; I was glad to be home and in the company of good friends. The hickory popped on the mid-century andirons, pulling my attention to the firescreen by Wilhelm Hunt Diederich. I had found the andirons at The Heart of Country Antiques Show in 1989. At $750, they were a bargain for the form: nickel-plated sitting dogs. I figured that they were worth more than twice as much now. For the firescreen, I had traded my Ford Econoline boxed truck and $5000 in cash after I had stopped doing antiques shows; I didn't need it anymore. Emma just about had a cow when I told her what I had done, but she calmed down when I showed her the auction results for Diederich stuff. The screen is worth about a hundred grand, I figured, and it complements 'the andirons. Pickers usually don't have a lot of money lying about because of upgrade opportunities like this, but material assets, eh, that's a whole different ball of wax.

In the living room, the three of us occasionally snickered at his commentary as we eavesdropped.

"Before I get too schnockered...." Thack said, and then he pulled an envelope out of an inner pocket of his tweed jacket and handed it to me "Here's the check."

Emma moved over behind me, put her arms around my neck, and watched as I opened the envelope to see a check for $6000. It was what Peter and I had agreed on: principal plus half of the net profit. Peter sold them for $9000. We got back our initial investment of $3000 and then we split the net.

Thack looked impressed. "Pretty good deal, isn't it?"

I reminded him, "Half of this will go to taxes. You realize that, right?"

He nodded, "Yeah, I know. Same for us, too."

"Thank you guys for handling it," I said, looking from Thack to Peter who was watching in the kitchen.

"The pleasure is all ours, Charles," said Thack.

I probed. "By any chance, was Fred Hoar the lucky buyer?"

Peter dropped something in the sink. "How'd you know that?" Wearing Emma's favorite apron with a panda sewn on it, Peter walked over to us and leaned on the stone chimney. "How do you know Fred Hoar, guys?"

"We have our sources," I teased. Emma giggled.

"Sir Frederick Hoar is his name, actually," said Thack, who was surprised, but patient enough to wait for an explanation as to how we could have known about Fred. "Fred was delighted with the set of books, by the way, and he told us that the set was the finest example he'd ever seen. In fact he said that he already had a private buyer for it in Hong Kong."

"Oh, really?" Emma was surprised by the fast turnover. It may have crossed her mind how much more we could have gotten had we known the sources Fred apparently knows. I suppose it is human nature; it crossed my mind, too. "You see," Emma continued, "we met him in Charlottesville at a restaurant. He must have received your call about the books while he was having drinks with us because he excused himself at the table to take a call."

"You're joking," Peter said, standing in an apron with one hand on his hip and gesturing with a wooden meat tenderizer in the other.

"No, not at all," I added. "It was completely coincidental. We were having dinner with friends in town and Fred happened to overhear our conversation regarding the state of the antiques business. He introduced himself, and he fell into our conversation stream like an old hat, which in fact he is as it turned out. And he charmed Emma due to his likeness to Eric Clapton."

"He is very charming, isn't he?" crooned Peter to Emma from afar as we heard something clatter across the heart pine floor, which was a sound, that for Grace, meant an employment opportunity had just presented itself; she responded rapidly. Thack told us all about stuff going on in Santa Barbara and with their friends in San Francisco and L.A., and we were surprised when Peter finally declared dinner ready. "Well, boys and girls, belly-up to the bookman's feast. I have it all laid out on this wonderful Hudson River Valley painted huntboard. Serve yourself!" By then, all of us were starving. We paraded past the blue six-legged masterpiece and loaded down our gilded Doulton plates. It was a feast to behold; a German smorgasbord. Peter had made my most favorite meal: plate-sized Wiener schnitzel, parsley potatoes, cucumber salad, and if all of that wasn't enough, he informed us that he had an apfelstrudel baking in the oven. Emma had no doubt provided Peter with this culinary intelligence; he'd never have known my favorites without her help. I grew up eating this menu made lovingly by the hand of my redheaded Austrian mom.

Emma and Peter each lit a sterling, five-cup, Unger candelabra in the middle of our newly acquired farm table, which was dressed with a white linen runner atop an ivory-colored lace tablecloth that we'd found in Romania. Thack and I sat in two of the six matching continuous arm black Windsors at opposite ends. Emma and Peter sat across from each other between the candelabras on the long sides. The discussion that we were having was replaced with oohing and ahhing for Peter's spectacular spread, and then Peter noticed the cutlery that Emma had set the table with.

He crowed, "My *goodness*, these are beautiful! Who are they?"

Emma smiled and looked to me to answer his question. Thack had begun gorging and was totally ignoring us. I said, "It's the 1875 Egyptian Pattern by the Whiting Division of Gorham."

He attempted to read the marks, but failed, and nodded a question, "Whiting was a Gorham division by then, right? It's rare, isn't it?" He was referring to the consolidation of silver companies in the late 1800's and early 1900's. The way we have witnessed banks gobble up each other in our time, silver companies consolidated early on.

I reached for the cucumber salad, and replied, "Yes and yes. This serving spoon is $400, give or take."

"Oh *my*," he said, and then appeared to scan the table inventory of its five-piece place settings and serving pieces. "How'd you find so many pieces?"

I smiled. "You're looking at fifteen years and half a million miles of road picking, one piece at a time, usually, my friend. If you think books are tough, you ought to try flatware."

We got down to the business of eating, which was interrupted irregularly with small talk, but eventually the inevitable question came up; Peter asked me, "So how's business been?" This question can't be avoided when in the company of dealer friends.

I shrugged and replied, "Until recently our pickings were slim to none, but recently, and I mean like in the past week or so, things have begun to turn around. The Audubons were part of that turnaround and we've managed to find quite a few others things, too, but business hasn't been well in general since January of 1991. It's probably too complicated to go into detail about tonight."

"Go ahead," Peter encouraged, motioning with a slice of hot bread in one hand and a Whiting fork in the other.

I took a sip of water from an Orrefors stemware goblet by designer Martti Rytkönen. "You want the short version or the long?" I asked.

"The long, while our attention span lasts." Peter reached for the remaining bottle of Dom Pérignon.

Thack, now mostly sated, asked the $64,000 question. "Why do you think the antiques business has been so poor and when will it recover?" He took a sip and pushed his plate away.

"Well, just remember you asked for it." I smiled.

The two men chuckled. Emma did not. She got up and began taking the plates away.

17 Market Analyses

For several years I've been advising my appraisal clients with the same market analysis I told our California guests, but it is mostly unappreciated. The general population won't read what I have posted on my website, and when I deliver lectures to nonprofit groups, they glaze over in less than fifteen seconds. Antiques and art dealers seem to last longer, maybe five minutes, but basically it's always the same: I might as well be reading the label on a paint can.

Emma was at the sink washing the fine dishes and silver by hand. She'd heard it all many times before. Peter and Thack, now seated at one end of the table, looked at me expectantly. I sighed and gave it to them slowly, so as to delay their comas for as long as possible.

"The current market trend, in a word, is caution," I chanted. "There are several negative factors at work influencing the market, such as, our massive national debt and the Euro debt, runaway government spending, leveraged Wall Street debt, cheap Fed money, and the push to loan money to anyone with a pulse, which is basically negligence."

Thack growled.

I nodded to him. "Yep." Thack grinned, and I continued, "I believe that the market is going to crash sometime soon and the economists will be pointing their collective fingers at those factors over the past twenty-some years."

Peter commented, "It's going to be big, isn't it?"

I nodded. "It's going to ruin everything as we know it and usher in a New World Order. It'll the beginning of the end."

Peter tapped the table with his finger. "The beginning of what end?"

I sat back in my chair and replied, "Of business as we know it."

Emma brought us a silver pot of Major Dickason's Blend coffee and the strudel on a matching Gorham tray. The fragrance of the Pink Lady apples, cinnamon, and nutmeg all wrapped up in delicate Phyllo dough evoked Pavlov's response in all of us. Everyone's attention was diverted while Emma cut the strudel and passed portions around, and then poured us all coffee in the Gaudy Welch cup and saucers.

"Wow! Peter," we definitely must have you stay more often, and as a pun, I added, "And of course you are welcome to bring Thack."

Everyone laughed, including Thack who was wolfing strudel like it might escape. After three portions he did slow his rate, stopped, and crossed his massive arms on his chest. He asked me, "What's this, this, ah, New World Order thing going to look like, Charles?"

I looked at him and then at Peter. "Ever read "1984" by George Orwell?"

The men both nodded but Emma shook her head. She'd grown up in Lima, Peru. The leader she was most familiar with was Alberto Fujimori.

I continued, "From what I have read, and I intend to believe it, our situation isn't static isolationism inclusive of Europe and Britain. Our situation is greatly affected by changes in the rest of the world, like rise of China, India, and Brazil as economic powerhouses. Their expansion is creating a demand that is causing the rise in cost of oil and the depletion of water and organic reserves."

Emma sat next to me. "What about global warming?"

I nodded at Emma. "That, too, is a concern, but the larger immediate concern is for an economic meltdown in Europe."

"Beginning with whom?" Peter inquired.

I thought for a second, shrugged one shoulder, and answered, "My guess? Greece I think will probably be first, but Italy and Spain are wilds cards, too."

Thack's jaw was tight, Peter began rubbing his temples. Emma burped. I thought to interrupt the philosophical tension, but I realized that she was genuinely embarrassed. She had even turned red. "Please excuse me," she said demurely. It's one of her traits I that like the most.

Peter chuckled at her, burped in sympathy, and then asked me, "Why a European calamity now?"

I sighed, "Because Europe has reached its tipping point. This scenario will likely come to a head in the next thirty-six months, in my opinion."

"What's the future of the antiques trade?" Peter asked.

I shrugged, "This threat will have a stagnating effect in the short term, but the larger consequence is the change in demographics."

"How so?" Thack wondered.

"Well, we Boomers are inheriting our parents' stuff which we sell at auction because we don't need it and because our kids don't want it. Diminishing demand and increasing supply is a perfect storm."

Peter interjected, "That will go on for twenty more years, right?"

I nodded, "Yep. Maybe longer."

Emma said, "But not everything has weak demand."

"True. There will always be a handful of categories that will appear to defy the new norm. I do not, however, expect the popular collectibles of the 60's, 70's, and 80's to recover, like Cracker Barrel primitives, carnival glass, and the other similar categories, to name a few. Fine art, folk art, and designer styles will likely prevail in the storm, especially if a piece is signed by a listed artist or recognized maker, such as Picasso or Wiener Werkstätte."

Peter sat back and crossed his arms on his chest the way Thack had a moment ago. "Jeez, does he always rant like this?" Peter said, making a face at Emma.

Thack ignored his partner. "That's OK, Charles, I think you're right."

"Charles," Peter interjected, "surely you have experienced other major changes in the antiques business in the years prior to the end of the previous boom, the 80's boom, wasn't there a slack off?"

For a moment, I paused in thought, and then continued. "Yes, there have been some notable fluctuations in my time. The gasoline shortage of 1973 was the first one that I was old enough to recognize. It had a major impact and realigned the industry. People were shocked by the cost of gas at fifty cents per gallon!"

"Only fifty cents?" Emma exclaimed. In 1973 she was a humble sixteen-year-old girl. She would have been unaware of the situation.

Peter added, "I remember it at twenty cents a gallon in the late sixties."

"My grandpa worked for Royal Shell before WWII," commented Thack, "he told me that gas was ten gallons for a dollar in Texas in the 1930's."

I took a sip and reflected.

Peter flapped a hand in my direction. "Go on, Charles," he encouraged. "Tell us more."

The others nodded. "Well, as a result, in the mid-1970's collectors drove less and not as far for a while until they became used to paying higher prices for gas or until their income caught up. The result was a reduction in the number of individual small shops for a few years and a coalescing of dealers into antique centers where the budget-conscious could see more stuff with less driving. Today gasoline prices are higher than ever, but the situation is different. People just keep on driving and are now willing to pay the piper."

Thack asked, "What happened after people got used to the increased cost of gas?"

"The number of antique centers stabilized as the nation went into upward-spiraling inflation in the mid-seventies. Viet Nam had just ended. Boomers were beginning to collect, and they had young and college-aged kids. They learned the collecting habit from their parents who were Depression Era babies. Depression Era babies tended to never throw anything away. When I moved my parents to a smaller place ten years ago, I discovered that Dad had about fifteen Maxwell House half- gallon coffee cans full of bent nails. Naturally I was curious and asked him why the nail collection. He told me that one day he intended to straighten them out and re-use them."

Thack asked, "What'dja tell him?"

Peter chuckled.

I smiled, "I told him that I would take care of it, and I did. As soon as I moved them, I took everything to the dump. I took it myself in twenty-five pickup truck load trips that included stuff like balls of baling string, empty tin cans and glass jars, cardboard boxes, and more.

"Some of the Depression parents and a lot of the Boomers were into the Back-to-the-Earth Movement, which fueled the antiques business. The primitive furniture craze was on. Supply and demand coupled with inflation made what was bought one day, worth more the next. It was difficult for dealers to re-supply. The craze went off the scale in the 1980's."

Thack was making a sandpaper noise stroking his chin as I spoke. "So, what you're describing is a classic economic bubble, right Charles?"

I nodded.

Emma suggested, "Let's sit by the fire and enjoy our coffee with more strudel."

We stood from our unpadded chairs and retreated to the upholstered furniture by the hearth. I threw a few sticks on the embers before taking my favorite brown leather club chair to watch the sparks chase the smoke up the chimney. For a minute, no one said anything. Grace waddled over and plopped down in front of the fire to watch the sparks, too.

Peter stared into the fire, and said, "You're right. When you explain it that way, all of the pieces fit together like the continents before they drifted apart."

Emma, who had been concentrating on what I had just said, motioned with her hand. "If there was a boom in the 1980's, then why aren't you rich, Amor?"

I laughed. "The apparent ease of sales of antiques didn't go unnoticed, Pretzel."

Peter cooed to Emma, "I like it when he calls you that."

Emma beamed.

I responded, "As I was saying, everyone jumped on the bandwagon. No one made a lot of money. It became difficult for anyone to depend solely on antiques for a living because there were too many dilettante dealers who didn't have to support themselves selling antiques; they had a working spouse or a real job. It was a hobby for them or a way to improve their own collections. Everyone had become a dealer. The margin of the make-a-living dealer was adversely impacted. Similar scenarios exist outside of the antiques business."

Peter inquired, "Oh?"

I looked to Emma, and she responded, "Well, for example, the food cart business. In D.C. around the Federal Square there are these trucks with kitchens that sell ethnic foods at lunchtime. If one businessman establishes a successful cart business, long lines form and long lines signal to his competition that he has chosen a good spot. More food trucks come until eventually no cart owner makes money.

I added, "At least not enough to justify his trouble, investment, and risk."

Peter and Thack stared understandingly at Emma.

Peter commented, "Sounds like the books business."

Emma nodded, "Too much business ruins it for all."

"And," I interjected, "in this country there isn't anything that we can do about it. It's free enterprise. However, in other countries, Austria, for instance, small enterprises are protected from too much competition. My maternal side of the family operates floral shops all over Vienna. In Austria, businesses are given market jurisdiction so that they will thrive. If they didn't have protection, then some would fail which would lead to vacancies that would accumulate and become dead economic zones, like our inner cities. Over there, their urban areas are bulwarks of their country. Vienna is probably in the top one percent of all cities. In our opinion, Emma's and mine, it is the most civilized capital city of all."

Emma nodded in agreement.

Peter mused, "But that's protectionism."

"Yep," I said. "That's one of the good/bad aspects of the European system, isn't it?"

Thack redirected the conversation by quipping, "You know, I've never met a doctor's wife that didn't have a tax number."

Peter laughed, "Or if they're not a dealer, then they're a lawyer's wife with a tax exempt number pretending to be an inferior desecrater."

Everyone chuckled.

"So, the most recent boom for antiques dealers was during what? The 1980's?" Thack asked me.

"Correct."

Thack rubbed his chin again, "But we had a 90's boom, too, right?"

I nodded *and* shook my head, "Yes *and* no. The perfect economic storm was brewing hot in the 90's, but the antiques trade had begun its downward spiral due to changing demographics. The Back-to-the-Earth, WWII generation slowed their collecting habit because they were then in their late sixties, and that's what's happening to the boomers now; their leading edge is now beginning to downsize. In another ten years they'll be in full bloom."

Thack looked at me with understanding.

Peter commented, "So what was the single most important contributing factor for where we are today, April 2005?"

"Overbuilding the US's military," Thack said.

"Yes," I replied. "That strategy won the Cold War."

Thack snorted, "It helped that crude was $10 a barrel in those days."

I nodded, "Yes it did. The USSR was poor as a church mouse then. That strategy wouldn't work today. Oil is more expensive and they have a lot of it. Although the Iron Curtain has fallen, the Russians are stable and growing richer as long as oil remains in demand."

Thack added, "Lucky for us Russia is run by thugs interested in self-enrichment rather than on some ideological pursuit."

"At what cost to future generation?" asked Peter.

"You mean how much did we run up the national debt?" I asked.

Peter nodded, "Yeah, at the end of his second term."

I replied, "To a record $2.7 trillion."

"And now it's over $8 trillion," Thack said.

There was silence for a while.

"Do continue," encouraged Thack. "Worst case scenario in ten years."

Peter was beginning to nod off. It was about midnight. Emma was sleeping in her chair. Only Thack and I remained open-eyed. I looked at him and wondered what he might think of me if I told him what my innermost fear was. And then I did.

His jaw fell open. "Jesus! You gotta be kiddin' me?"

Emma awoke and yawned.

Peter moaned, "I've got a headache. See you in the morning, darlings."

Thack shrugged, "Good night, Charles."

I couldn't sleep. My mind was still busy. Grace and I went for a walk around the neighborhood on past Fred Nichols' studio, and then back again.

18 Space Available

"Amor, it's time to get up," Emma said, trying to shake me out of my dream state.

I heard what sounded like muffled voices ... of submariners cheering ... all around us ... and Brigadier General Fleetwood Pride was shaking my bleeding hand. I awoke with a start on my belly and raised my head up off the mattress. All the pillows were missing and I was spread out perpendicular. Emma was shaking my shoulder and Grace had a hold of my hand in her mouth as I lay buried in a briar patch of Vera Wang sheets, my arm dangling over the side.

"Huh?" I managed a croak from an alcohol-dry mouth. Emma opened the drapes letting in blinding sunlight. I pulled the covers over my head and moaned.

"Come on, Amor. Rise and shine. Breakfast time. It's a glorious day!"

The cogs of my brain vibrated. "How can you be so bloody chipper? You had more to drink last night than I did," I rasped.

"Oh, I've been up for hours, Amor. Already I have been for a walk with Thack and Peter and Grace. Come on now. It's 10:30 in the morning. Get *up*!"

"OK, OK." I untangled myself from the sheets.

"You must've been dreaming again last night. You were thrashing like a fish."

"So I see." I managed to untangle myself. "I was visiting Fleet when you woke me."

"What?"

"Fleet. He was just about to congratulate me again when you *nuked* me with those open curtains," I complained, shielding my eyes with an outstretched arm.

Emma gave me a thoughtful evaluation, her hands on her hips. She looked like she was about to tsk, tsk me. "Sounds like your PTSD is acting up again. Maybe you should go to the medical center and tell them about your dreams."

"You know what I think of doctors," I said, as I sat on the edge of the queen-sized bed. I scratched my head and tried to focus on the darting figure of Emma dressed in a pair of form-fitting cobalt blue Ann Taylor ankle pants that my mother had found for her at Goodwill, a Raga animal-pattern sweater I had given her for her last birthday, dark silver metallic leather Salvatore Ferragamo Ballerina flats that she'd gotten on sale at Nordstrom's, and her favorite bill cap, the one she found washed up on the beach in Corolla. The hat sports the official logo of the North Carolina Ferry Service. Under the logo is the name of one of its boats, the *Chicamacomico*. I groaned in exasperation at myself when I realized that my brain was already at work processing visual stimuli even though it was still half- asleep. I know it's not normal, but I can't stop it. It processes provenance like a Cuisinart.

"I'm beginning to worry about you," she said, gesturing with one hand, the other on her curvaceous Bond Girl hip. Through the window, the low morning sun gleamed off of her red nails. She raised an eyebrow and pursed her matching red lips expecting an intelligent reply.

"So?" I screwed one eye with a fist, yawned, and farted.

She made a face. "*Cochino!*" She has cause to use that expression often. It means pig. Exasperated, she bustled about the boudoir tidying.

"That was a dry one," I said, and then burped.

"*Qué cochino!*"

"Huh?" I grunted, as I stood and stretched.

"*Cochinazo!*" she said, and spat something else in Quechua too fast for me to comprehend.

"Ahhh, both ends." Feeling relentless this morning, I stood scratching my hairy belly with both claws.

"Amor, *please!*" she complained, but I perceived a twinkle in her eye in spite of my boorishness.

"*What?*" I feigned innocence.

She finished what she was doing, whipped her long hair, and stalked out of the room. Over her shoulder as she left, she said, "Open a window, and make an appointment to the hospital."

"Yes Dear," I surrendered.

After a while she hollered at me from the kitchen, "Amor, you want to come to breakfast, or not?" I could hear our guests talking and the clatter of silverware in use.

"*In a minute*, I yelled back. "You-all start without me." By the time I made it to the breakfast nook, the three of them were clearing the table.

"Oh, sorry folks. I'm a bit groggy this morning. Couldn't sleep last night."

Peter smirked at me for being absent from breakfast. "Past demons?" he asked.

I gave him a false smile. "They were driving me nuts all night long."

"That's OK, pal," said Thack. "With the end of the world scenario you got bouncing around inside your head, it's no wonder you can't sleep."

"Just take it easy this morning," Peter comforted me.

Emma was less charitable. "We have important guests, Amor. You could be more courteous."

"Don't hound him, Emma, he looks like crap," Peter said as if this was some kind of compliment.

Emma and Thack chuckled.

Emma pointed. "Food's in the warming drawer and the mail and paper are on the breakfast table. The coffee is still fresh."

"Thank you, Periwinkle," I grunted, and the three of them scurried out of sight without explanation.

From the pile of mail Emma had left for me in the painted buttocks basket on the end of the counter, I grabbed a newspaper for what is to us pickers the *Wall Street Journal* of the Antiques business, the *Maine Antique Digest*. Once a month, our letter carrier risks a hernia by lugging the behemoth to our door. It's three inches thick and takes me all month every month to read because I savor it like a platter of fried merkels. From my early days in the trade, I learned from its pages. Its articles are written by legends in the trade and its advertisements are placed by our gods, some of whom are telecast on PBS from time to time. I ripped off the protective plastic cover, dropped two halves of a Bodo's Bagel in the red toaster and then took a peek in the warming drawer where I found scrambled eggs and Kite Country Ham.

Mr. Kite's hams are a local delicacy. They're made in Wolftown, and shipped to the far corners of the globe. The Japanese import a lot of them, I've been told. Others I have tried, from Smithfield to Barcelona, but Kite's got them all beat by a mile.

My foggy mind was about to traipse off on a geography tangent when the bagel popped from the toaster. I buttered it and sat down to nosh and read about a big heist in Ohio that made a cover headline in The Digest.

In the pile of mail there was also a FedEx envelope from Randal Cunningham. It included a check for $3000 and a note praising my good luck; the Coca-Cola collection transaction had gone well. In the past few days our luck had changed considerably, especially with the key basket; however we weren't yet on Easy Street. I flipped open the Mac and added those dollar numbers to my Excel spreadsheet. By my reckoning, we'd netted $22,500 or so. I set aside forty percent for self-employment taxes and paid a few of our outstanding bills online, applied $5k back to the line of credit which offset the recent advance to buy Lenny's stuff. And that left us *no* dollars ahead.

Great. Back to Square One.

I slumped in my seat and exhaled loudly – *but* then I remembered that we did still have loot to show for our efforts, and fresh inventory in the pipeline: books. And, we had retained some keepers, too: the Aylor rocker, the Quervelle server, the Spratling brooch, the Charlottesville sword, *Half of Paradise* by James Lee Burke, and Patricia Cornwell's first novel,

Post-Mortem, plus the farm table upgrade. All that was worth something but it wasn't cash.

Such is the life of a picker, I thought as I finished the last of the bagel and coffee and stuffed Randal's and Peter's checks in an envelope to go in the day's mail to our bank in Gordonsville. As I was finishing up, the trio came through the door making a happy racket.

"Eeeee, Amor, look at our new swim suits!" exclaimed Emma. The three of them, Emma, Peter, and Thack stood in size order on display, waiting for my critique. All had on the briefest and loudest things I'd seen since our trip to Rio.

The sight was too much. I leaned back into the cushion. "It's March. Why are you in swim suits?" I asked reasonably.

"It's April, actually," corrected Peter.

I thought a moment. "Hum, I stand corrected."

"We wanted to surprise you," Emma pirouetted on her tippy toes. Peter followed Emma's lead ridiculously. For a moment it looked like Thack would, too, but then he saw the look on my face and resumed his muscle-man pose.

"So, why are you three gomers in swimming attire when it's," I glanced at the outside thermometer, "forty-one degrees outside?"

"Come on Charles. Be a sport. How do we look?" Thack insisted.

I sighed. "Well, you all look just fine, I suppose," said I, knowing full well that my praise was insufficient for their enthusiasm. Their faces drooped.

"*Just* fine? You *suppose*?" Peter sniffed, "We worked all morning on this, come now, tell us we're gorgeous."

I'm not much of a romantic, so says Emma regularly, but diplomacy is one of my Libra strong suits. "OK, OK, I've never seen such stylish dental floss in all my born days." The three of them snorted in unison.

"I guess that'll have to do," Thack said, shaking his mane.

"Let's go to the beach," Emma said, stalking closer to me and squeezing her cleavage together with arms enticingly outstretched towards me,.

"What beach?" I asked.

"Key West," Thack replied.

I concentrated and looked past Emma's canyon. "Florida? I thought you hated Florida," I argued with Emma and remained nonchalant.

Emma's enthusiasm wilted. She stood in front of me with her arms crossed supporting her attributes and toe-tapping one gilded flip-flop. "*Come on*, Charles, you need some sun. You're as white as fish-meat," she insisted.

Her strategy was having the desired effect on me. Cleavage is like catnip to hetero men. We can't help but want to roll in it. I did a mental lip-flapping brrrr, but snapped out of it in the nick of time. I forced myself to look at Thack. I said to the barely clad, "What, you guys want to drive all the way to Key West? Are you *nuts?*"

"No, *fly*, silly," she said. I realized that they probably had engineered this surprise while I lay sleeping too late. I knew that I wasn't going to be able to avoid their plan.

"OK, Dulles or BWI?" I asked.

"Charlottesville," Peter said.

"Huh?"

Thack was leaning against a doorjamb trying to get a word in. It creaked. I imagined the cottage falling like a house of cards.

Finally, Thack succeeded. "I have an NFL buddy who owns shares on a G5. It's on the tarmac at the airport in Charlottesville. That's why we decided to deliver the check in person."

My mouth twisted as I harrumphed a reply, "And I thought you two loved us."

Peter replied, "Of course we do, darling, now do you want to come with us or stay here and garden until we return?"

I blinked at Emma who had her hands on her hips. She should have been an intelligence officer. *This is some form of entrapment*, I thought to myself. I asked Peter, "You have a private jet waiting for us here, right now, in Charlottesville?"

"Yep, Thack's buddy has directed the pilot to pick him up in Key West, so it's flying there empty to get him," Peter explained.

"Space available," I mumbled, remembering my military hops. That particular perk would not be available to me again until I turn sixty-five, when my retirement pension takes effect, because I had retired from the reserves and not regular service.

"Correct," he replied.

"Thack wants to do some fishing, don't you Thack?" said Peter. He looked at his partner and then to Emma for support. "And we want to get a tan, right Em?"

"Yes, of course, darling," she dramatized by unfolding a reflecting lampshade-looking thing which resembled what George Hamilton whips out for effect anytime a camera comes in range.

"Well, …I suppose….," I guessed.

"Well then let's go," Emma insisted.

"What about Grace?"

"The dog sitter is coming to get her now," Emma explained patiently.

I must say that if you have to travel, a private jet is the way to go. The Brits use the term "posh" to express expensive luxury. Until I saw the inside of the Gulfstream 550, I guess I never really knew what posh meant. At 562 miles per hour, it took longer for Emma and Peter to get their stuff together than it did to fly the 958 air miles from portal to portal. By lunchtime, we'd parked our rented Cadillac and were checked in at the Marriott Hotel in Key West.

19 Knuckle Thumpers

Emma bombarded me with brochures provided by the way-too-helpful concierge the next morning. I didn't feel like sitting by the pool, fake rock wall climbing, parasailing, or snorkeling. She can be relentless. I was desperate to do nothing.

"I don't like swimming pools," I whined.

Puzzled, Peter asked, "Why?"

"Because they remind me of The Beverly Hillbillies," I said, standing on infirm ground.

"*What?*" she exclaimed, and started rattling at Peter for an explanation faster than I was able to comprehend. Emma had grown up poor in Peru and thus had pretty much missed all of the popular American culture that was old hat for the guys and me. They stopped conferring and looked at me, waiting for an explanation.

I clarified, "...They're nothing more than 'cement ponds.'" The two stared at me and withered like vines. I expounded, "Collecting solar radiation is a waste of valuable time when a *real* man could be picking antiques or fishing or smoking cigars and drinking beers."

Thack rescued me in the nick of time. "Yeah, that's right," endorsed Thack, with his thumbs in his waistband.

Peter sniffed and expressed his opposition with a head-flip, a signal of contempt he had evidently taught Emma because she demonstrated the same proficiency.

Thack quickly calmed the waters with a solution. "Emma why don't you and Peter go do your thing at poolside, and Charles and I'll go fishing."

Thack had joined my squad of one.

Emma knew when she was defeated. "OK," she sniffed, and then copied Peter's body language. "Let's go Peter." And with a tandem flip of their hair, they both sashayed down the Yellow Brick Road as Thack and I bumped knuckles like the cavemen we pretended to be. When they were out of sight, I turned to my fishing buddy and gave him a onceover inspection. "You'd better get some more clothes on if we're going fishing," I warned. "The UV reflection on the water will fry your ass."

He looked down at himself, realized what I was talking about, and began back-peddling himself toward the door. "Right. You're right. Be back in a jiff, Charles."

While Thack was getting dressed, I made use of the time to use the Blackberry to check on our bank deposits, email, eBay, website, and all of the other stuff my then-twelve-year-old niece had taught me how to do. Everything seemed to be in good order. A few minutes later Thack appeared, dressed like he was Humphrey Bogart on safari. I almost laughed at him, but I managed a poker face of astonishment instead.

"Ready?" queried Thack, as he stood for re-inspection.

"Geez, Thack. One extreme to another."

He ignored my comment, cracking his knuckles. "So, Charles, how do we go about this?"

"I suppose that we'll do it whichever way the locals do it. Let's go down to the wharf and find out."

"Just like that?"

"Yep, even though you're dressed like a safari guide and will no doubt stand out like a sore thumb."

"Yeah, so what. The fish don't care one way or the other. Besides most of the population here won't mind a bit," Thack smirked.

"True enough. Just tell them to shove off if they come at *me*, will ya?" When Emma and I walk around Key West, I get more stares and uh-hums than she does. It bothered me when I was younger but I've gotten used to it. It doesn't trouble me any longer unless they're rude.

We discovered that most of the flat-bottomed skiff captains were out with their bookings because they typically take their clients out at first light. We'd missed the early launch. After asking around for a minute or two, I managed to hail one who looked like he'd just come back from a half-day session. He was a big salty type, bronzed by the sun, wearing cutoffs, a white T-shirt, a red bandanna around his neck, and an oversized bill cap with ear and neck flaps. As we approached, he was kneeling at a piling tying a rope from a fairly large boat to a horn cleat. His skin glistened from the sunscreen that he had applied. The smell of coconut, cigar, and salt was in the air.

"Captain," I greeted. He looked up. "Would you be free to take us out for half a day of fishing?"

He looked up at us. "Sure, man, no problem. Just let me straighten up my boat. I need to get some more ice and grab a sandwich. My name's Mott Perry, by the way," he threw the introduction over his shoulder as he worked to ready his outfit.

I was astonished. I realized that he must be Bubba's nephew. "Boy! It sure is a small world, Mott. I was told to look you up in Roanoke." Mott suddenly looked rather startled.

"My name's Charles Dawes and this is my friend Thack Shupp."

"Dawes?" Mott said, visibly relaxing a bit. "Bubba called and told me that he met you all." He gave me a wan smile.

"That's right. My wife and I met your uncle Bubba a few days ago up in Lexington."

"Sorry, you sort of startled me for a moment. I'm a retired cop. I made some people unhappy along the way, especially in Chinatown. I can't stop looking over my shoulder if you know what I mean."

Thack and I understood his meaning.

"Well it's good to meet you."

We shook hands with the gruff gumshoe.

"Was Chinatown your beat?" I asked.

He adjusted an unlit cigar stub in the corner of his mouth with his lips. "Yeah, and I lived there, too. I had a Chinese gal at the time." He changed the subject. "Bubba said you were good customers and that you might show up at the bar, but I didn't figure I'd see you all down here."

I replied, "It's entirely coincidental, Mott. I didn't expect to meet you down here either. Bubba told us about your place in Roanoke only a few days ago. We were on our way to Roanoke and had planned to stop by to introduce ourselves, but that day we were diverted by something and ended up returning home instead."

Mott pushed back the bill of his hat, extracted his cigar, and studied the burnt end, "And now you're here."

"Yeah," I replied. "A couple of days later, Thack and Peter showed up on our doorstep with an invitation to R&R in Key West." Thack was reviewing the bevy of men circulating about the boats as I explained to Mott the circumstances.

Mott chucked his cigar stub at a nearby seagull and fished for something red in his shirt pocket. "Actually," he explained, relaxing a bit. "I leave my day manager in charge of the bar in Roanoke and live on the 'Origami'," he gestured a thumb at the boat he had just tied off. "I spend part of my winter down here. Come spring I'll travel up the Intracoastal Waterway back to my berth on the Occoquan."

"I don't blame you one bit for escaping the snow, Mott," I said. Thack's attention had wandered off in the direction of some young waiter flitting around the outside seating at the tavern nearby. "Right Thack?"

"Huh, you kiddin'?" Thack demonstrate his ability to do two things at once, and replied correctly. "Winter sucks. That's why Pete and I live in California."

I squinted a warning at Thack because I didn't know Mott's beliefs, and continued the dialogue with the boat captain. "Emma and Peter are either at poolside or out shopping right now, I'd imagine, but Thack and I are on a mission. We'd like to hire a boat."

Mott looked from me to Thack as he unwrapped a stick of cinnamon Dentyne. "Oh, I see. What do you want to fish for?"

"The legendary bonefish," was my reply.

"Bonefish, huh?" He adjusted his jewels, put one foot on a big cooler, and leaned on his knee. "I don't know about bonefish, boys. It takes some doing to land one of them. You think you can handle one?" He gave me a superficial onceover but his scrutiny lingered on Thack.

"Absolutely," Thack huffed, chagrinned to have anyone question his physical prowess.

Mott continued, "I have several different boats down here. The 'Origami' is too large for what you have in mind. Bonefish live in the shallows."

I nodded, "Yeah, I know. We're going to need a skiff."

"We'll take my Chittum Legacy," he pointed, "over there."

Thack and I turned. "That'd be perfect," I replied.

Thack agreed with a grunt. "What's it, eighteen feet?"

Mott nodded. "OK, you guys hang out here for a minute while I get us some sandwiches and ice. If you want anything special now's the time to say so. Jax, Pepsi, or bottled water is provided."

We stated our preferences and then Mott disappeared into the convenience store on the dock next to the tavern for a few minutes leaving us to man-talk about gear and go over the behavior characteristics of bonefish as we watched gulls swoop in and out between the boats and pilings. Half-day captains were tossing scraps to the gulls as they cleaned their clients' catches. Onlookers had congregated near each returned boat to ooh and ahh over the catches as they were revealed. Most of what was caught had come from farther out in the blue water, not where we were headed. It appeared that dolphin and tuna were the most numerous species caught.

"I'm back," Mott announced. "You guys ready?"

"Ready," echoed Thack.

"Okeydokey, all aboard," Mott ordered. "I'll take you the long way around through the mangroves to the flats. It's kind of a scenic route. I have the best place. It's my secret fishing area. You'll catch all you want there."

We piled in and were off, slowly at first until we left the harbor area, then Mott opened the throttle, and we nearly flew along through some of the most beautiful water that I'd ever seen. Thack and I were speechless because of the wind rushing at us. It wouldn't have made any difference anyway though; the outboard motor was too loud to talk over. After ten minutes or so, he slowed the boat and maneuvered very slowly, hardly making a ripple. The air was still and the water glass smooth.

20 Bonefishing

"Either of you do much fishing?" Mott asked, quietly.

We both nodded. Thack looked to me to answer first. "I fly fish mostly mountain streams back home with a Tenkara rod."

"What's that?" asked Thack.

Mott answered for me, "It's a rod that telescopes."

"And a reel is not necessary," I added. "You tie the line to the rod's tip. The length of the line matches the rod length, and then the tippet is attached to the end of the line. It's a Japanese style of fishing meant for small mountain streams. You can use dry or wet flies, even live bait if you prefer. The compatibility of the rod is perfect for backpackers hiking the backwoods."

"He's right," Mott said. "What do you fish for, Thack?"

"I like big game, billfish, mostly," he replied. "I go to Cabo and Ixtapa as often as time permits."

"Charles, what about you?" Mott asked. "Ever go after big game?"

"Sort of," I answered.

Mott squinted. "What's that mean?"

I smiled modestly with one side of my mouth. "I hold the freedive spearfishing world record for Atlantic Bluefin."

Both of their heads snapped towards me, their jaws open.

Thack said, "I didn't know that."

Mott said, "No way. How big?"

I replied, "Oh, about 655 point 2 pounds."

That information was food for fodder for the two of them for a couple of minutes. They went on and on about their own big catches until finally coming back around to ask me to tell them my story, and I did. Free diving, by the way, is done without air tanks but the sportsman wears a wet suit, flippers, mask, and snorkel. The point is to stay down for as long as possible and as deep as possible and return to the surface undead. It's a sport popular in Italy. Big game spearfishing is similar but it's a separate sport that strains the same physiological limits of the diver. Hunters employ a kinetic speargun and line. The target must be within the speargun's effective range, which is about twenty-three feet. The objective is to kill a trophy fish *and* return to the surface undead, but it is not easy.

The two were all ears.

I began, "Spearing a fish that weighs as much as an Angus heifer is one of the scariest things that I've ever done. I was hunting at 400 feet deep off the coast of Silveira Island with a three-band Riffe gun. On the way up for air, I saw it. So I quickly surfaced, took a couple of deep lungfuls of air, and then went back down. It must have been curious. It had followed me from the depths to near the surface. We swam alongside each other in the current for a minute about twenty meters apart. It was so graceful and beautiful, and then it turned and flew at me, with the intent to bump me as it would a predator. I jerked to one side, deflecting its trajectory with the butt of the gun, and fired off a shot as it swept by, hitting it behind the eye."

"Then what happened?" Thack bared his teeth.

With his mouth open, Mott turned off his Evinrude, grabbed a long pole and stood on the high, tilted platform over the engine.

I adjusted my prescription sunglasses with one finger and continued, "Its momentum kept its mass going past me, but I had hit it solidly with a lucky shot. The spear went all the way through. It shuddered and moved erratically. I swam over, grabbed it by the spear and directed it toward the surface. There was blood everywhere. Its shuddering tail helped to propel us to the surface. I signaled the boat, and the rest is history."

The two of them asked me a few more questions as Mott maneuvered us to his favorite spot; everyone was psyched to do some fishing. The water was nearly perfect: glass smooth, clear to the white sandy bottom, and less than waist deep. It was a sunny day about two o'clock. Neither of us had used flies before in salt water or fished for bonefish. Mott gave us a quick lesson. Luckily, I had read a bit online about the sport to have a grasp of the essentials, and I knew enough to dress in long UV-armored pants and sleeves to protect myself from the reflecting sun which beat down on us mercilessly and up off of the water.

"Alright you guys, spray on some sunblock," advised Mott, "and be especially sure to cover the areas under your chin and eyes because the rays reflect up off of the white sand bottom. Then wash your hands before handling the flies or the line. The fish don't like the taste of it."

"So tell us what to expect, Mott," Thack requested as he wiped his giant hands with tiny Towelettes, and I opened my rod case.

Mott popped a stick of gum in his mouth and began his memorized lecture, "Pound for pound, bonefish fight harder than anything else in these waters. They school together in groups of at least a half a dozen or more, usually more and they tend to travel with their backs to the sun. When the sun's at its zenith, they head for deeper waters to feed." Mott was scanning the water with binoculars. "Once we've located a school I'll stay the boat. Then you-all can have a try at 'em. Use your newfound casting skills to get a streamer in as close as possible." It took a few minutes for the two of us to ready ourselves. Meanwhile Mott scoped the water from his high perch for the elusive bonefish.

Mott whispered, "Thar she blows, gents, at ten o'clock. Don't get too close, now. They's got eyes in the back of their heads. Just about anything will scare 'em off."

"Bloody hot," I murmured, as I whipped a tan Mantis Shrimp streamer overhead on #7 line, using an 8-weight Z-Axis rod. It landed two feet to the left of where I had in mind, but it was my first cast. I blamed the inaccuracy on the wind, like any fisherman would.

"I hear anglers from around the world come here to try to outwit these fish," Thack whispered.

"You do this often?" I inquired quietly.

Mott whispered, "I have five local employees that help. Today it's my turn to operate one of the skiffs. I never ask my people to do anything I wouldn't do myself. I prefer to guide half days, like what I'm doing now."

I reeled in my fly.

"I've guided people from all fifty states and just about every country on the face of the planet," Mott said without moving his lips through gritted teeth, "Alright now. Get close. Be quiet. Cast it so it lands like a feather about six feet in front of 'em."

After some struggling, I managed to cast the line toward the general vicinity of where I'd wanted it to go, but before I ... *Wham!* What felt like a comet grabbed a-hold of my bait, emptied the reel before I had sense enough to apply the brake, and snapped the line before I could recover my wits. I stood there flustered like Don Knotts, my mouth open. I gulped, "Good God! What the heck was that!"

"That was a bonefish, dude," said Thack, laughing his fool head off.

"Now you see why people travel here from around the world," said Mott. "And you'll like it even better if you can manage to actually catch one."

"*Good grief!*" My hands were shaking like a Big-5 hunter on his first safari.

"You'll do it," Mott encouraged, "now that you know what to expect."

"Mott," I attempted to explain, "it was like a covey of quail exploding at my feet for the first time when I was twelve years old. I nearly wet my pants."

"Well, you ain't no virgin no more," Thack laughed.

Mott directed, "Tie on another streamer and try it again. You'll bring one in this time." He used his push-pole to reposition the skiff, taking in consideration the shadows, the wind, and everything else. My hands were too shaky. I just couldn't do it; I handed the end of the tippet to him to tie on the streamer. I took the long pole from him and hopped up on the high perch as he stepped down on the flat deck.

Mott was right. Both Thack and I had the time of our lives after we got the knack of it. It's not like bass or trout fishing at all. Catching bonefish is like trying to rope an in-coming artillery shell, or hunting geese with a rake; it was *really* difficult. Each of us managed to be successful though. We caught three or four each and released them without harming them or us. Time went by quickly. Pretty soon, the shadows were long. "Man Charles, this is something isn't it?" exclaimed Thack, wiping his forehead with a cool Jax while holding his rod in his other hand. "I've never seen fish fight so hard."

21 Break Even

All of us decided to freshen up before dinner. While Emma took a shower, I had time to check my messages again. There was a text from Jane Hickam, our real estate agent and lawyer: *sold! call me 1st chance.* I wasted no time and dialed Jane.

"I've sold the properties," she said before I even spoke.

"That's great! Has the check cleared yet?"

"Yes, everything has been finalized." She had discretion in this matter. We trusted her explicitly. I went over some of the finer points, including the bottom line, before Emma reappeared from the spacious bathroom suite drying her raven hair with a white towel. She gave me a, *"who is that?" look* as I spoke to the phone in my hand, "Jane, wait a second, I'll put you on speaker. Emma is here now, too."

Jane hooted, "Hi Em. I sold your properties!"

Emma jumped for joy. "Yippee!" She stopped hopping for a second and asked, "How much?" A cruise ship horn sounded as Jane answered.

I butted in holding my hand up, "Emma, long story short, there's enough to pay off the mortgages on the two commercial buildings and to clear the line of credit for the first time ever, plus a little left for working capital."

She hugged me. "What a relief," Emma said. She looked at me excitedly and pushed away to hop some more.

"Where *are* you guys?" Jane asked. "I've been trying to reach you all day."

Emma answered, hopping, "We're in Key West with some friends."

"Key West? Charlottesville or Florida?"

"Florida," Emma stopped her hopping and replied breathlessly.

"Must be nice!" she exclaimed.

Emma flopped backwards on the bed.

"Jane," I interjected, "what do you need for us to do?"

"Nothing. I have it all under control. BB&T in Gordonsville is working with me to pay off the mortgages. I'm on top of it and will take care of everything until you get back, which is, by the way, *when*, exactly?"

Emma looked at me and shrugged, smiling like a possum.

"We don't know yet, Jane," I said, "perhaps a few more days...probably...maybe. It all depends on our friends, and what they have in mind. We're using their transportation."

"OK, that's fine. I'll keep you apprised via email and text messages," she said, with a few more addendums, and then hung up.

"What do you think about *that*, Amor?" Emma exclaimed.

I sighed, "What a relief! And just in the nick of time, too. I think the economic bubble we're in is going to burst at any moment. I'm glad that we'll be out of real estate when it bursts, except for the bungalow, of course." With that part of our lives now in the past, the future suddenly looked brighter ... and yet unfocused. What, exactly, *would* we do now? I turned to talk to Emma but she gave me a look and then hugged me again despite my fishiness, and kept kissing me. It took us a little longer than we expected to meet the guys at the restaurant, but the delay was worth it.

22 Tactical Saling

The four of us hung out in Key West for two more days luxuriating in the warm weather, eating too much, and getting a better tan but eventually, alas, we said our goodbyes. Peter and Thack flew back to California and Emma and I drove up the Gulf Coast for cheaper lodging. Hotels around Ft. Myers are less than half of what they are in Key West. Although we were no longer on the water, our Ft. Myers hotel was only a couple of blocks away from the causeway to Sanibel Island and the winter estates of Thomas Edison and Henry Ford. We visited both and they were worth it. Edison's banyan tree was particularly wonderful. And along the Gulf shore of the barrier islands is some of the best sea shelling in the world. After a storm, the beaches are strewn with a kaleidoscopic blanket of shells. Emma was frantic with enthusiasm when she saw the shelling smorgasbord. She filled four one-gallon Tupperware containers of shells with which I was to make lamps when we got home but three days of shell hunting was enough for me. I was ready to get back to hunting antiques.

It was time to hit the road again.

We followed picking leads gleaned from the Internet, classifieds, and even tips provided to us by gas station clerks along the way. Picking requires patience, which requires stopping *everywhere*, and that's what we do. We pull over at every antiques store and flea market, pawnshop, thrift shop, and even every time we see a hand-painted "Junque" sign along the highway. As usual, our efforts were mostly fruitless but it's part of the job description. It must be done. The one lead that we pass on might be the one that reveals an unidentified treasure.

After hours getting in and out of the car I found only one figural head humidor of an Indian chief, a cast iron Victorian hand paperholder, and about a half-dozen first edition novels; of the latter, all were of small consequence. Emma had better luck. She picked up two pieces of silver studio jewelry by the French-American sculptor, Maxwell Chayat; both were marked "Chayat". The books would eventually pay for the gas. The Chayat pieces were keepers, of course, with long-term investment potential.

At a fueling stop I picked up a *Dollar Saver* hoping that we might snag a yard sale before the opening bell the following morning, which is a picker strategy: to scan the Friday ads for Saturday yard sales. If any ads appear to be promising, then we call the number in the ad to ask if we can come by Friday instead of waiting until the following morning. The excuse we use with some success to gain early access is: 'Because we're from out of town.' Usually they allow us early entry whereupon we pick the yard or garage sale before anyone else. Many professional pickers use this ploy even if they are not from out of town, but we use it only when we are.

It sounds simple but, depending on the area, there can be a page or more of yard sales with several hundred ads, so accurate intel is crucial in order to save time and gas. How the ad reads makes all the difference. Any ad that mentions clothes is a no-go, unless it states 'vintage clothes,' which is an altogether different matter. We do handle vintage designer labels. Typically though, the key words in the print that we look for are silver, jewelry, crocks, quilts, antique, and paintings, to name a few.

In the *Dollar Saver* I marked ten ads of interest and handed the paper to Emma instead of making the calls myself, because it's better if a prospect hears a female voice on the phone. A woman's voice is less threatening to women and a curiosity to men. Emma's mannerism and her telephone voice are perfect for this task, which is probably why The Rosetta Stone hired her to do voice-over work. I left her alone in the car for a while for her to do her thing, and asked the clerk if I could see his phone book. Gleaning intel from local "Yellow Pages" is a waning possibility but once-upon-a-time it was an important source for leads. In less than ten years, I figured, the print version will be gone. Already it's out-moded.

I went back to the car.

Emma advised, "Amor, of the ads that you marked nine answered the phone, but only four would permit early buying."

I nodded, "OK. That's par for the course."

She had folded the paper a certain way and said, "I made appointments for each of them through lunchtime."

"When's the first appointment?"

She looked at her notes, "In thirty minutes. Amor, we need to hurry to be on time."

23 Over the Threshold

The home was a white foursquare in a nice neighborhood. Mass-produced architectural elements from the Victorian era adorned its deep wraparound porch. Hanging moss draped massive evergreen live oaks that provided year-round shade on both sides and in the back where there was a garage, that probably began life as a small carriage house before automobiles were commonplace. We pulled into the driveway and stopped in the lane leading to the garage. I heard a screen door slam as we stepped out of the car and saw an older lady walk around the back and stand under a tall crape myrtle bush as large around at the base as a basketball. She had on a straw garden hat with a green cloth band, short sleeve white blouse, and yellow linen pants. I guessed her age to be about seventy-five. She smiled when we approached and spoke with a sophisticated Southern accent.

I said to Emma, "My sensors are *not* tingling."

"Amor, be patient," was her reply. "She may have something."

Emma and I helloed simultaneously and, as a courtesy, we removed our sunglasses so that she could see our eyes.

"How do you do?" she replied sweetly and likewise removed her sunglasses to reveal her blue eyes. "I am Mrs. Lam."

Emma and I shook hands with the lady. "May I offer you some iced tea?" she said.

I answered for the both of us, "No thank you very much, Mrs. Lam. Not at the moment. We are on our way back to Virginia today. We read your ad for tomorrow's garage sale. I hope that we're not intruding too much on your Friday morning." It's important to talk to prospective clients to allay their misgivings and fears. Small talk is essential if a picker wants to get over the threshold.

"No indeed," she replied. "I enjoy having someone to talk to. I'm a widow, you know."

Emma responded by touching her forearm. "I'm so sorry," she sympathized. "How long has it been?"

"No need to worry about me, Dearie, he's been gone ten years," she told us. "I have gotten used to the loss."

"Mrs. Lam," I interjected, "you mentioned in the newspaper ad that you have 'bottles, crocks, and vintage clothing….'"

"Yes, in the garage I do. Go on in love, and have a look."

Inside were open-top cardboard boxes, on top of and piled under six- and eight-foot long folding tables, old armoires filled with hanging and folded clothes, and racks of pine board shelves against the back wall on either side of one small window. Under the window was a workbench with tools stuck in slots and holes in the back along the wall and in trays under its thick maple top. Mrs. Lam sat down in a folding aluminum chair and watched us sort through her possessions. Emma gravitated to the clothes and I went for the manly-man stuff. It took us about twenty minutes to make two piles: Emma made one and I made another.

Mrs. Lam priced everything: a 1940's men's long-sleeve rayon Hawaiian shirt ($10), a 1970's men's long-sleeve disco shirt ($5), a pair of 1930's silver sandal-style shoes ($15), and a 1950's yellow brocade dress with a green floral print ($15), plus half a dozen pieces of designer costume jewelry ($60) by Yves Saint Laurent, Christian Dior, Christian Lacroix, Schiaparelli, and yet another piece by Miriam Haskell. And then Mrs. Lam priced my treasure pile, which included a Greenlee mortise chisel ($5), an apple wood plow plane marked John Bell ($50), and a scarce plow plane by Quebec maker Dalpe ($15). All in all, not a bad pick in twenty minutes if one didn't include the prep and travel time required. The clothes were destined to become stock for our eBay store or website.

It would be my job when we got home to clean and wax the tools, while Emma will take the clothes to be dry-cleaned. The shoes, she'll polish herself. The tools, I will offer first to One-Eyed Jack, a dealer friend of ours who I've known since I was a corporal; he lives in Williamsburg, Virginia and handles tools and other manly-man smalls. The couture, will first be offered to a film studio costume designer acquaintance of ours in Hollywood. If she doesn't need them for her inventory, then they will ultimately go on our eBay. Both categories are examples of niche collectibles that defy the demographic trend.

"Is that all you two are going to buy, Mr. Dawes?" she asked.

"I am afraid so, Mrs. Lam," I replied. "Unless you have sterling flatware or paintings that you wish to sell." She thought for a moment as I peeled off twenties while Emma folded the vintage clothing.

"We're traveling light. Normally we have a minivan, but we flew down and are driving this rental sedan back. If you were closer, we might buy larger pieces, but not on this trip."

Mrs Lam pulled on her ear lobe. "You know, Mr. Dawes, I do have some silverware that I'm willing to sell if the price is right," she raised an eyebrow and let go of her ear.

I looked at Emma; she shrugged OK. "Alright ma'am, let's have a look."

"Come on in." Mrs. Lam motioned for us to follow her and offered us something to drink again, which we accepted this time. In a golden oak sideboard, she had a load of flatware in a plain pattern. Emma pulled out her ubiquitous loupe and read the mark.

"Towle sterling," Emma declared.

I counted the pieces, assessed the variety of serving pieces in the pattern, and the dozen or so of miscellaneous pieces not of the same pattern in the same box. "Would you like to sell all of it, ma'am?"

She replied, "Maybe. Depends on what it's worth."

"Emma, if you please – " I didn't even have to complete the sentence.

Emma replied, "The scales."

I explained to Mrs. Lam, "She'll be right back. She's just going to get the scales."

Mrs. Lam nodded and shifted in her seat.

"Thank you," I said, as Emma went out to the door to get the kit we carry for such occasions. I explained to Mrs. Lam that silver is a commodity that fluctuates the same way that the stocks and bonds markets do. Patterns, forms, and makers may or may not be a value attribute; it depends. Tiffany, for instance, generally trumps other makers except for a few other notables like Georg Jensen, Cartier, and William Spratling. All things being equal, if one had one spoon by each of these four makers, then pattern would be the deciding attribute, and likewise form. My lovely returned after a minute and set up the electronic scales.

"Mrs. Lam," I explained, "silver value is calculated by Troy ounce. There are 31.1 grams in a Troy ounce. My scale is set to weigh in grams, which I will convert to Troy ounces; the calculation is more accurate in grams than if the scale were set to Troy ounces. I'm going to weigh all of the solid pattern pieces together by form to get a total weight per form count. That means the weight of all of the teaspoons, and then all of the dinner forks, etc. The hollow-handled knives I'll figure separately; their silver weight is approximately half an ounce each. The solid serving pieces, like this ladle and this asparagus server," I held up each, "I'll calculate separately because these forms have added value because of what they are. Typically, a young bride acquires a service of X-number of place settings with each place setting having four or five pieces, but the initial service typically includes no or very few serving pieces. Not until later in life when the collector is more settled and affluent does she add more serving pieces. It is this 'later demand' that adds additional value to serving pieces in general, for all makers and all patterns. I'll weigh each of your serving pieces individually and calculate their worth based on their respective pattern and form."

It took less than ten minutes all told. "OK, Mrs. Lam, you have sixty ounces of silver in the Towle plain pattern. Emma, look on your Blackberry to see what sterling is selling for today."

Emma punched her keypad numerous times and then declared, "Spot metal right now, today, is $6.25 a Troy ounce…multiplied by sixty, equals $375 total."

I looked to Mrs. Lam for her reaction, and added, "Plus three dollars each for the hollow handled knives."

She did not look impressed.

In the end, Mrs. Lam decided that she would keep all of the silver and so we had in fact wasted our time. We did, however, file away her contact information for the day when silver prices were high enough to make it worth her while. Sometimes you have to spend time and money now in order to harvest a bountiful crop later. I just hoped that she lived long enough to see the day.

24 Intangibles

"Where to?" I asked Emma.

"A place call Spuds."

I crinkled my face in a closed smile at the amusing name, squinted in the bright sunlight, and realized that we were not on a northerly heading as we had planned, but that's picking for you. We never know where a lead will take us next. "So, what does this appointment have?"

She shuffled through the tattered *Dollar Saver*.

"'A Civil War hat,' the old man said," Emma replied. "Can you tell if it really is one? What if it is a repro from the movie, *Gone With the Wind*, or something like that?"

I shrugged. "I can usually tell. Did he say what kind it is?"

"A kepi," she replied. An American Civil War era forage cap is called a kepi. It is round on top, sags in front, and has a shiny sun visor. "What's it worth?"

"That depends on a lot of factors: condition, whether it's Union or Confederate or from an old movie set, and on the furniture it bears." Emma looked at me quizzically.

"What?"

I explained, "In the front it may or may not have a thin sheet brass insignia like crossed cannons, or something like that."

"Oh," she said. "Got it. It's blue, by the way. That would mean that it was Northern, right?"

I made a sound of uncertainty. "Usually but not always," I explained. "The Confederates were Southern and their uniforms were usually gray, but not all Southern units wore Southern Gray uniforms in the beginning of the conflict. Before the war began in April of 1861, a few State militias in the South wore blue and some in the North wore gray. It all depended on the eye of the wealthy, ego-centric officer that had outfitted them. It wasn't until both sides realized that the 'Little Embarrassment,' later known as the American Civil War, would become a protracted conflict and that uniform and equipment standardization might be required."

I drove around and around through back alleys and down a long dusty driveway. *Tina*, the GPS voice, *must have taken us the scenic route*, I thought. Finally, across a cattle guard, we got to a shack with an oyster shell gravel parking spot under the shade of a big crape myrtle. A pack of yipping, flea-bitten Chihuahuas rushed the car. Dominique and Rhode Island Red chickens ignored the miniatures and continued scratching for breakfast bugs and seeds in the mowed yard. Six strands of high tinsel-wire fence framed the shack in need of paint. White Brahmas grazed the tall green pasture on the other side of the fence. The bovines lifted their heads when we crunched to a stop and then returned to their grazing as their ever-present sentinels, white egrets, kept watch hoping for fleeing insects as the beasts stirred the tall grasses. It is a common scene down South, one I have enjoyed countless times in the tropics across the globe. I knew enough about cattle to recognize a pure-bred herd when I saw one. These bovines were beautiful and, I surmised, too valuable to belong to the residents of the shack we were visiting. I guessed that the shack was probably a rental property let by the land and cattle owner.

Resting in a black wicker rocking chair on the right side of the porch was a shirtless old man in worn bib overalls. What I recognized as a Henry rifle leaned against the wall beside him to his left, and on a small round wicker stand on his right was a pitcher of lemonade and three 1960's cartoon glasses. I turned the engine off and opened my door, ignoring the barking roaches. A big coonhound on the porch opened one eye, feebly lifted his head, and then resumed his coma. Fearful of the noisy dogs despite their diminutive size, Emma stayed in the car. The dogs stopped barking when the old man cleared his throat and spat a dark stream into the dust of what passed for a front yard in Spuds, Florida. I greeted him with an "Ahoy, there!" I use nautical terms out of habit and because it tends to disarm landlubbers with a peculiar curiosity. It worked.

He stopped rocking and squinted. "Was y'all the ones that called?"

"Yes sir," I replied. "May I come aboard?"

"Permission granted," the old man said.

As I climbed the weathered steps to the porch, my little ones began to curl; something was nearby. The old guy motioned me to a chair next to the lemonade. "Hep yursef, sir," he said without his dentures, and then peered at Emma stranded in the car with his pack of Chihuahuas circling her, peeing on all four tires. Emma stayed put. She's allergic to anything with feet. She was even allergic to Grace and me in the beginning of our relationship. I looked her way and she waved me encouragement. "Yourn misses kin join us if'n she likes, sir."

"Thank you, sir. Maybe in a minute." I invented an excuse for her. "She needs to make business phone calls."

"Okeydokey," he mused, and spat once more.

"Nice First Model you have there, sir," I complemented, pointing to the rifle. I figured it to be causing my effect; both fingers throbbed.

He looked at it with his walleye. "Yep, .44 Rimfire. Not many 'round no more. Saw me a coyote spying the chickens this morning. Hopin' to get a shot sometime today."

Small talk is important in rural settings. Rushing a seller is not wise. I took him up on his hospitality with the libation to break the ice so that I could gain his trust and to find out more about the strange coincidence that I was beginning to assemble in my mind. There was something suspicious pertaining to this leg of the pick. My suspicion began when I noticed the rifle. A Henry is rare. So are kepis. The two rare pieces together do not make a suspicious puzzle, but when they appear in tandem with a recent posting in the latest edition of the *Maine Antique Digest*, it does tend to make one suspicious. I figured that I might be onto something bigger than a routine pick.

I took a sip of the pink lemonade and mulled the news article around in my mind. "Mmm, hits the spot," I complimented the old guy. He nodded and returned a toothless smile.

MAD is a trade paper that nearly everyone in the antiques trade subscribes to. I grew up around it in my parents' house and can't ever remember it not being around. I grew up around it in my parents' house and can't ever remember it not being around. I think it first appeared on the scene in the 1970's. We brought the latest issue with us to read on the plane. In it, there was mention of a theft at a prominent auction house in Ohio. I couldn't remember if it was at Garth's or Cowan's, but I managed to remember some of the items that were mentioned as having been stolen in a daring midnight raid: a Henry rifle, an 1861 Union blue kepi, a WWI M-8 experimental helmet, a Confederate D-guard Bowie knife, and a 17th century German lobster-tail helmet.

I'd run into stolen property on numerous occasions. When I had an open storefront on Route 29, hot merchandise was especially common because a lot of con artists and racketeers traveled the thoroughfare pedaling their goods to the numerous antiques shopkeepers along the highway. For some reason I have a sixth sense about crookedness in general. The coincidence of the two items made the short neck hairs on my neck stand up but the naïveté of the old man made them lie back down again; he didn't seem the type. But something wasn't right. I studied the old man's composure. He just didn't seem to fit the mold. He was Old School.

I tested my sixth sense by asking him if I could examine the Henry, and he handed it over without hesitation. If he had refused, I might have suspected him. "Mighty fine rifle, Henrys," I complimented him. The throbbing in my pinkies halted and I noticed that they straightened with a mind of their own. "Did this come down in the family?" The rifle was loaded with one round in the chamber.

"No sir, my nephew left it with me not long ago, and the kepi, too. That's what you come to look at, right?"

I handed the rifle back to him and he returned it to the same spot. "Yes, sir, and anything else you might like to show me."

"Yep, there is. Wait here a moment and I'll go get it." He creaked up out of the wicker rocking chair, almost tottered backwards before stepping forward and then over the hound, and ambled to the screen door. The loaded rifle he left against the wall, which was yet another sign that he was unaware of the situation he might be in. Other than my standing hairs, I didn't have proof of anything. He returned carrying a cardboard box and set it on the tongue-and-groove porch floor.

"So, what else do you have in this banana box, sir?" He showed me by slipping off its lid. Sure enough, the articles that I remembered, and some that I had forgotten, were in the box. I examined them with interest for ten minutes or so as the old man watched and commented. Inside was the corroborating evidence that proved my supposition was accurate. I signaled Emma by looking her way. She responded by calling my cell.

"Yes, Amor?"

I replied in Spanish. "*Do we still have the* MAD*?*"

Emma continued the dialogue in Spanish. "*Yes, Amor. Why?*"

"*The kepi hat and the other stuff that he has were stolen from an Ohio auction house last month. I saw pictures of the stuff in an article about the robbery in* MAD. *Look at the last paragraph of the article; there will be the contact*" *information for a police department. Call the investigator now and explain to him that we have discovered some of the missing articles here in Spuds, Florida. Tell him that we will stay on site until he sends local law enforcement to relieve us. Give him this address.*"

"*OK, Amor. I have it and I'll call now.*"

The old man looked at me for an explanation as to why all of the Spanish. "My wife is afraid of dogs," is all I told him. Emma kept the engine running while we waited because it was hot even in the shade in Florida in April. I stretched the small talk as well as I could until I saw in the distance the approach of a dusty turmoil that startled egrets to rise and relocate before I could hear the approach of a car on the gravel road. The barking roaches moved to fresh meat as the marked car pulled in beside Emma with its flashing lights off, which I thought portended familiarity. A tall man in a straw fedora and brown uniform dismounted from the passenger's side, spat, and then growled at the yappers which caused them to scatter with tails tucked. The deputy sheriff driver got out and leaned against the squad car as his boss ascended the porch steps.

The old man and I stood and I introduced myself to the lawman. Old Man Givens seemed curious why the lawman was visiting and looked to me as if I might be the one the sheriff was there for, but all he said was, "Howdy Sheriff," as the lawman shook my hand and then his. They obviously knew each other.

"I'm Charles Dawes. My wife is in the Caddy, sir," I said a little nervously. Being in an unfamiliar area in the Deep South always makes me a little anxious. Where I grew up in Virginia it was not so

Southern any longer, and becoming less Southern every year.

"Well, Mr. Dawes, you say. I'm Sheriff Williams, and hello again, Mr. Givens," He glanced at the rifle against the wall. "What do we have here?" he said as his eye was drawn to the stuff in the box.

The lawman pushed his hat back and moved stuff around in the box with an index finger. He examined the kepi carefully and then told Mr. Givens why he was visiting. "Sir, I'm here again about your nephew. We think that he may have been involved in a break-in up north. I got a call from a detective in Ohio. It seems some of the things here in this box may be stolen, and the rifle on the wall over there, also."

The old man turned to look at the rifle with his mouth open. "I was goin' to shoot me a coyote with it. He been stealin' my striped hens, done got my red rooster, already." His head snapped to the sheriff. "Is it really stolen?"

"I believe so," replied the sheriff. The lawman ambled over to the firearm, handled it, mindful of its muzzle, and ejected a round onto the seat of the old man's padded rocker. He then took his bifocals out and looked closely at the gun's serial number. "Yep, Mr. Givens. This is the stolen rifle that we've been looking for. I'm going to have to confiscate it and the contents in the box, and if you don't mind, I'm going to have my deputy look around a bit, too?" The old man nodded acquiescence. Without being told, the deputy hopped up the steps and went inside.

"You goin' to take the Henry from me, Sheriff?"

The lawman looked regretful. "I'm afraid so, Mr. Givens. I have no choice."

"My nephew lent it to me when I told him about the coyotes," said the old man.

"Yeah, I know sir," replied the sheriff. "Do you know where I might find Clarence?"

"He tolt me he in Miami, Sheriff," said the old man. "But I don't believe much of anything he tells me no more."

The sheriff asked him, "Who placed the ad in the newspaper to sell tomorrow?"

The old man didn't understand the question. "I don't get no newspaper, Sheriff. Cain't see to read no more, and if'n I could I wouldn't want to."

The sheriff looked at me and then back to Old Man Givens, and leaned in on him a bit with a hand on the arm of his chair. "Mr. Givens, how did Mr. Dawes know to come here to look at the kepi?"

Givens shrugged, "Clarence said he told some people to come buy it, and he told me the final prices..." he strained to remember. "...he told me to get cash only. Dat's all I knows, sir."

The sheriff stood up straight with one hand holding the rifle pointed at the floor and with the other, he took his hat off. Givens offered him lemonade. "Thanks, Mr. Givens, don't mind if I do." And he handed the Henry to me to hold as he poured himself a glass, drank all of it, and then poured half of another. "What do you think, Mr. Dawes?" the sheriff asked me.

I shrugged. "A man can't choose his family, Sheriff Williams," is all I said to the man wearing gold eagles on his collar.

"That'd be the truest thing I've heard all day," he replied with a smile. About then the deputy returned with a report.

"Sheriff, looks like there's a roomful of stuff and it may be all from Ohio," the deputy advised.

The sheriff nodded and then turned to me. "Mr. Dawes I want to thank you for your assistance in this matter. Not many people would have done what you and your wife did."

"You're welcome, Sheriff. Semper Fidelis, sir. I have learned that the only things that really matter are the intangibles."

The sheriff stood straighter when I said 'Semper Fi.' "You were in the Corps, Mr. Dawes?"

"Yes sir," I replied. "Retired a few months ago from the reserves."

"What grade?"

"Major."

The sheriff stood practically at attention.

"I was a Master Gunny, sir." A Marine warrior is a special occupation that generally outranks non-Marine occupations in the minds of Marines, no matter what. Once the sheriff identified himself as a former gunnery sergeant, I automatically elevated my respect for the man he had proven himself to be.

I smiled and shook his hand once more. "I am very pleased to make your acquaintance, Gunny Williams."

"Thank you, Major. A moment ago, what'd you mean about intangibles?"

"Well, Gunny, it's my opinion the only things that really matter are the intangibles, like fidelity, loyalty, integrity, honesty, and so forth – I call them my T's. It's the T's that count, nothing else matters as much. I do what is right even if it is not popular and not politically correct. In fact, if it is politically incorrect, you can bet one of the T's has been circumvented."

Gunny nodded his approval of my abstract and seemed to focus on something in his distant memory for a few seconds as I explained. "I like that, sir. I think I might borrow that idea for my next re-election campaign."

I chuckled, "You are more than welcome to, Gunny. Now, Mrs. Dawes and I need to hit the road again and head back north. What else can we do to help?"

"Sir, I need for you to stop by the office on your way out of town and make a statement. Shouldn't take more'n a few minutes."

"OK. I understand. Be glad to, Sheriff."

I thanked Old Man Givens and shook his hand, too, and then we took off with the three men on the porch watching us go. As I promised, we stopped by the Sheriff's Office and left a statement and then we hit the road again.

Emma said, "I called the other two picks and told them we'd be late."

I turned my head to look at her. "Almost forgot about them in all of the excitement."

"You want me to call them to say we're not coming by?"

"No, no, let's go check them out. You never know what you're going to find next."

25 Louis Vuitton

North of St. Augustine, in Ponte Vedra, we picked up a 1939 first edition by Marguerite De Angeli, titled: *Skippack School Being the Story of Eli Shrawder and of One Christopher Dock, Schoolmaster, about the Year 1750*. It was only ten dollars.

I bought it because the title mentioned the regionally renowned Early American celebrity teacher, Christopher Dock, and I had become interested in him after reading a book about folk art in which he was mentioned.

Dock was a Mennonite schoolmaster, scrivener, community leader, and farmer. He gained prominence in the Colonies by emphasizing personal character and discussion instead of obedient silence. Unlike his contemporaries, he employed the carrot instead of a stick and was rewarded with remarkable results.

He was a radical.

Dock was also a maker of fraktur, or a scrivener, and the plural of fraktur is fraktur. Fraktur were/are illuminated paper documents commemorating a rite of passage, such as a birth, marriage, or death. Early fraktur were drawn in ink and hand-decorated with watercolors and calligraphy. Usually the text was in German because most scriveners were Germans making fraktur for their German constituents. Typically, early fraktur were sixteen inches by thirteen inches in size and most were scribed vertically.

Any information on Dock or anything identified as being by his hand has torrid demand amongst folk art collectors in the modern marketplace, especially in eastern Pennsylvania. Teacher Dock was known to have rewarded his well-performing students with small illustrations on paper of a bird or a flower that he drew himself. Over the years, I had seen three or four "rewards" that were attributed to him but I had never actually owned one. Nor had I ever owned this title before, but after a quick search on Bookfinder dot-com, I figured that we could flip it for $300 by making a phone call when we got home, but I wanted to read it first.

Emma punched in an address on the GPS. The next pick was supposed to have old trunks. We went around the Jacksonville beltway, took the exit onto State Route 17, and then headed north to Melbourne, a small community of 70,000 people.

"What are we going to see at this pick besides trunks?" I asked her. "You know we don't have room for trunks unless we pull a trailer, right?"

"'Trunks,' is all she told me," Emma replied.

"We don't have room for trunks, Periwinkle," I repeated.

"They may be Louis Vuitton, Amor." Emma turned her head and raised one eyebrow.

I snapped my head in her direction and then back. "We'll make room," I replied, just as we arrived.

The driveway was white pea gravel mixed with oyster shells, separated by a mowed grass center for a hundred yards. It was flanked by a tunnel of crape myrtle bushes leading to an old house on the edge of town amidst enveloping live oaks. In the world of trunks, Louis Vuitton is crème de la crème. *We'll tie it on top if we have to*, I thought to myself. One of my fantasies is to go back in time and extract the Louis Vuitton luggage that went down on the *Titanic*.

In the back yard stood a wiry old gray-haired lady working on a camelback steamer trunk atop a sheet of three quarter-inch plywood resting on old wooden sawhorses. As we approached, I could see that she was prying tacks from one end where a leather strap-handle once had been. It was a common Stagecoach Era trunk, not a Robber Baron Era Louis Vuitton.

"Ahoy!" I said loudly, thinking that she might be hard of hearing. Emma followed.

The old lady looked up from her task and gave me a squint. "I ain't deaf, you know."

Emma and I looked at each other. I chuckled. "We are Charles and Emma Dawes, ma'am. How do you do?"

I was beginning to tingle on the left.

She put down her pliers and took off one canvas garden glove to offer us her hand. "I'm Margi Smith, I am, yes." She spoke in a peculiar manner with a Brooklyn accent long modified by Southern living. "And I can't get this daggone nail out."

I bent over to take a closer look, took the pliers from her hand, and promptly removed the stubborn fastener. "There," I said cheerfully.

"While you're at it, pull this one, too, uh-huh," Mrs. Smith requested gruffly, pointing to the other end of the trunk.

I pulled it out, too. On her makeshift bench, she had two new hand-sewn leather straps and the trunk's four old original cast iron end caps. I pointed the pliers at the straps and asked, "Renovator's Supply?"

"They don't have them anymore, no," Mrs. Smith replied, shaking her head. "I got these online from Constantine's, I did. Have you replaced handles before, Mr. Dawes?"

I smiled. "Once or twice, Mrs. Smith. My mom used to drag home trunks for me to work on when I was a teenager. That's how I earned my allowance, before I could even drive."

"You mean you had to *work* for your allowance? It wasn't just *given* to you, no?" she had a twinkle in her eye and a look of growing respect.

"Yes ma'am. My allowance was a dollar a week if I did my chores without complaint, and for every trunk I restored, I'd get two dollars more."

Emma looked at me. "You never told me that."

I chuckled. "Well, now you both know."

"It's good for children, to learn the value of work, yes," Mrs. Smith said.

I nodded and looked at the hardware on the worktable. "I'll be glad to put these on for you if you like," I offered.

The old lady blinked. "I don't mind if you do, Mr. Dawes. Yes, thank you ever so much. Please be my guest, uh-huh."

And with those words of encouragement, I let my hands do the work they remembered as routine as the three of us had a nice conversation about trunks, antiques, and travel. In the ten minutes it took for me to install the new straps we learned a few things about each other, especially after Emma mentioned being from Peru. After that there was no stopping Mrs. Smith. She had to know all about Machu Picchu, Lake Titicaca, Peru's capital city, Lima, and all of the countries south of the equator that we had been to; the wines and cuisine, and so on. Investing time with a client, whether you're selling to them or buying from them, matters. And it matters a great deal. It's a very easy, pleasurable, and gentlemanly way one can earn trust, which often leads to larger mutual gains.

Mrs. Smith looked at each strap and smiled. "Perfect! Exactly the same on both sides, yes. Thank you so much, Mr. Dawes."

"My pleasure Mrs. Smith." I redirected our attention. "Now, Emma told me that you have a Louis Vuitton trunk that you might want to part with?"

She squinted at me and nodded. "Yes, indeed, sir, I do, uh-huh. Right this way, please, yes." She wobbled a bit and clutched a lady's walking stick that she had leaning against the worktable within reach. Emma grabbed her arm to steady her as we were taken to the detached garage flanked with a riot of flora that I recognized as firebush, fire spike, shrimp plant, and salvia. Three or four ruby throated hummingbirds were darting about amongst the blossoms. By the time I crossed the threshold, both digits were in rigor mortis. Inside, Mrs. Smith pointed to a tattered white sheet covering something in the back corner behind an old riding lawn mower. "Take that sheet off, Mr. Dawes, if you don't mind, yes, and open the door to let some light in." She moved over near the lawn mower and took a seat on an old wooden chair facing the white-sheeted stack.

I did as she directed, using my thumbs and the remaining three fingers on each hand. Like a crab, I opened the door and then removed the sheet to reveal a graduated stack of trunks and suitcases illuminated by the subdued light filtered through a mimosa tree behind the building. The largest piece of luggage was on the bottom and the smallest was on top. It was a wonderful display. I gulped and stood with my mouth open and my pinkies screaming bloody murder for probably a full minute admiring the collection before I thought to touch the nearest piece with one index finger. Immediately, I felt relief.

All were in very good condition. On the bottom was a huge rectilinear wardrobe trunk with a retail value of between fifteen and twenty-five thousand dollars, depending on the market level. Smaller, less valuable trunks of the same shape were stacked on top to form a pyramid. All-told I supposed that we were looking at between thirty-five to fifty thousand dollars' worth of Louis Vuitton luggage; that would be retail and it would be dependent on how well-placed we could insert them into the market.

Market level is important; it is where something is sold. Yard sale would be the lowest level while Park Avenue would be at the top of the food chain. The higher in the proverbial ladder we inserted them, the more we would net.

"Wow!" I exclaimed, and Emma chimed in with equal enthusiasm. I could tell that Mrs. Smith really appreciated the fact that we knew what we were looking at, its value and all. "What a beautiful collection, Mrs. Smith," I said, and Emma was speechless.

"After seeing you put those straps on the camelback, I figured that you might like seeing my fancy stuff, yes, uh-huh."

"Are you sure that you're not going to travel much anymore, Mrs. Smith?" Emma asked.

"I'm sure, yes," she replied. "I seldom travel these days, and when I do, I travel light. Back in the day before air travel became commonplace, I used all of these, yes." She tapped the bottom trunk with the tip of her walking stick. "My husband was alive then. We often traveled on business, and for pleasure, uh-huh." She looked like she nodded to an imaginary image of someone in her mind. It was clear that she was lost in the moment recalling fond memories. "We liked traveling by ship, both the big liners and the small ones. We saw much of the world by freighter, too, we did. You know the small freighters will take on paying passengers, and it's quite comfortable although they are a bit slow, uh-huh. That's why I had so many pieces of luggage. I mean, we'd be at sea for weeks, in ports a day or two, yes, and then at sea again for long periods. One needed a lot of clothes then, one did, yes, I did." Mrs. Smith was charming with her old mannerisms. I looked past her wrinkles and imagined her at twenty and saw a young Candice Bergen with sculpted features and a penchant for living wildly, or maybe not.

We understood first-hand what she was telling us. Emma and I had traveled on small freighters around the Black Sea. "I am surprised that you still have these pieces so late in the day of a yard sale, Mrs. Smith," I said. "I would have thought someone would have bought them by now."

She looked at me and at Emma and then wistfully at the stack. "The newspaper ad I put stated trunks, not Louis Vuitton, it did. When people came looking I showed them the camelback and that flattop one over there." She pointed to a scruffy steamer trunk by the sawhorse. "I was saving these here for just the right person, or people, as it were." She turned, facing us. "And I think you are they, uh-huh, yes I do. Would you like to buy them?"

Emma was desperately trying to maintain her composure. She gave me an *"is she kidding?" look.* "Yes, Mrs. Smith," I replied, "we would very much like to buy them; that is, if we can afford them."

"I see, uh-huh," Mrs. Smith contemplated. "I'll tell you what, young-uns, I'll sell them to you for $10,000. How's that?"

"That sounds fine, Mrs. Smith," Emma answered too quickly. "Right, Charles?"

I gave Emma a stern look and turned to Mrs. Smith. "Yes, ma'am, but on one condition."

"Do sit down, Mr. Dawes," Mrs. Smith said. I sat down on an apple crate stenciled Granny Smith Apples, facing her. "What condition would that be?" she said, no longer looking up at me.

It would be easy for us to make off like bandits with this Louis Vuitton treasure trove, but that's not our style. I don't do that to people. Maybe that's why I'm a struggling picker instead of CEO of Lehman Brothers, or whatever. "We'll agree to the $10,000 now and if we manage to get more than $20,000 for the collection, we'll split the excess with you after expenses."

The little old lady got a little older and a little more shriveled before our eyes just then. She looked at the concrete floor and mumbled something unintelligible. I looked at Emma,shrugged, and then looked back at Mrs. Smith to see her streaming tears. Emma knelt before her and I stooped over her. "What's the matter, Mrs. Smith?" Emma asked.

Mrs. Smith dabbed her eyes with a lace hanky she kept up her sleeve and replied, "I prayed for patience and I got you, yes, uh-huh."

Crying women make me feel helpless. "You don't understand, Mrs. Smith." I said, thinking that she must have misunderstood my intent. "We are going to share the profit with you *after* we sell it. We will deposit in your bank half of what we make *over* $20,000."

She dabbed her eyes again. "Don't be silly. I'm old but not stupid. I understood you, I did, yes, and I am happy. I cry when I am happy, yes, and because I am old."

Emma and I both sighed with relief. Making old women cry is just about the worst feeling one can experience. We smiled and put hands on Mrs. Smith. I wiped my forehead with the red bandana that I keep in my right back pocket for such occasions and sat back down. Emma flipped over a white five-gallon bucket that once contained spackling compound and sat on it.

I smiled at Mrs. Smith and let her have a few moments to recompose before I explained the details. "OK, here's the plan. Emma is going to stay here with you and make a few calls to find a buyer." I looked at Emma. "Call Peter and ask him who on Rodeo Drive has been asking for Louis Vuitton." Then I turned to Mrs. Smith and said, "Meanwhile I'm going to go find a U-Haul trailer because all of this is not going to fit into our sedan. I think I remember seeing a dealer on the way here."

"You did, yes," Mrs. Smith said.

I nodded. "And, I'm going to stop by Staples and print out a Letter of Agreement outlining this transaction. How's that sound?"

"That sounds good but unnecessary." Mrs. Smith shook her head.

"Good, because it's the way we do business, Mrs. Smith. Emma, please write Mrs. Smith a check and I'll deposit it for her when I look for a trailer. Mrs. Smith, is your bank near the U-Haul place?"

"Yes, it is," Mrs. Smith replied. "It's at the next light past the rental place on the opposite side of the street, yes. Save me a trip, too, yes, good idea. Mrs. Dawes let's go in to the house to write the check and to make some tea. Help me up, please."

"Right, of course," I replied, sheepishly. *She's sharper than I am*, I thought. *There's too much churning around in my mind.* Admittedly part of my mind was enjoying the sea breeze at the rails of a long-gone *Titanic* as I gazed at our great trunk find.

Mrs. Smith's home was a white rococo revival Victorian masterpiece, inside and out. The gingerbread accents on the outside were outdone by master millwork artisans everywhere on the inside. Wainscoting, crown molding, wide cypress wood flooring, elegant dual-front staircases, and a spectacular paneled den to-die-for, all provided a splendorous backdrop for a collection of furnishings several generations old. It was a pleasure to see such an impressive and well-kept home. Emma got the grand tour while I was away securing a trailer and depositing our check into Mrs. Smith's account. The dealer had a trailer that was big enough, but the wait for the hitch attachment took way too long. I texted Emma the reason for the delay. By the time I got back, it was dusk. I pulled the trailer in close to the back door of the garage and manhandled the luggage into the box trailer, expertly padded it all with blankets, and tied everything down, and then drove around front to get Emma. It was almost dark.

"About time," Emma said when she saw me. Bugs were circling the porch lamps.

"I have everything loaded to go," was my response.

"Dinner is ready," Emma informed me through the screen door to the screen-enclosed back porch. "Mrs. Smith has invited us to stay the night and we accepted. Bring the suitcases in, Amor, please."

She left me standing in the dark with my hands on my hips.

26 Tricks of the Trade

Mrs. Smith was kind enough to put us up in her west wing suite with a canopy bed swaddled in white sheets that were as fine as our Vera Wang at home. Like most old homes of the period, this house had floor-to-ceiling high windows that open at the bottom and at the top in order to control temperature; a necessity before the advent of air-conditioning. Gilt and red floral wallpaper adorned the walls, a magnificent ca.1860 Persian Ardabil Mosque rug covered the floor, and ebonized American Aesthetic Movement furniture furnished the open space. American impressionist canvasses housed in ornate giltwood frames filled the three piers between the ceiling-high red silk curtains trimmed with gold braid. Two sets of French doors opened onto the open wraparound porch.

I dreamt all night that I was a stevedore on the pier loading Louis Vuitton luggage onto the *Titanic* at Cherbourg, the ship's second of three ports of call before heading on its doomed voyage across the Atlantic in April 1912. A ching-ching bicycle bell sound awoke me from my fantasy. It was punctuated by a thump against the outside wall of the house. I opened one eye and swung an arm over to feel if I was alone. I was. Emma usually gets up before I do. She says it's because she eats properly. I untangled myself, put on a white terrycloth robe, and stepped out onto the tongue-and-groove board porch floor in time to see a kid on a bicycle receding into the distance. At my feet on the deck was a rolled newspaper.

Emma saw me retrieving the paper as she entered the room. "Oh good, you're up. Breakfast is on. Come and get it." I mumbled a reply after she darted away. It takes me awhile to get my act together in the morning, unless someone's shooting at me, but that's not likely to happen anymore, so I've decided to just be myself – as long as I don't miss breakfast.

The ladies were all prettied up and bushy-tailed when I arrived to a spread of scrambled eggs, waffles, American buttermilk biscuits, fruit, orange juice, and coffee. "Ahh, this looks and smells wonderful!" I exclaimed. Emma and Mrs. Smith were delighted that I had finally made my appearance. The two of them chatted about a dozen different topics as they enjoyed watching a man eat. In the past few hours, they had become fast friends.

Staying overnight at a client's house is not something that we do very often because we both much prefer the anonymity and service of a hotel, but I once spoke to a show dealer who looked forward to staying with clients. It was part of his marketing strategy. He would personally deliver expensive large items that he sold at antiques shows to anywhere in the country and Canada, no matter how far away the customer lived provided his client was wealthy enough.

Most top-tier show dealers do not deliver. They prefer instead to direct their clients to the show promoter's sanctioned company that specializes in delivery. There are several reasons for their deference: liability concerns, convenience, the dealer's advanced age, busy schedule, or their ego. The latter motive would be a minority reason, but nonetheless it is worth mentioning. Snob is a capitalized word in the trade at the national level, and not just with the dealers. Customers are often worse.

Quite a few collectors masquerade as dealers in order to improve their personal collections, and they find it beneath their station to have to use the service elevator in order to make a delivery when their day job is millionaire doctor, lawyer, or Indian chief. But the dealer that I knew who actually liked to deliver to clients' homes and stay overnight had a different take. He believed that once one stays the night in a client's house and breaks bread with him the next morning, one has a devoted client for life because of the bonding and trust that naturally develops. Until now, I had never practiced his theory but I'd say that he's probably correct; judging from the looks of things, Emma and Mrs. Smith are as tight as ticks. I harrumphed to myself remembering a man named Woody who had told me this story, and smiled at the realization that I would be able in my old age to recount hundreds of such stories to amuse myself or anyone patient enough to listen. Here I am, forty years of age, and I am talking to myself about my distant old age.

I wondered, *Is this a sign of something?*

We were in no particular hurry so I took my time eating and helped with the dishes afterwards. The ladies disappeared to somewhere speaking animatedly to do whatever women do when they vanish. I contemplated calling Peter about the luggage but it was too early on the Left Coast, and so I washed the dishes instead. The evening before Emma had briefed me on Peter's response. Wisely, she sent him a photo of the stack so that he had a visual inventory of the merch. As soon as he saw the picture, he decided that he wanted to broker the luggage himself rather than provide the name of a broker, which was fine. It's good business to involve others and grow relationships. Peter agreed to a short margin of just ten percent because anything as strong as Louis Vuitton can be flipped with a phone call. There is little or no risk. Under like circumstances, most dealers are willing to work a short sale for the privilege of being included in the action, as well as a quick profit, and that is what Peter intended. It was left up to me to set the price and to arrange for delivery to California.

Hmm, a POD, *or van lines, or hauler?* I mulled the permutations and costs of the various venues. I went to the POD website to check on that possibility and discovered The Website From Hell; an absolute nightmare to navigate. A troglodyte must have designed it. To add disappointment to agony, the smallest POD, an eight-foot container, would have been nearly $3400. *That's out*, I thought to myself.

Next, I called Bruno, a formerly ornery Latvian dealer friend of mine – formerly ornery, that is, a Teddy bear now, and always a friend – who has a big shop in Strasburg, Virginia. Bruno looks like he might once have spent some time in a Russian gulag, and he has the accent for it. Being the curious sort, one day I asked him. Boy, was *that* ever a mistake! His ensuing explosion almost ended our business relationship. Humorously, the short of it was, yes, the old cuss had been locked up for being a political dissident in the USSR. In fact, he was a pal of

Solzhenitsyn. Being confined for years was probably
what made him such an ornery beast to get along
with, that is, until he had a coronary, which proved to
be a life-altering event. It miraculously turned him
into one of the nicest Theodore Roosevelt lookalikes
one might imagine. Bruno handles period American
neo-classical furniture – the heavy stuff – as well as
paintings, porcelains, sterling, architectural elements,
and folk art.

I knew Bruno shipped antiques and art to
Chicago, St. Louis, and California, so it stood to
reason that he had a long hauler guy that went coast
to coast.

Haulers are truckers who own their own truck
and work as lone operators, or with one other person;
sometimes it's their spouse. They usually drive a
circuit that includes regular stops for the same band
of clients. Most established antiques dealers, art
gallery owners, and show promoters use haulers.
There are several that Emma and I use, who travel up
and down the east coast -- one who does the northern
tier to the Dakotas but no farther, one who does the
middle tier to the Mississippi but no farther, and one
who does the southern tier to New Orleans but no
farther -- but we did not have a coast-to-coaster. Not
many haulers want to do the long-haul all the way
cross-country; after all, it is 2,700 miles from DC to
LA, and nearly 4,000 miles on the diagonal from Key
West to Vancouver.

Bruno had a load scheduled to be picked up
by his man three days hence. I told him how much
space I needed and where it had to go, and he agreed
to make it happen. So Emma and I had a couple

more days of yard saling before we had to return to the deep freeze, which was just fine by me.

I didn't know where the women went to but that didn't matter. I found a comfortable Heywood Wakefield wicker settee out on the side porch in the sun and settled down with the *Jacksonville News* and MAD until they reappeared. The sun was getting warmer, the hummingbirds were flitting from feeder to feeder, and I was feeling pretty good about everything.

27 Backscratchers

Mrs. Smith bade us farewell before lunchtime with a picnic basket full of goodies to nosh en route. We hit the road again with me behind the wheel and Emma beyond inconsolable. She had grown very fond of Mrs. Smith in just the few hours we had known her.

"Amor, how can you be so callous?" she complained.

Oh boy, here we go, I thought. "I am sorry, Periwinkle, but we couldn't stay forever, now could we? We live in Virginia. We need to at least move in that direction. Besides, just think how Grace is missing us."

"I want to go back." She crossed her arms under her breasts and faux-pouted.

"But Periwinkle, we just left."

She thought hard for about three shakes and then asked, "Alright, then when can we come back?"

I sighed and tried not to roll my eyes. "I don't know, Pretzel, but right now our short mission is to get the luggage to Bruno."

She looked at me, pleadingly.

I sighed, "In the Fall, maybe?" I searched for reason in a field of wrong answers.

"I *miss* her. She's so like my mom," she sniffed.

Rather than argue the point I soothed her grief with kind words. "Yes, I know dear, but we have a life and Mrs. Smith has a life. Each of us must make our own way and everyone needs to get back to their routine, including Mrs. Smith. You can stay in touch via email and Skype, if you like. Now then, let's go forward and check out Savannah! What do you say?"

For an answer, she sighed and looked out her side window. Emma had lost her mother five years earlier, just before we got together; I never got to meet her mom. They both had a very hard life, but Emma made it and managed to extract herself, her mom, her sister, and her three kids out of poverty. Under unbearable circumstances, she pulled herself up and out of the squalor of a Third World ghetto by her imaginary bootstraps and prevailed against all odds to become a self-made professional woman of distinction without losing sight of the T's that I value so much. When I read Emma's bio on Match, it was love at first read. I knew she was the one, and I was right. I have never been happier. After having been in a relationship with a psycho for five years followed by a marriage to a drunken control freak for seven, Emma is a true blessing. What we have is not perfect, but it's close enough to paradise.

We took Georgia State Route 301 to 17 and picked along the way, without much success, to the southern door of one of the most splendid cities of the Old South, Savannah, Georgia. She is a slow-motion architectural masterpiece that no one forgets if they've ever visited her. Twenty-two park-like squares comprise one of the largest National Historic Landmark Districts in the United States. Live Oaks draped with Spanish moss are everywhere, as well as palmettos and palms and flowering plants. Restored old homes frame the squares, and there's a constant salt breeze from the ocean. It's a beautiful, genteel place where sterling silver flatware is still in daily use and both white and black debutantes expect to be introduced to society in the traditional and fashionable manner. Most of the old racial prejudices have subsided here, as they have in Virginia.

What madness the previous hundred years of stupidity was, I thought. *I hope no one ruins it. O.J. Simpson almost did.*

We checked in early to the Savannah Marriott Riverfront with a view of the water, and walked the river walk as the sun set. In the old part of the revitalized wharf area, the cobblestones were worn smooth from steel-rimmed wagon wheels driven by teamsters plying shod horses, mules, and oxen over hundreds of years. Overhead gulls screeched constantly and in the distance, boats sounded their horns intermittently over glass-smooth water that reflected a blue sky and billowy white clouds.

One of the bistros down an alley caught Emma's ear and my nose. We read the menu posted outside and entered to find a raucous crowd enjoying a Latin beat. Young and old alike were dancing and drinking and having a wholesome good time. Emma picked a booth farthest from the band and ordered a frozen margarita without salt. I had a double Woodford Reserve on the rocks. Emma soon forgot about her sorrows from earlier in the day and got into the mood. Before long, we were both on our feet doing our best to keep up with the local yokels.

After we'd had enough exercise, we ordered from a menu we can't get back home. For me it was marsh hen and Chicken-Andouille Gumbo with a side of ripple fries. Emma chose seared octopus, dirty rice, and black-eyed peas. It was mighty fine dining for a hole-in-the-wall joint but it's what we prefer most of the time instead of white linens and a stuffy maître d'. Just about any place I'd ever been in that had dirty rice on the menu has had 'good eats' as they say Down South. When I asked the waitress how the chef knew how to make the dirty rice so well when we were so far north and east, she informed me that the chef was a Cajun transplant from New Iberia on the Bayou Teche. "Say no more," I replied. "That explains everything. My compliments to the chef."

***

We would have loved to spend more time in the Deep South, especially nearby Charleston, which is just as enchanting as Savannah, but the Louis Vuittons had to get to Bruno before his hauler departed for California in two days. As much as we wanted to pick the area, there wasn't time, so we took the fastest route north out of Savannah, Interstate 95. By lunchtime, we were north of Raleigh, but home was still four hours away and Strasburg, Virginia was even farther. I realized that we weren't going to make it all the way in one day, so I called Bruno.

"Where are you?" he asked.

"We stopped for a bite to eat somewhere near Rocky Mount."

"You're not going to make it here today, are you?"

"No, it doesn't look like it unless you want me on your doorstep at 9:00 PM."

"No need for that, Charles. Tomorrow before quitting time will do just fine. Look, since you're in

Rocky Mount, how about doing me a favor if you have the room in your U-Haul."

"Name it."

"There's a clock collection I need for you to pick up in Petersburg. I'd be much obliged and I'll make it worth your while. Bring the collection and I'll foot the cost of the space on my hauler's truck for the luggage to California. And a second favor…I'd like to add a couple of pieces of my own Louis Vuitton to yours, if you don't mind."

I agreed, and Bruno texted me the name, phone number, and address of the Petersburg clock collector. These kinds of favors are common in the business amongst the smart dealers and everyone is better off. In this transaction, Bruno and I not only scratched each other's back, but we both added important contacts for future use. Bruno got my West Coast contact and I got his clocks contact here in Virginia. It was a fair exchange of intel, and the barter was mutually beneficial because it kept both of our overheads down.

28 Time Peddlers

Anselm Tupper was my point of contact in Petersburg. His storefront was on a side street in downtown Petersburg. I parallel parked in front of it and rubbed the tingle in my hands. 'Tup,' as he insisted on being addressed, met us at the door with a smile. He is a tall, lean gentleman, with a New England accent softened by living on the Southside for several decades. We liked him immediately. Tup had loads of clocks as well as barometers and other mechanical things that I found absolutely fascinating.

"Tup, what is this?" Emma asked, pointing some sort of miniature contraption.

He replied with pride, "Oh, that. It's a salesman's sample of a reaper, one of the best that I have ever seen, by the way." I touched it hoping that the tingling in my hands might subside. It did a bit, but there was so much to gawk at in Tup's store that I just shoved my complainers deep into the back pockets of my jeans.

I stood next to Emma as she flipped the tag on the piece to see its price. It was priced $12,000. I looked at him, "You really like this one a lot, don't you?" I commented to Tup.

My incredulousness amused him. Crow's feet appeared at his eyes. He replied, "Besides clocks and scientific instruments my strong suits are miniatures, patent models, and salesman's samples." He lifted his face in a nod, pointing at the model. "It's priced about right."

"What's a patent model?" Emma asked.

Tup answered, "It's a three dimensional, twelve-inch working example of what an inventor has submitted with a patent application. The model demonstrates how the invention works. The requirement remained in practice until 1880."

Emma and I both encouraged him to tell us more.

Tup smiled and continued his lecture, which seemed practiced by the way it just rolled off of his tongue. "An English gentleman bought the entire collection of patent models in 1925 with the intent to establish a museum, but The Great Depression ravaged his fortune before he could act. The collection went through a succession of private ownerships after his death. Most were sold. About 4,000 are in the Rothschild Patent Museum."

"Very interesting, Tup," I said. "I didn't know the details."

"Thanks Charles," he replied. "Actually, I wrote the book on them."

I looked at him. "Really?"

And he responded by handing me a copy. "On the house," he said.

"Well, thanks Tup. That's very kind of you. I'll leave feedback on Amazon for you, too."

Tup smiled at that. "Thank you Charles. I'd very much like it if you did."

Emma picked up what looked like a toy street sweeper with a worker riding on top. She looked at it and the other miniatures and asked, "How can I tell …"

"A patent model from a salesman's sample?" Tup anticipated.

"Right," Emma grinned. "And what is a salesman's sample?"

He pulled a tape rule from his trouser pocket and held it to the reaper. "There are several ways to distinguish the two, size for one. All patent models had to be not more than twelve inches. Tag, secondly. Like this one's tag." He pointed to an official-looking inventory string tag. "And then there are references one can utilize." He turned to another miniature with his measuring tape. "A salesman's sample was similar to a patent model: it was an easily portable product example, but it could be larger than twelve inches. Rather than carry around a giant machine, a traveling salesman would carry a miniaturized version, like this." He held his tape to what might be a wringer washing machine about fifteen inches in height. "This was back in the day when the literacy rate was low. Often a picture was worth a thousand words, and a model was even better."

Emma seemed quite intrigued with the dozen or so miniatures. "Which is more valuable: patent models or salesman's samples?" she asked.

Tup looked to me, and so I answered. "The two categories have essentially equal demand amongst collectors, right, Tup?"

"Correct," he agreed. "It varies from specimen to specimen, according to subject. There is no set rule."

"You know, Tup," I said, "while standing here, I couldn't help but notice the tall case clock over there. What's the story on it?" An ebonized seven-foot tall folk art clock that looked homemade had caught my eye. It had reeded columns, and what we refer to as a broken arch pediment on top, a squat wooden center finial, and matching flanking wooden finials. A glazed hood stood on top of a blind thorax door over a plinth base that rested on bracket feet. Oddly, the face was paper on metal with a paper moondial. I walked to it for a closer look. My fingers began throbbing, but stopped altogether when I touched it.

"Oh, that's a C.C. Colley," Tup replied. "I just got it in this morning. Colley was a Confederate veteran. That may be why he glued a Battle Flag and General Lee on Traveler on it above his name."

Except for this Colley clock, Tup's clocks collection was what I expected it to be, comprised of both cartel and mantle timepieces from the first four decades of the nineteenth century. All were Yankee-made innovations from the Connecticut River Valley with key-wound works housed in fine wood cases.

"Charles," he asked, "you ought to read an article by a guy named Joseph T. Rainer. He wrote a piece about Yankee peddlers and how they transformed the market landscape. When clocks first appeared on the scene, it was consumer love at first sight from New England to Texas to Cuba."

I was curious. "What's it about?"

"You got a minute? Let's sit," he motioned to upholstered chairs.

I nodded.

"I'm going to look around," said Emma.

Tup grinned and began.

"Clocks were one of the first American consumer crazes that swept the country. Eli Terry brought the cost of a timepiece within the reach of most of the population when he began mass-producing wooden key-wound mechanisms for small wall and shelf clocks. Demand was strong and he immediately filled the distribution system that had been in place since the 1740's.

"Before the American Revolution, a tinsmith in Connecticut developed a peddling scheme for his vast tinware product line. As most men did, in the summer months, he farmed the land, but in the winter months he made utilitarian tin wares for the home to sell. When his winter business overtook his farming activities, he employed other seasonally idle men to increase his volume. Eventually demand for his products waned as New England became saturated, so he extended his range south and west by enlisting young men in their twenties to hawk his products on commission. This took his scheme to the next level. Much of the settled continent was covered in a very short period. His agents only returned for the winter, or when their inventory was exhausted.

"Fortunes were made in peddling tinwork but even greater fortunes were made selling clocks. The cost of manufacturing one clock was less than four dollars. Peddlers often had the latitude to set the price for as much as the market would bear. A price of $40 to $70 in the 18-teens was commonplace. There are even reports of the not-so-savvy being beguiled into paying over $100 in the Deep South before Yankee Peddlers saturated the region. Between the Yanks gouging Southern customers on clock purchases and tinware salesmen selling polished tin as silver, the Southerner's ill impression of Yankees in general was set well before the advent of the Civil War in 1861."

I listened intently the whole time, and said, "I had no idea, and I've been dealing and collecting clocks since college."

"Pretty cool, isn't it, to know the mechanics of the marketplace?" he said.

I nodded. "Yeah, I'll say. I appreciate the in-depth briefing. It dovetails smartly with my geography background and what I've learned from experience. Not to change the subject, but I was wondering: what'll you take for the Colley clock, Tup?" I asked him suddenly.

Tup put one hand on his chin and thought deeply for a few seconds. "It needs work, Charles."

That's what I'd expect to hear from an honest dealer, full disclosure of all apologies. It's my policy, and it's the ethical thing to do, and I was glad Tup was that way, too.

"I know. I can tell but thank you, Tup."

Emma gave me a quizzical look. "Amor, why do you ask? Do I like it?"

I chuckled, "Yes, dear, you like it."

"I'll take $1,500 for it," Tup finally answered.

We barely got it in the U-Haul. In fact, we had to wrap it in packing blankets and wedge it on top of everything else. And the only way we could get the clock collection on board was to put some of the clocks inside the luggage pieces. The load wasn't very heavy, but distributing the weight over the trailer's single axel took some ingenuity; it always does. An improperly packed trailer can press the rear of the car down or pull it up, which is dangerous and makes the car difficult to drive. Time invested up front usually saves time later.

Emma and I paid Tup for the longcase clock, said our goodbyes, and headed home to Barboursville.

"Amor," Emma wondered, "why do I like the big clock?"

"It'll be perfect, Periwinkle," I smiled at my novice, "in the living room between the two windows in line-of-sight of the dining room, kitchen, and the desk in the den."

She was silent for a moment, thinking. "Or, at the top of the stairs on the landing so that when we come in the front door it can be seen."

"Yes, that is a good place, too. We'll keep it for a while until another we like better comes our way. In the meantime, I'll see if I can do Colley's genealogy. The more interesting his story, the more we can get for it when we decide to sell it."

29 Newlyweds & Nearlydeads

I had a restless night with little sleep. Between the recent success and the next day's delivery to Strasburg, my mind churned all night, and I had another one of my Coventry dreams. *Will they haunt me for the rest of my life?* I wonder.

"You tossed and turned all night, Amor," Emma cooed to me in the morning as she straightened things around the master bedroom.

I opened one eye and surveyed the nest I had squirmed for myself on my side of the bed. Flashes of Emma went past my line of sight. She was dressed in white jeans and a pink sweater. Bright-eyed and bushy-tailed, she had already retrieved Grace from the dog lady. Grace slobbered my open eye, *Ick*, making me roll over defensively. Face-up, I read the time projected by the radio clock on the ceiling, 0730, and sat up.

The sun was higher on the eastern horizon at this hour in the morning in nearly mid-April than when we had left for Florida. Spring was definitely here. I am convinced annually by Mother Nature's display, that nowhere is Spring more beautiful than in Virginia. The maples were past blushing, the poplars and redbud, too, and the forsythia and daffodils were amplifying the golden sunlight across the tiny neighborhood we've called home for two years now.

The drive home had actually been a push back into the seasonal shift. If we had kept going north I am sure that it would have been replaced altogether by winter in another three hundred miles. *Ever more the reason to live in the Mid-Atlantic rather than points farther north*, I thought, as I scratched my belly and fended off Grace from sniffing my crotch.

"Amor, I'm going to stay here and do some paperwork," Emma suggested. "Do you mind delivering to Bruno by yourself?"

I rummaged the logistics in my mind for a few seconds too long.

"Charles?" she prodded.

"Ah, yeah sure. I was just thinking of how I should drop the car off."

"Call me when you're near Rio Hill Hertz and I'll pick you up. Then we can get some things from Whole Foods."

"Right. After my breakfast, I know you've had yours, how about we take the longcase clock off and then I'll be on my way?"

"Perfecto."

***

I pulled on to Route 33, which is about seventy-five yards from the front of our little white house, and drove west through the junction at Ruckersville and on past Stanardsville up the steep winding road into the Shenandoah National Park and down the other side into Old Dominion's third largest county, Rockingham. About halfway down the other side is a fine panoramic view of the magnificent Shenandoah Valley with Massanutten Mountain in the distance. *I wonder how many times I have taken this route*, I thought to myself.

In Harrisonburg, I picked up I81 North and barreled along at 70 miles an hour until I saw signs for Strasburg where I exited at 298B. Two minutes later, where it intersects The Valley Pike at the bottom, I coasted to a stop right in front of Bruno's Antiques Shop. It was still closed. I figured that it might be because of his show schedule, but as I turned off the ignition, he rolled in with coffee and doughnuts. I waved to him. He held up the goodies and motioned to me with his shoulder to come inside.

"Don't mind if I do," I said, as I dismounted.

"You still look like a fit Marine," he mumbled with his mouth full. "Let's see if we can induce Type II diabetes in you this morning."

I laughed, "Don't tell Emma or we'll both be in trouble."

The exterior of his store is deceptively modest, but the interior is something to behold. Bruno's shop is one of the best of its kind in the United States. Interior designers routinely drive down from DC and New York City to pick for their celebrity clients, and more than once his inventory has been seen on the Big Screen as decorative elements on movie sets. In the world of antiques, Bruno is a big fish in a big pond, but you'd never know it. He patiently serves kindness to all, from newlywed young couples without a clue in the world, to the nearly dead who remember when everything cost just a dollar.

Ours was a friendship of trust and respect built on an intimate knowledge of each other's personal and business history over decades. We were now friends, although we'd had our moments early on. Once upon a time when we were young and foolish, there was tension between us in our marketplace, but now that we were in our middle age neither of us could remember what "it" was all about. We both realized that what matters to the cock-crowing youth, matters little or not at all to the latter-day wise.

Bruno looked at me over his coffee cup with an eyebrow raised. "What's the latest trend in the business, Charles?"

I froze in thought for two ticks and replied with a shrug, "I think the demographics are ah-changing fast," I replied, noshing down on another glazed pastry.

He paused before stuffing another bite and said, "You're talking about the Boomers, right?"

"Yep," I nodded and replied, "the smart ones are trading in their McMansions for rooms with a view all on one level in a warmer latitude."

We noshed a half minute or so in silence. I knew he was thinking.

He sipped on his coffee and asked, "You and Emma got plans to move on south?"

I shook my head, no. "How about you?" I mumbled, still with food in my mouth.

He thought again for a moment before replying. "The way I figure it," he said, "if we were Canadians or New Englanders, we'd be happy to move to here, so, we're already living in a warm enough climate."

His logic made sense to me. But part of me wondered just where in life we were heading after the sale of our storefronts. We were happy where we lived and enjoyed a fine network of business contacts. Yet I could feel in my bones that my life was, yet again, taking a new direction. *Where?* I asked myself. Where to *this* time?

30 Schoolgirl Chirp

Rather than take the time for a game with Jerry at The Strasburg Emporium, I took the Valley Pike south and stopped in to see my favorite dealers along the way. Janet's Spring Hollow Antiques shop was my first stop on Main Street in Woodstock. I hadn't seen her in six months or more and it didn't matter because she hadn't changed one bit; she is always calm and delightful. Over a spot of Earl Gray tea, she brought me up to speed on business gossip like what had sold and for how much and to whom, etc., and we picked each other's brains for market trends, too.

Jan got her start about the same time I got mine, and we have similar taste in antiques, too, especially furniture. Her painted inventory has always been at the top in the Lower Valley. By the way, the term "Lower Valley" is a misnomer; the northern part of the Valley is actually the "Lower Valley" because rivers in the Shenandoah Valley flow north. Early settlers used rivers as transportation routes because overland travel was so difficult; this was before roads. So, going downstream meant going north, hence down the Valley, Lower Valley.

In the upper part of the Valley (south by Lexington) there's David Gee's Old South Antiques in Brownsburg. At the opposite end of the Valley (north near Strasburg) is Janet's Spring Hollow shop and, before I closed it there was my shop on the eastern side of the Blue Ridge Mountains, Spring Hill Farm Antiques. Our three shops made a triangle on the map and comprised Virginia's triple crown of American country antiques shops, but I had no regrets. For me it was time to move on. I just hope Janet and David would eventually realize that 'the times are a-changing.' Naturally, I found no sleepers at Janet's, as I had not at David's. I never expect to. Both know enough not to let a sleeper slide through their fingers.

Janet sent me down Route 11 a ways to Bob and Rob in nearby Edinburg. Smaller than Woodstock, Edinburg is like all of the other minor municipalities in the Valley; it's a bedroom community for the greater Washington Metro Area. The city folks have their weekend retreats here in these quaint hamlets for a variety of reasons: scenic beauty for one, escape from the rat race is another reason. But since 9-11, the motive that I hear most often is safety. The Shenandoah Valley has become a bug-out destination for the worried metropolitan types. They are buying second homes here now because it's out of the blast zone and upwind from the prevailing weather patterns that move NBC hazards (nuclear, biological, chemical) west to northeast. If something goes boom in DC, the city preppers who survive, plan on bugging west to their over-the-mountain retreats. Harrisonburg's mayor was the first to mention the tendency to me last year. It makes sense, but I figure if it's a really big boom it won't matter where we are, and if it's a little firecracker then we'll be fine in Barboursville.

Like Janet's shop in Woodstock and Dave's in Brownsburg, Bob and Rob's shop has 'Inventory of the Better Sort.' They are avid collectors, I'd say, especially if something has a Valley origin. At auction, watch out! When they attend a local auction sale, it always means something Southern is on the docket and the sale will most certainly turn into an event that will make the trades. I've learned to stay on my side of the mountain because between David, Janet, and the Edinburg Boys, there's no way I'm ever going to end up carrying anything home. They close ranks and make sure of that, but there's no lasting animosity. It's just business, and in the Boys' case, it's just collecting – which is more of a condition than an avocation. I used to be afflicted in the same manner as they, but no longer. Now it is just business. I am usually emotionally detached, but the typical collector is not. He is as invested as a lover is in a tryst. When asked how I defeated the monster, I smile now and tell them that I've successfully completed a 12-step program. I'm kidding of course. Twelve steps wouldn't even come close to being a cure.

Bob and Rob plied me with home-baked cookies and iced tea amidst a swarm of little dogs and caged parrots in their kitchen. Outdoors they have yet another swarm: goats, geese, and a llama or alpaca; I don't know the difference. All I know is that every time I visit I leave with a smile on my face and hair all over my trousers.

The Edinburg Boys deal in fine period American furniture, the heavy stuff: corner cupboards, high chests, stepback cabinets, etc. Rob does the conservation and restoration. Bob handles the business end of things. I have known them for a very long time and I identify with them as fellow stalwart dealers and because they abide by the same virtues as I do.

Like at Dave's place and Janet's shop, there were no sleepers at Bob and Rob's shop. I expected no less. Not all picking has to do with making a profit. Socializing and networking is just as important. In the country taking the time to talk and catch up is expected; in the city, not so much. I prefer the more relaxed pace of the rural setting. Besides, smelling the roses is part of my new job description; Emma insists and I agree.

After I'd had enough cookies, petted all the pooches, and approved of the new inventory pieces with which they live within their brick home and the new pieces out in the carriage house, I bid farewell and worked my way out to the Caddy in the gravel parking lot. But at the last moment as I closed the door of the car I thought of the clock. I rolled the window down. The two of them were about to wave bye.

"Guys, I bought a longcase clock a few days ago that you ought to see," I foolishly said. For someone who was trying his best to get back on the road, mentioning one of their favorites was not so smart. They practically jumped onto the car, both talking so fast with a myriad of questions, that I said, "Whoa! Hold your horses."

Rob insisted, "You must come back in and tell us all about it."

"I can't," I whined. "I have to get back to Emma. We just got back last night from Florida."

Bob pleaded, "I'll cook you dinner?"

I thought, *How stupid of me. I could have emailed them all about it.* "No, thank you. Really, I have to go.

Look." I got out my phone and showed them the two pictures I had of it through the open window of the car, one of the hood and the other of the whole long case. They oohed and awed. Both are avid collectors of Southern stuff. The clock was about as Southern as a collectible piece can be.

Holding the phone so that they could see, I pointed to the text on the face of the clock in the photo. "It has a paper face, guys, a moon dial, and right there," I adjusted my finger point, "it's marked by the maker, C.C. Colley."

They pulled the phone out of my hand. *Oh boy*, I thought to myself, *I'm really not going anywhere now for sure.*

I sighed patiently, "See there, where it reads "C.C. Colley Marion Virginia"? He was a Confederate cavalryman. The clock is, maybe ca.1900, I'd guess. Obviously he survived the war. It needs some work but —"

Together they stepped away from me before I could complete my thought and began jabbering to each other by a white picket fence. I heard snippets and bits and pieces of their conversation as to where it would look best in their house — ceiling height, color of drapery, etc. After some lengthy whispering they pattered back to me, looked from each other to me, and Rob asked me coyly, "How much?" Oh boy, I calculated. If Rob is the one who asks instead of Bob … then they are both really serious because ordinarily Bob does the negotiating.

"Guys, Emma and I have owned it all of two days," I moaned.

They lurched closer and insisted.

"It's in our house, in the most perfect spot," I looked up at them.

The two of them bent at the waist like toy soldiers, placed their four hands on the door of my open window, and exclaimed in unison, "Charles!"

I flinched and the hairs on my neck freaked out.

Bob insisted, "We must have it!"

I backed up as far as my shoulder strap would allow and managed a schoolgirl chirp, "I want my phone back."

Rob handed it back as if it were a scalpel, with a slap, whereupon I yelled over my shoulder, "Sorry, guys, you'll just have to speak to Emma." And then I did what any battle-hardened Marine decorated for valor would have done under the same circumstances, I peeled out of there with the two of them and their pack of West Highland terriers chasing me down the driveway.

31 Eye of the Needle

I continued on south towards Harrisonburg via Interstate 81 with the intent to pick The Rolling Hills Antiques Mall since it was on the way home and only two blocks from where I picked up Route 33 East to go home. My cell rang about at the midway point. I knew it was Emma even before I looked at the phone's screen. No doubt Rob had communicated my escape in vivid detail. *Oh boy*, I thought, *I'm going to get the third degree.*

"Hi Periwinkle," I answered nonchalantly.

A raft of Spanish language streamed from the Blackberry.

When Spanish and German are spoken at 33 RPM, I can understand it well, but Emma was redlining beyond my capabilities and her lung capacity is substantial. Like me, she's a free diver. Both of us can hold our breath for over three minutes. I knew that her rant could go on for miles so I lodged the chattering cell phone between the spokes of my steering wheel and drove on. The Route 33 West exit appeared before me just about the time my darling came up for air.

"You're not saying anything!" she gasped at me in English, finally.

Rather than pointing out that she had been dominating the airwaves for two counties, I answered, "I love you, darling."

"Amor, I hate it when you do that." I heard her smile-crack coming.

"You are my feather," I cooed.

"Stop that!" she giggled.

I went to the heart of the matter. "How much have you decided to sell the clock to Bob and Rob for, my love?"

She sniffed, "I thought I liked it too much to sell?"

"Yes dear, it is a nice clock but we'll find another we like just as well one day. In the meantime we can make two friends ecstatically happy and some profit at the same time."

She accused, "You did this on purpose, didn't you?"

"Did what, my feather?" I replied coyly. Leaders don't always reveal their strategy. Suffice it is to say that an effective leader need only to make the right decision at the right time and delegate the remainder to others. Often this is done on the fly and a considerable amount of luck is involved. For a very good leader this is second nature. The clock was a case in point. It was all totally random karma, but each segment of the adventure led to the next in the sequence.

Emma snorted, "You gave them the hook, fly, and sinker."

I corrected, "You mean 'hook, line, and sinker,' don't you?"

She was frustrated. "You understand my meaning, *Charles*!"

"I should get my Tenkara rods out again. The trout are probably biting."

She nearly shouted, "*Did* you tell them a price?"

I imagined her with one hand on her hip.

"You mean the clock?"

She replied in too fast Spanish, and then an intelligible, "Uh-huh."

She was tapping her toe. I could hear it. This, I realized, was not a good sign. I was baiting a bear. I answered cautiously, "No."

She interrupted, "They said that you fled 'like a scalded cat.' What is that?"

"It's just a figure of speech, dear. I couldn't help it."

"What do you mean, 'you couldn't help it'?'

"They chased me," I sighed, knowing I had lost the argument. She was never going to accept the fact that I ran from anything.

"What's a scalded cat, Amor?"

"Look, just sell them the clock."

"I will. You're the one who likes it. How much?"

I thought for a few moments. *At auction, like at Green Valley or Brunk's, it would probably fetch twenty grand*, I figured.

"Well? I don't have all day," she tapped. "Amor?"

"They can have it for eighteen thousand."

"They won't pay that much. Will they?"

"If they want to own it they'll have to. There aren't that many Southern clocks and even fewer that come onto the market, and they know that. I think that they can handle that amount, and if they ever decide to sell it, which they won't, Bob is probably brave enough to double it. For Pete's sake, people come from all over for their Southern stuff. Jackie-O and Robert Duval used to shop there."

Silence. I looked at the phone to make sure we were still connected. I could hear her think, she was so quiet.

Before we met, Emma had headed marketing divisions for three companies in the Americas and Europe. In each instance she was lauded for soaring sales where others before had failed. She's a fixer, a trainer, and can thread a storm through the eye of a needle. I've seen her speak calmingly to a kindergarten full of squirming kids and to an auditorium full of fidgeting executives. When she speaks all listen, all remain engaged, and all are on their feet when she finishes. My wife is the consummate marketer.

They ended up buying the C.C. Colley clock for a lot more than I suggested.

Epilogue

I saw the dogwoods were blooming across the landscape outside our kitchen window as I greeted the day. For some reason that I cannot explain, I think of Indians when the dogwoods are in bloom.

Years ago, I read somewhere that in the olden days Indian boys used to harvest the straight suckers from the base of dogwood trees to make arrows. Trivia like that fills my mind and many would say it is not much good for anything, but that is not true. The minutia is useful when I write appraisal reports. Tidbits like that end up as part of a description: 'Bow and matching set of ten arrows, ca.1840's, Comanche, Southern Plains, Osage orange wood and sinew-backed bow, with three-feather dogwood arrows.' Why trivia like this enters my mind and remains permanently lodged when Emma's grocery-buying instructions do not, I can't say, but it does.

Sometimes, however, I know the trivia comes from other times, other lives. The woven double-sided blanket we use in the bedroom, for instance. Its subtle patterns of florals on one side, in soft lavender tones has, more than once, brought to memory the rolling purple heathers outside the town of Coventry in my life as Randolph West. And, sometimes the facts of antique objects I have picked while traveling in England in this life are facts only someone who has "been there" could really know. Obviously I don't reveal the source of that knowledge at those times. People consider antiques dealers a bit of an oddity as it is -- no point in widening that perception. At least Emma understood.

I wondered where Emma was; Grace was gone, too. I assumed that the two of them were on a morning walk. In the kitchen, my love had left me a warm Kite Ham biscuit wrapped in aluminum foil in the warming oven and five oranges on the counter in a ca.1890's buttocks basket. She knows how I enjoy squeezing my own juice, and I did, as I watched the morning news on the small flat screen. When the coffee was ready, I sat at the table and checked my messages on the laptop as the heads on WAHU Channel 27 rattled on.

Since the sale of the storefronts, life had taken on a new perspective, more focused, I liked to think. Still we had our picking to do in order to acquire the items we could then sell to our extensive network of dealers and collectors or on our eBay store. The latest round of events had garnered me more contacts, from Fred Hoar in old books to the Petersburg clock collector. I'd made more alliances and traded more favors among those I already considered friends. And I'd had the joy of bonefishing at Key West along the way. Life was good.

Yet there was always that part of me that wriggled a bit at periods of transition. I don't fight changes, at least not as much as most people I know, but still … there is that slight itch in the soul when heading into lesser known territories. Would I be able to sustain us on our picking for private collectors and dealers? Would my appraisal services, now picking up again in the couple of weeks since we'd been back home, continue to increase, or fall off like the antiques business in general? It was all a throw of the dice in a way. An educated one, I felt, but still.

I'd reinvented myself so many times already, that making a change should feel like second nature. From a miserable couple of past relationships, to life-threatening combat situations, to watching the inevitable decay of the business I dearly loved, life had taken turns on me. I sighed. Just one more step along the way. But … on the way to where or what?

I popped the last bite of biscuit into my mouth as someone was saying something on the news about a winning lottery ticket. A winner had failed to collect the winnings from some months back. It was a significant amount.

A motion out the window caught my eye and I saw Emma and Grace were coming. I loved to watch them. I could see them in the distance, out by the mulberry tree.

Another TV head more or less repeated what the first one had just said but the words registered this time. And then I remembered having an old ticket in my wallet from months ago. Vaguely, I remembered purchasing it at D's…no, it was at Bobby's country store over at the junction of Route 20 and Turkey Sag Road. *I must have been over there to pick up or to drop off Grace at the dog lady*, I thought.

I opened my twenty-year-old wallet and looked at the folded ticket. I studied it for a few moments, my head moving up and down comparing the numbers on the TV and the ticket.

None matched.

I sighed again, wondering when my ship would come in. Or if I was on the deck of the *Titanic* and didn't realize it.

Grace bounded in, checked her food dish first, and then greeted me. *Priorities*, I grinned. Emma looked at me oddly and sensed something was wrong. She backed up one step and looked around furtively. "What's wrong?" she whispered.

I glanced about our kitchen furnished with its Shaker cabinets and Valley of Virginia pottery. We had just enough in the bank to carry us into our next period of life, whatever that might hold. But for now, Grace had flopped unceremoniously at my feet, her deep brown eyes giving me an adoring but exhausted look. And in front of me stood the most caring and loving woman I could know. I stood up and held Emma in my arms and said, "Nothing dear. Nothing at all. I was just thinking we are on our way ... to somewhere."

"We are?" she asked, leaning back with another curious stare.

I grinned. "Yes, we are. I was just thinking that we should take some time off, maybe go to Mexico." We both loved the Riviera Maya.

She looked up at me and smiled back. "Spoil me, *Amor*," she said.

Glossary

A Day to Remember (real)
The author's wedding day went pretty much as written, except for the adoration in the courthouse and the Marine/Pentagon twist. The real Emma & Charles' anniversary is August 4th, and they did meet on Match dot-com.

Albert Aylor (real person) (American: 1832-1922)
A regionally renowned maker of chairs, cabinets, and violins. Aylor was a Confederate Civil War POW imprisoned in Delaware. He survived the war to become a rural postmaster in the Haywood area of Madison County, Virginia, and a local legend.

Alberto Fujimori Fujimori (real person) (Peruvian: 1938 -). President of Peru from 1990-2000, now serving 25 years for serious charges even though his methods for fighting the drug cartels were effective.

Allen Edmonds Shoes (real)
An upscale American domestic manufacturer if fine quality men's shoes since 1922.

American Aesthetic Movement (real)
A style with its origins in Britain, it became a dominant style and the precursor to the Art Nouveau style. Ebonized woods with gilt highlights, organic elements, and incised line-and-dot adornment were some of the attributes used on all forms of decorative artifacts of the 1870's in the U.S.

Antique (real)
One hundred years old. A standard set by U.S. Customs.

Antiques Associates at West Townsend (real)
One of the finest antiques venues in the United States.

Antoine Gabriel Quervelle (real person) (French-American: 1789-1856). Cabinetmaker, Philadelphia from ca.1817, known for ornate mahogany and giltwood pier tables and cabinets often decorated with ormolu mounts mirroring the style of his elite contemporaries in France (Empire) and England (Regency); both are similar very high-styles. Surviving pieces by Quervelle today are sought by serious collectors and often fetch high hammer prices at auction.

Ardabil Mosque Rug (real)
A style of Azerbaijani carpet from the province of Persia by the same name dating to the Safavid Dynasty in the 16th century. A pair is on display in the Victoria and Albert Museum, London.

Baltimore Painted Screen Society (real)
Dedicated to the folk art tradition of painted screens.

Barboursville Gift Gallery (real)
Fictionalized for this story, this is a real store located near Barboursville, Virginia.

Barboursville Vineyards (real)

Located in Barboursville, Virginia.

Barboursville, Virginia (real)
The hamlet in which the Dawes' live.

Bayou Teche (real)
A culturally significant 125 mile-long waterway in rural southern Louisiana.

Blind Doors (real term)
Refers to furniture doors with a wood panel instead of a window pane.

Blitz (real)
An intense combat campaign pitting overwhelming forces against weaker forces.

Blue Whale Books (real)
Fictionalized for this story, this is a real book store located in Charlottesville, Virginia.

Bob & Rob (fictional persons)
See the Edinburg Boys.

Bodo's Bagels (real)
The authors' favorite bagels.

Bombay Hook Wildlife Refuge (real)
A national wildlife preserve in Delaware.

Bookfinder.com (real)
An emporium for booksellers.

Brunk Auctions (real)

Fictionalized for this story, this is a real business located in Asheville, North Carolina.

Bruno (fictional person)

This character is a fictionalized friend of the author's. Bruno is a Latvian dealer friend of Dawes who has a big shop in Strasburg, Virginia. Bruno is a Theodore Roosevelt lookalike who once spent some time in a Russian gulag. He has a thick accent.

Bubba Baxter (fictional person)

Southern Squire Antiques on Preston Street in Lexington, Virginia.

C&O Restaurant (real)

Fictionalized for this story, this is a real restaurant located in Charlottesville, Virginia.

Cartel Clocks (real)

Wall-hung clocks as opposed to mantel clocks.

Castle Hill (real)

A plantation in Albemarle County, Virginia.

C.C. Colley Clock (real)

In the author's living room.

Charles Horatio Dawes (fictional person) (US/UK: 1954 -)

This character is a fictionalized version of the author with almost all of his negative attributes omitted and many positive attributes added. Charles is an antiques dealer, picker, appraiser, collector, conservator, and connoisseur. Until he sold them, he owned and operated an antiques shop and antiques mall in rural Madison County, Virginia. In this storyline he lives in a Craftsman bungalow in nearby Barboursville, Virginia with his Peruvian spouse, Emma. ★ Charles' military service: Major, USMC Ret., Pilot; Force-Recon: Panama, Grenada, Bosnia, Iraq, Afghanistan. ★ The author's actual military service: USAF Aeromedic A90150 1972-1976; U.S. Army ordnance officer 1983-1987, and he was designated an "Honorary Leatherneck" by the U.S. Marines in 1984 for not having pissed anyone off while he was assigned as a platoon commander for a month as part of his own Basic Officer's Course at Aberdeen Proving Grounds. He cherishes that bit of paper on his office wall that his Marine Major awarded him.

Charlottesville, Virginia (real)
The closest city of any size to where the Dawes' live in Barboursville.

Chicamacomico (real)
One of the ferry boats that run between Hatteras and Ocracoke Islands, North Carolina.

Chickamauga (real)
An American civil war battle that occurred in Catoosa and Walker Counties, Georgia September 19-20, 1863 between Union Federal forces and Southern Confederate forces. It was the most significant Union defeat in the Western Theatre and it marked the end of Federal efforts in the entire region. Only at the Battle of Gettysburg were there more casualties.

Christopher Dock (real person) (American/British subject: 1698-1771). Dock was a Mennonite school teacher in Skippack located in south-eastern Pennsylvania. A Mennonite high school in the Towamencin Township today bears his name. Dock is a major fictionalized protagonist in *The Serapis Fraktur* , and a spinoff series is planned by the author in which Dock will be the protagonist in a fantasy series because readers seem to like him best.

Clarence Givens (fictional person)
Nephew of Mr. Givens in Florida who had the stolen Henry rifle, kepi, etc.

Clay Hill Forge (real)
Fictionalized for this story, this is a real forge in Waynesboro, Virginia.

Collet Foot: A round domed base.

Clore Furniture Company (real)
Fictionalized for this story, this is a real furniture manufacturer. E.A. Clore & Sons was established in 1830 in Madison County, Virginia.

Confederate Air Force (fictional)
There is actually a Commemorative Air Force that was affectionately referred to as the Confederate Air Force.

Constantine's Wood Center (real)
A retail supplier of restoration products.

Coon's Age (real term)

Refers to the age of a type of canine that hunts raccoons, typically 4-6 years.

County Albemarle, Virginia (real)
The County has a total area of 726 square miles (1,880 km).

County Culpeper, Virginia (real)
The County has a total area of 382 square miles (989.4 km).

County Madison, Virginia (real)
The County has a total area of 322 square miles (830 km).

County Orange, Virginia (real)
The County has a total area of 343 square miles (889 km).

County Rockbridge, Virginia (real)
The County has a total area of 601 square miles (1,557 km).

County Rockingham, Virginia (real)
The County is Virginia's third largest with a total area of 853 square miles (2,210 km).

County Wythe, Virginia (real)
The County has a total area of 465 square miles (1,203 km).

Coventry (real)
The UK city where Dawes grew up in his first incarnation and died in 1942 from the Blitz.

Cowherd Mountain (real)

Its elevation is 1196 feet (365 m) and it is in sight of Barboursville, Virginia.

Crystal Diamond (fictional person)

Wife of a Charlottesville picker Lenny Diamond who is a perpetual student: BS, MA, MS, PhD, JD, MD, etc.

Culpeper, Virginia (real)

Twenty miles north of where Charles Dawes had a business.

David Gee (fictional person)

Greta Gee's antiques dealer husband. Brownsburg, Virginia. He is a fictionalized friend of the author.

Dirty Rice (real)

A Cajun dish comprised of delectable edibles that make white rice turn brown and flavorful.

Edinburg Boys (fictional men)

Edinburg, Virginia antiques dealers with inventory of the better sort. They are fictionalized friends of the author.

El Charro (real)

The author's favorite Mexican restaurant in Harrisonburg, Virginia.

Emma Dawes (fictional person) (Peru/US: 1957 -).

Charles Dawes' spouse. She is a fictionalized version of the author's wife, Chany. Chany is a certified interpreter who works in the justice system and she is one of two female Spanish talents that have worked for Rosetta Stone. Her company is Linguistic Services, LLC.

Felix
The Jack Russell terrier that Charles Dawes believes was his in an earlier incarnation.

Firsts Magazine (real)
Established in 1991. A periodical dedicated to collecting first edition books.

Fleetwood Pride (fictional person)
Commander of the Confederate Air Force Museum. He's a leaner version of the actor from the Quaker Oats commercials. He earned his star after Desert Storm, where, as a Marine jet pilot, he was one of the few to be shot down.

Fleming Kean Rich (real person) (American: 1806-1861). A regionally famous furniture maker known for his pie safes. He lived in Wythe County, Virginia. Active ca.1830-1845.

Flying Tigers (real)
A group of American pilots recruited from the various branches of the US military, and some wildcat civilians, who were under the command of General Claire Lee Chennault who formed the 1st American Volunteer Group (AVG).

Fraktur (real)
A document commemorating a life transition such as a birth, marriage, or death. It is hand written in

ink and hand decorated with watercolors. Usually the text is in German because most of the fraktur makers were Germans making fraktur for the German market in America. The plural of fraktur is fraktur. Typical size: 16"H 13"W.

Fred Nichols (real person) (American: 1948 -)
Known for wilderness landscapes. Active in Barboursville, Virginia.

General Claire Lee Chennault (real person) (American: 1893-1958). The iron-fisted, charismatic, and extraordinarily effective commander of the world famous Flying Tigers.

Glazed (real term)
Refers to the glass in doors.

Grace
The Dawes' old yellow lab.

Grand Luxxe (real)
A five-star resort enterprise on the Riviera Maya, the author's favorite.

Green Valley Auctions (real)
Fictionalized for this story, this is a real business located in Mt. Crawford, Virginia.

Greta Gee (fictional person)
David Gee's travel agent wife. Brownsburg, Virginia.

Hard Image (real term)

A photo on metal or glass or some other hard surface other than paper.

Harrisonburg, Virginia (real)
Headquarters to the Rosetta Stone Company and where Charles Dawes and the author once attended college at James Madison University.

Harry Watts (fictional person)
Taxi driver and odd jobs man in Madison, Virginia.

Hebron Lutheran Church (real)
Located in Madison County, Virginia.

Henry Compton (fictional person)
Owner of Sambo's in Leipzig, Delaware.

Heywood-Wakefield (real)
An American furniture company.

Hood Store (real)
Fictionalized for this story, this is a real store in Hood, Virginia.

Hood Mercantile Store (real)
Fictionalized for this story, this is a real store located in Wolftown, Virginia.

James Lee Burke (real)
The author's favorite mystery writer. Burke is a two-time *Edgar* winner.

James Madison University (real)
Located in Harrisonburg, Virginia.

Jane Hickam (fictional person)
Charles' real estate agent and lawyer. She collects stereo cards and Imperial German steins.

Janet (fictional person)
Woodstock, Virginia antiques dealer.

Jazzman Fry (fictional person)
Modeled after a childhood friend of the author's, Jazz is a Black Vietnam vet, retired CID army E9, antiques dealer in Culpeper who Charles mentors. Jazz sometimes works odd private detective jobs from for local law enforcement.

Jerry Houff (fictional person)
This character is modeled after someone the author actually knew and he did own and operate The Strasburg Emporium at one time.

John Arnold (fictional person)
A picker Charles met at Tobacco Barn who handles only tribal Oriental rugs. John's about six-feet-six, two-hundred-fifty hard pounds, a retired Marine Colonel, and looks kind of like Johnny Depp.

Joseph T. Rainer (real)
A contributor to the book, "Cultural Change and the Market Revolution in America, 1789-1860."

Judge Derry (fictional person)
The circuit court judge who witnessed Lenny Diamond chuck a phone into the street.

Ken Neumann (fictional person)
This character is modeled after a freelance journalist who actually does write for the *Maine Antique Digest*.

Kite Hams (real)
Processor of the best Virginia hams. Located in Wolftown, Virginia.

Lenny Diamond (fictional person)
This character is modeled after a picker extraordinaire that the author has known since the early 1980's. The fictional Lenny is a retired late middle-aged second story man in Charlottesville. He swears that he never carried a gun on a caper and only took from the super-rich when they pissed him off. He probably got caught at it about as many times as he's been married. Lenny's operated a coin-and-stamp shop on a side street for the three years since his latest release in this story. Originally from Las Vegas, he wears too much gold and diamond jewelry, and spends a lot of time at the track.

Lisa Blue (fictional person)
This character is fictionalized from the real person. Lisa was the token black integration girl at all-white Waverly Yowell Elementary School in 1965. Her circumstances really did happen. The author was witness.

Louie's Backyard (real)
Located at 700 Waddell Avenue, Key West, Florida. (305) 294-1061.

Macallan Scotch Whiskey (real)

Extravagantly expensive libation from the 21st century.

Madison Antiques Center (real)

Owned and operated by the author, SEP 1991-AUG 1994. It had 65 dealers from 13 states and Washington, DC. Barbara Streisand and Kathleen Turner stopped by once shortly after Bill Clinton visited Monticello before his first inauguration. Eugene McCarthy was a regular patron and a friend.

Madison Eagle (real)

A local newspaper for Madison County Virginia.

Madison, Virginia (real)

The county in which Charles Dawes (and the author) owned and operated an antiques shop and antiques mall for 25 years (from 1979-2004).

Maine Antique Digest (real)

A monthly trade publication equivalent to the *Wall Street Journal* of the antiques business.

Major Dickason's Blend (real)

Purveyed by Peet's Coffee & Tea. It is their signature blend of coffee and the author's favorite.

Marriott: Key West Marriott Beachside Hotel (real)

Located in Key West, Florida, USA.

Marriott: Savannah Marriott Riverfront (real)

Located in Savannah, Georgia, USA.

Martti Rytkönen (real person) (active 1994 -)

A series designer of fine crystal glass for <u>Orrefors</u>.

Massanutten Mountain <u>(real)</u>
Is an end-cap mountain on a synclinal ridge in the Ridge-and-Valley Mountains located in the Shenandoah Valley of Virginia.

Maxwell Chayat <u>(real person) (French-American: 1909-1982)</u>. A sculptor and maker of Jewish ritual art objects and retro silver jewelry. Maxwell Chayat was born in Paris in 1909. He received a BA and MA from Columbia University and headed the Art Department at NM State Teacher's College. Later in life he moved to NJ where he had a studio and another in Forestburg, New York for the summer season.

MI <u>(real term)</u>
Military Intelligence is an occupation specialty with the mission to collect and analyze data on all enemies for advantage.

Miriam Haskel <u>(real person/company) (American: 1899-1981)</u>. She was a designer of affordable costume jewelry from 1920 through the 1950s. Her namesake company continues today.

Mott Perry <u>(fictional person)</u>
Ex Frisco cop runs the Valley Bar & Grill on Delancey in Roanoke, Virginia. Nephew of Bubba. Was the flat-bottom skiff captain in Key West when Charles and Thack went bonefishing.

Mr. Givens <u>(fictional person)</u>

Had the stolen goods from the Ohio auction company.

Mr. Yowell (real person)
Helped the author's dad mow the lawn at Spring Hill Farm in 1965.

Mrs. Lam (fictional person)
The seventy-five-year-old lady in Florida with vintage clothing, tools, and silver flatware.

Mrs. Margi Smith (fictional person)
Had a pyramid of Louis Vuitton luggage in Melbourne, Florida.

News-Gazette (real)
A legendary Rockbridge County periodical with roots dating back to 1801.

Ogee
A double-S curved molding.

Old Man Givens (fictional person)
See Mr. Givens.

Old Soul
A reincarnated entity.

Old South Antiques (real)
Fictionalized for this story, this is a real store in Brownsburg, Virginia.

One-Eyed Jack (fictional person)

This character is a fictionalized acquaintance that the author has known since the late 1980's. One-Eye is a tools dealer Charles has known 'since back in the day.'

Openwork
A surface with sections removed for a decorative effect. Found commonly in chair splats and in silver serving pieces.

Origami
Mott Perry's boat in Key West.

Ormolu
A gilt metal ornament, usually gold over bronze.

Orrefors (real)
A fine crystal manufacturer based in Sweden since 1898.

Ovoid
A potter's term. A pot that is narrow at the top, broadening outward on descent to just above the first third and then tapering inward to the bottom which often has the same diameter as the top.

Ovolo
A round, quarter section of a circle.

Palladio Restaurant (real)
Fictionalized for this story, this is a real business at the Barboursville Vineyards in Barboursville, Virginia.

Paresthesia (real term)
A sensation of pins and needles.

Pateræ
An inlaid oval embellishment on decorative objects e.g. furniture and silver.

Personal Property
Any tangible object that can be moved: toys, jewelry, fine art, crops, chattel, furniture, yachts, weapons, starships, etc. In the British vernacular these are referred to simply as property and appraisers are known as valuers or surveyors of worth.

Peter Shupp (fictional person)
This character is an amalgamation of real people that the author knew when he was stationed at Ramstein Air Base in West Germany in the mid 1970's. A book dealer who lives in in Santa Barbara, California, Peter is wildly flamboyant, rich, brilliant, and the top antique bookseller in the country. Married to Thackery, the two know everyone who is anyone on the Left Coast. Peter was one of Charles' JMU ROTC instructors.

Peters Mountain (real)
A sign pretending to be an AT&T facility marks the entrance of a government facility at the foot its base on Turkey Sag Road.

Picker (real term)
One who supplies another with antique or vintage merchandise.

Pier (real)

The wall space between two windows, hence pier table.

Professor Ian Stevenson (real person) (Canadian-American: 1918-2007). A paranormal research psychiatrist who worked at the University of Virginia for 50 years. His seminal work, *Reincarnation and Biology: A Contribution to the Etiology of Birthmarks and Birth Defects* (1997), reported 200 patients with birthmarks. He believed that the birthmarks were a result of a wound in the respective patient's previous incarnation, as recalled by the thousands of child-patients that he interviewed and studied as his life's work.

Provenance (real term)

The origin and history of ownership or the source of an object back to its place of origin.

Quechua (real)

It is the most spoken indigenous language in the New World (6.9 million).

Randal Cunningham (fictional person)

Coca-Cola memorabilia dealer from Atlanta.

Randolph West (fictional person)

The person Charles Dawes believes he had been in an earlier incarnation.

Rebecca West (fictional person)

The name of Charles Dawes' wife in an earlier incarnation.

Renovator's Supply, Inc. (real)
A retail supplier of restoration products.

Rick Waggener (fictional person)
This is fictionalized acquaintance known to the author. He is an expert and dealer of hard images and other categories of the better sort in Gaithersburg, Maryland.

Robber Baron Era (real) (American: 4th quarter 19th century). A short period of extravagance practiced by successful industrialists and their scion who, as a result, became larger-than-life targets of literary criticism.

Robert Tolles (real person) (American: ca.1820's-1883). Inventor of microscopes and other ocular instruments.

Rolling Hills Antiques Center (real)
Fictionalized for this story, this is a real antiques mall in Harrisonburg, Virginia.

Rosetta Stone Company (real)
A language teaching company based in Harrisonburg, Virginia.

Sabots (real term)
Shoes on furniture feet, often metal.

Sambo's (real)

Fictionalized for this story, this is a real restaurant located at 283 Front St., Leipsic, Delaware. (302) 674-9724.

Shenandoah National Park (real) [pronounced: shen-ann-dough-uh]. A major national park in Virginia. Shenandoah is an Iroquoian Indian word derived from the word 'deer.'

Shenandoah Valley (real)
Situated between the Blue Ridge Mountains along its east and the Appalachian Mountains on its west side, the ancient Valley of Virginia runs north-south the length of the state encompassing many of the western counties of the Old Dominion.

Sheriff Williams (fictional person)
Recovered stolen property from Mr. Givens in Florida.

Signal Knob (real)
A mountain 2106 feet in elevation overlooking the town of Strasburg, Virginia. It was used by both Union and Confederated forces during the American Civil War because of its strategic advantage.

Sir Frederick Hoar (fictional person)
Has a rare bookshop in London. Went after the Audubons when his New York office called him.

Skippack, Pennsylvania (real)
Where Christopher Dock taught school in the 18th century.

Sleeper (real term)

Slang for an undervalued object.

Smalls (real term)

Slang for objects smaller than a breadbox; i.e. ceramics, jewelry, books, etc.

Southside (real)

A geographic area in Virginia south of the James River, east of the Blue Ridge Mountains, and west of the tidewater region where the sons of early tidewater gentry went to entrepreneur.

Spring Hill Farm Antiques (real)

Fictionalized for this story, this was the name of the author's actual antiques business in Madison County, Virginia. It was located at the junction of U.S. 29N and 230W from 1979 to 2004.

Spring Hollow Antiques (real)

Fictionalized for this story, this is a real store in Woodstock, Virginia.

Strasburg Emporium (real)

Fictionalized for this story, this is a real super-regional antiques mall in the Valley of Virginia located in a town by the same name.

Synesthesia (real term)

An extra-sensory ability to discern with one sense a different sensation; e.g. colors have flavor, sounds have scent, etc.

TDY (real term)
A military acronym that stands for 'temporary duty assignment.'

Tenkara Fishing (real)
A traditional Japanese method of fishing for trout in mountain streams with a telescoping rod and no reel. The line is attached to the tip of the rod and it is only as long as the rod.

Thackerey Shupp (fictional person)
Peter's husband. Former NFL linebacker. Body builder. He's only thirty-five-years-old, six-feet-six, two-hundred-eighty-five pounds, Irish-Mormon background, with a physics degree from Yale. After only three seasons, he washed out of football with a nest egg that helped propel Peter to the top of the book world. He and Peter have been a couple for six-and-a-half years in this timeline.

Timeline
The period when the story begins for *The Madison Picker*: Spring 2005.

Tobacco Barn Antiques Show (real)
Defunct. Once held in a tobacco warehouse in Upper Marlboro, Maryland.

Tom Tanner (fictional person)
Owns Turkey Sag Farm, collects turkey calls, and was a witness to strange events.

Tup, or Anselm Tupper (fictional person)
Clocks expert in Petersburg, Virginia.

Tupper, Anselm (real person) (American: 1763-1808). Was a lieutenant in the American Revolutionary army at the age of 17, having been in uniform since age 11.

Valley Bar & Grill (fictional)
Owned and operated in Roanoke, Virginia by former San Francisco policeman, Mott Perry.

Valley of Virginia (real)
See Shenandoah Valley.

Valley Pike (real)
A thoroughfare running north-south in the Shenandoah Valley.

Value Attribute (real term)
Any feature that contributes to the sum of values an object possesses.

Vera Wang (real person) (American: 1949 -)
Figure skater turned fashion designer.

Virginia Book Shop (real)
Fictionalized for this story, this is a real business located in Charlottesville, Virginia.

Vogelzang Stoves (real)
A brand of wood-burning stove.

Whitehurst, Jessie Harrison (real person) (American: 1823-1875). Daguerreotypist, photographer, and entrepreneur with galleries in

New York, Washington D.C., Baltimore, Richmond, Norfolk, Petersburg, and Lynchburg. He lost a fortune speculating on Caribbean guano mining.

Whole Foods Markets (real)
A supermarket chain.

Wiener Werkstätte (real)
A production community of visual artists in Vienna, Austria established in 1903.

Wilhelm Hunt Diederich (real) (American: 1884-1953). An artist extraordinaire, cowboy, adventurer, and traveler who had a style of design which set a new standard that few have matched and all have emulated.

William Oktavec (real person) (Czech-American: active 1913-1930s). Invented door screen painting, a form of folk art in the greater Baltimore area.

William Spratling (real person) (American: 1900-1967). A veritable giant in the world of jewelry design who transformed the silver jewelry industry in Taxco, Mexico.

The Author's Thoughts

If you liked "The Madison Picker," you may be happy to know that "Picker" is the first title in the series. More adventures are in the works including the sequels, "Some Kind of Good" and "A South Boston Beauty." And for those of you who enjoy science fiction, Charles Dawes is also the protagonist in "The Conglomerate Series" which is a series in the 25th century. Fancy that. He's in the present *and* the far future. The first and second titles are already available in print and as eBooks. Check out "<u>The Serapis Fraktur</u>" and "<u>Attack on Orbital 454</u>."

If you have enjoyed this story, which I first began writing in 1993, please consider leaving positive feedback on Amazon or wherever else you may have discovered it. My greatest reward is to know that you have been entertained. It is enough to keep me writing. Thank you for your support.

★★★★★

Finally, for my brothers and sisters who wear or have ever worn a uniform with honor, I salute you and thank you for keeping us all safe.

Semper Fidelis
★★★★★

Proof

Made in the USA
Charleston, SC
01 March 2014